THE SPOILS OF WAR

"We had not intended that you should observe such terrible things, Arbiter Renamos," Princess Zia said. "The passengers are victims of the Green Union's attacks . . ."

Curved door-ramps were being lowered from both sides of the spaceship. A steady stream of shiny "cocoons" was floating down the ramps, guided by techs in gray and white. Renee craned her neck as the first one went past. A Niandian male lay inside. He was nearly naked, and a shimmering transparent bandage covered his gaping wounds. The dressing kept out dirt and germ-laden air, but it couldn't hide the gore . . .

By Juanita Coulson
Published by Ballantine Books:

STAR SISTER

Juanita Coulson

A Del Rey Book

BALLANTINE BOOKS · NEW YORK

To Bruce Coulson,
who has been very patient and knows
these things must be done delicately,
or you break the spell.

A Del Rey Book
Published by Ballantine Books

Copyright © 1990 by Juanita Coulson

Library of Congress Catalog Number: 89-91896

ISBN 0-345-36522-4

Manufactured in the United States of America

First Edition: March 1990

Cover Art by Richard Hescox

chapter
1

TRAFFIC was awful, a gut-tightening, brake-riding, 70-miles-per-hour madhouse—except for an occasional slow-moving vehicle which threatened to cause a massive pileup. Renee leaned forward and gripped the steering wheel more firmly, cursing the mess under her breath. As she did, an import with a broken or nonexistent muffler pulled out recklessly, almost sideswiping her aging Chevy as he zipped into the passing lane.

"Man driver!" Renee yelled, adding several pithier comments on the driver's character. A waste of breath. He was far ahead of her already. She couldn't even vent her rage by throwing him "the bird"; he'd never see it.

Calm down, she thought. The object is to stay alert and stay alive. I have to concentrate on the job at hand.

Difficult. Her thoughts kept drifting to that afternoon's hearings at Metro Council. For several long hours there, Renee had feared that, too, was going to be an exercise in wasted breath. She'd been only one petitioner among many, and a very unimportant petitioner, at that. A dozen not-for-profit organizations were scrambling for the available public funds Metro parceled out on a semi-annual basis. In theory, the various groups were allies, all working for the "commonweal." In actuality, they often ended up at each others' throats during these sessions. The financial pie was limited, and each group wanted a major chunk to service *its* particular clients. There never seemed to be enough to go around, and every organization feared being left out in the cold.

Renee's group, the Social Outreach Sisterhood, boasted a savvy committee chief, fortunately. Evy's experience dated back to the early '50s. The middle-aged black woman had learned a lot of the in and outs of the "do-gooder" business, including patience. She was trying to instill that quality especially in the younger members of Outreach.

I've sure got a hell of a long way to go yet, compared to Evy, Renee thought. Sometimes I think the only reason she put me on the funding committee was to give me some extra instruction. Very much needed! After all, what have I got to offer, really? Damned little. I'm the token WASP among Outreach's regular staff. Average. Not from a deprived background. Not from a rich, expensively educated background, with all the connections that could deliver to SOS. Every other committee member outranks me, has a better reason for getting involved in the work we do. Evy's got those tons of experience in the black civil rights, feminist, and poverty protest movements. Susan's got her Jewish background and dozens of crucial contacts in the academic community and service organizations. Maria comes right out of the Hispanic section of the city; she, like Evy, has had to put up with prejudice and its consequences in a way I've never even come close to. And Tran Cai? Third World. Boat person. Talk about background in being able to empathize with Outreach's needy clients!

A sputtering pickup towing a U-Haul was laboring slowly in the lane in front of Renee. She steered carefully around it, glancing at the driver and passengers as she passed. What she saw made her wince. A gaunt man and his haggard wife. Sad-eyed, woebegone kids. Goodwill furniture heaped precariously in the bed of the pickup. Obviously, the family was part of the exodus from the near-downtown area that was being razed. A developer was putting in brand-new housing and a mall there. Progress. And the project *would* pump badly needed money into the inner city's economy. But while the low-cost housing was being built, lots of families like this one were being pushed out onto the streets. Who was going to help that human jetsam?

The Social Outreach Sisterhood was, among other groups. In fact, SOS had made a heavy pitch in exactly that direction this afternoon at Metro.

Typically, Deputy Mayor Delores Lupez, SOS's friend on the Council, had been in their corner. Equally typically, that old pol Janike had fought them tooth and nail. Looking out for his buddies in other Metro departments, and their greedy relatives who wanted to grab a chunk of the financial pie. Evy had warned Renee and the rest not to bite on Janike's insults. The councilman was baiting them deliberately, hoping to provoke an outburst so he could persuade his fellow board members to deny funding to SOS. Renee still seethed, remembering how she had to hold her tongue and endure Janike's taunting questions. The man was antediluvian! A total Archie Bunker type. "SOS. Isn't your title the Social Outreach *Sisterhood*? Didn't you start out as a bunch of radical, braburning feminists? I don't think Metro ought to be giving you girls money for special-interest projects. We shouldn't cater to these questionable outfits, not when we're obligated to serve the *general* public . . ."

Evy had outmaneuvered him brilliantly. Yes, SOS had begun as a feminist association. It had since developed, and now served all sorts of people: battered women; abused children; the chronically unemployed and handicapped, men and women both; needy veterans; the elderly; displaced homemakers and entire families, like the one Renee had just passed. Evy finished by saying politely that she hoped Metro Council had also updated *its* goals, as the Sisterhood had. Gradually, she, Susan, Maria, and Tran Cai had swayed key board members, winning the desperately needed funding.

And what was I? Cheering section. Well, that's the best a probationer can expect, I suppose. But, dammit, I want to contribute. I feel guilty. Evy and the others, they've been through the real conflict. I didn't even know what prejudice and poverty were, while I was growing up. I've got so much catching up to do!

Later, rehashing the Metro session as they had trekked their way out to the parking lot, the sisters agreed they'd accomplished *most* of the day's agenda. Not all, by a long shot, but most. "It seems slow," Evy had said to console them. "Just remember where we came from. Don't let the haters like Janike beat you down. Back in the fifties and sixties, a lot of the people in the movement were afraid none of the walls would ever go down. But plenty of 'em have. Plenty more will. We have to keep pushing. Or figure out how to bypass them—and obstacles like Councilman Janike. Otherwise, we go nowhere. Worse, we might go backward. So hang in there. We owe it to the little people. It takes time, though. You gotta learn patience."

That's what it's all about: The Little People. The ones who get stepped on and shoved aside. SOS has to help them. We simply must!

If only I had a magic wand, I'd change Councilman Janike's bigoted opinions so fast I'd . . .

Renee sighed. Who was she kidding? A probationer wasn't in a position to effect much change at all. She'd just have to keep plugging, as Evy and the others had for so long.

And if she didn't watch what she was doing, she'd end up as an accident statistic. She couldn't afford even a fender banger, much less a few broken bones. And SOS wouldn't be able to carry her through a recuperation period if she goofed up and had to spend weeks on the disabled list. Money was too tight. The clients came first. And in that case, she'd be reading the classifieds, again . . .

Where in the hell was she?

She sat up very straight and lifted her foot off the accelerator. All of a sudden, she was alone, driving into a thick cloud of smog. She'd never seen this part of the expressway before.

Oh, hell, I took the wrong exit ramp!

The smog was swallowing up the beams thrown by the Chevy's headlights, and Renee poised her foot over the brake pedal. She couldn't see any other cars around her. Not ahead. Not in the one lane remaining to her left. Not in the rearview mirror.

Wait just a damned minute, she thought. *I don't care*

what exit this is. There has to be someone else getting off here during rush hour.

But there wasn't. She looked for barricades. That *had* to be the explanation: She had pulled onto an uncompleted ramp by mistake. Any moment now, shc'd see flare pots and sawhorses ahead, blocking her way.

Mingled with irritation at her error, Renee felt a growing sense of disquiet. The endless vista of city lights and skyline was fading, as if a curtain were dropping between her and the rest of the world. The smog no longer seemed offensive and ugly. In fact, it was becoming almost beautiful, a golden cloud, suffused with green.

Green? The smog's really weird this evening. Only it doesn't look quite like smog. It looks like . . .

The road vanished. So did the Chevy's hood. She stomped hard on the brake, but the car didn't stop. Nor did it feel out of control. It continued moving on into a universe that was crumbling.

No, "crumbling" wasn't the right word. Instead, everything she saw was like a wirephoto seen close up, composed of millions of tiny gray-green-gold dots.

Renee used the clutch, shifting down, grateful she'd bought a car with a manual transmission rather than with a more expensive automatic system. Engine drag would halt this crazy ride . . .

The gray-green-gold invaded the car's interior; blotting out the dash lights and the steering wheel. She choked back a scream and braced herself for impact.

Funny, in other wrecks she'd been involved in, everything had happened in split seconds. Why was the crash taking so long this time? Surely, any moment now, she had to hit something, traveling blind as she was. Well, maybe it wouldn't be too bad, as slowly as the Chevy was moving. And this was a tough old car. It could take the knocks . . .

What car?

With stunned amazement, she realized she couldn't feel the frayed seat covers, the shoulder harness, the brake pedal . . . nothing whatsoever was touching her.

Had she already hit something? Was she being hurled from the car, flying through the air, heading for an agonizing collision with the pavement or another vehicle?

She wasn't airborne, though. No, those weren't the sensations. Renee's reactions were oddly detached, and she wondered dreamily if she were dead. Had it ended, minutes earlier, when she'd let her concentration slip? Perhaps she was lying back there on the expressway beside her wrecked Chevy. Just one more gory statistic.

It will be okay, she thought with chilling practicality. My insurance will clean up the messy details. If only no one else was hurt . . .

She was sitting on something cold and wet and hard.

Renee groped about cautiously while she stared into the gray-green-gold smog. There was no engine vibration, no whistle of air past her face, no forward movement, though she couldn't pinpoint exactly when her impressions of forward movement had disappeared. Her fingers touched stone, wet stone, and a fine mist began to spatter against her skin and clothes.

Well, maybe she wasn't dead, yet. Maybe she was merely lying on the pavement, injured.

Dammit, she wasn't lying; she was sitting. And seeing.

She finally *could* see something besides that damned smog. Gray crowded out green and gold, and bit by bit, the gray took form: walls. Big, chunky blocks of gray stone stacked into high walls. A scene out of beautiful downtown Machu Picchu.

No car. No expressway. No off ramp. Nothing resembling a modern road with lane stripes and embedded safety reflectors. No city lights. No skyline. Only the stone surface she sat on, gray walls, and mist. Even the smog was evaporating.

She could see something else now: a man. He stood about twenty feet away from her, near a bend in one of the walls. The stranger shifted nervously from one foot to the other and glanced around. But when he looked toward Renee, he didn't seem to see her.

The man appeared to be in his mid-twenties, Renee's own age, and wore a cloak and a floppy hat. Rain was pouring off the front of its brim.

Rain? But where she sat, it was merely misting. Was she in some kind of limbo? He couldn't see her, and she couldn't feel his rain.

Renee's next thought was considerably more pleasant: He looks like he'd be fun to know. The young man had a slightly turned-up nose and enough worry chasing over his regular features to add maturity to what might otherwise be classified as a callow face.

Maybe he could hear her, even if he couldn't see her. Renee took a deep breath, preparing to shout a "Hello."

An odd noise stopped her before she could utter a sound. The young man jerked his head, peering to Renee's right, and she turned that way, too. Whatever the noise was, at least they could both hear it. It grew louder, rising in pitch to a shrill whine, as painful as a rock band's amp feedback. Then there was a loud pop.

Where there had been nothing, two men now stood. One was a thin, fox-faced guy with a thick mop of black hair. The other was a rangy, muscular blond.

Abruptly, Renee was no longer sitting in mist. She was being soaked by Floppy Hat's downpour. Her teeth chattering, she moved onto her hands and knees. The gray-green-gold smog had vanished completely. She was crouching on a narrow stone street or alley, midway between Floppy Hat and the two new arrivals.

The three men gaped at her. Floppy Hat gestured wildly to the others and shouted. Renee couldn't understand a single word.

"No! Stay there, Prince Chayo!" That was Fox Face, waving urgently at the man in the hat and cloak. The big blond divided his attention between them; his wrestler's mug was remarkably vacant, devoid even of curiosity. Fox Face started to speak again, then clutched his temples. A strangled shriek burst from his mouth, and he pitched his length onto the puddle-filled street, writhing in pain. Blondie knelt beside him, his empty expression suddenly contorted with concern.

Reflexively, Renee got to her feet and moved toward them. Out of the corner of her eye, she saw Floppy Hat doing the same. Their Good Samaritan impulses were cut short by Fox Face. He roared at them, motioning them back. Puzzled, they watched Blondie help the smaller man to his feet.

Fox Face sagged weakly against his companion and moaned, "They found us. Already! So much for arriving in an isolated area to forestall detection. I warned HQ about these damned porous networks." Panting in agony, he fumbled at his shirt. It took Renee a few seconds to figure out what he was doing—tearing a strip off his shirttail. All the while, Blondie, who still hadn't said anything, propped him up. Fox Face wiped the rag across a twinkling pendant he wore, muttering, "Transfer . . . essence . . . away. Tae!"

Blondie, continuing to support the other man, seized the rag in his free hand, wadded it into a ball, and hurled it a startling distance off into the gray stone scenery. It had hardly traveled out of sight in the rain when a burst of blue-white incandescence exploded from that spot.

Renee flinched, flinging her hands protectively over her head. Nothing happened. No follow-up explosions. No being pelted by shrapnel—or even by rag fragments. Apprehensively, she lowered her arms and peered around. Fox Face was no longer in pain, and he was glaring at her, making her feel naked. Then Renee sensed that wasn't solely an emotional reaction. Her blouse and skirt had undergone a sea change; they seemed to be made out of moth-eaten fishnet. She wasn't totally into a "sky clad" morality, and she fervently hoped her clothes weren't quite as transparent as she suspected they now were.

By now, Fox Face's mood was approaching outrage. Renee adopted an innocent pose, trying to look apologetic. The man acted as though she were responsible for his pain, though she couldn't imagine why.

"Tae."

At that command, the big blond advanced on her. Renee backpedaled. Tricky going. The pavement was rain-slick, and among other things, she was now barefoot. She'd barely congratulated herself on avoiding a nasty fall when she saw that she'd been maneuvered into a cul-de-sac. Squeaking, she tried in vain to crawl inside the stones.

Floppy Hat was arguing with Fox Face. She still couldn't understand anything the former was saying. The skinnier man at first ignored the protest, then growled, "Oh, all right. All *right*! Tae!"

The blond—obviously "Tae"—froze, looming over

Renee. He was a hawk-nosed giant whose hair appeared to have been cut with a butcher knife, giving him a boyish, ragged fringe. His mouth was froggish, wide and thin-lipped, and presently split in a grin, perhaps one of sadistic anticipation. A pendant, a twin to Fox Face's, swung against Tae's dark, belted tunic. The jewel inside the metal cage glowed with a green fire. The only thing encouraging about the crazy situation was Tae's stare. He had lovely big blue eyes, bright with humor. Was that humor benign or vicious? As if in answer, his grin broadened, and he put two long fingers against her lips.

No talking? No screaming? Renee received a powerful impression that he had replied, "Yes." But he hadn't spoken.

Well, what did it matter, anyway? She was lying on the freeway, delirious. Inevitably, another driver would run over her and this wild dream would end in an excruciating flash. So why not go with the flow while it lasted? She might even get to know Prince Chayo before reality finally intruded. There'd be time, soon enough, to wake up in an ambulance or emergency room, having needles stuck into her and medical staffers discussing frightening possibilities over her semiconscious form.

Tae removed his fingers from her lips and grabbed her wrist in one of his paws. The men closed ranks, running, and Renee was towed along with them. Not roughly, but firmly, and at considerable speed. Cold rain plastered what was left of her clothes to her skin. She thought wryly that if she had a ten-rated bod, about now she could win a wet T-shirt contest.

Not that these guys would give me a glance if I did, she thought. They're in too much of a hurry. Are we going to a fire? I hope so. I'm cold.

She quickly became grateful she'd been enrolled in self-defense classes for months and was Outreach's top base runner in the city softball league; otherwise, she'd never have been able to keep up with the pace the men were setting. Once, when she stepped on a pebble, all of them stumbled to a temporary halt while she howled and clutched her instep. "Quiet!" Fox Face ordered in a loud stage whisper. Then they resumed their flight, Renee hobbling and hopping, being towed by the big blond man.

Why the hell was she putting up with this nonsense? It was turning out to be a lousy dream, and after such an interesting beginning, too. About now, being run over on the expressway would be an improvement. That, at least, would guarantee her a ride in a nice, warm, dry ambulance.

But if it was a dream, it was awfully damned logical in some respects. For one, she was trying to keep up because she didn't want to stay where she was—with the threat of more mysterious explosions.

Chayo was leading the way. His floppy hat and cloak afforded him some protection from the rain—the other three now resembled drowned rats.

Are these damned walls going to go on forever? she wondered.

Maybe. But the foursome didn't. Chayo came to a stop in another cul-de-sac and opened a door. Fox Face moved forward. Chayo shoved him back and bowed to Renee, inviting her to go first. She wasn't sure she wanted that honor. It meant walking further into the unknown, and was patronizing, to boot. SOS's charter included lots of caveats against tolerating patristic courtesies—those demeaning pats on the head designed to placate women while actually keeping them "in their places" when it came to equal job opportunities and full social status.

Everything hung fire as she dithered. They were a quartet of dripping statues. Fox Face studied Renee calculatingly, then seized the lead, hurrying on inside. Renee was relieved that he'd broken the impasse—and paradoxically irked with herself for being so relieved.

The heavy door was made of intricately carved wood with brass hinges, and the panels were wet, of course, from all the rain. The entire thing was very, very solid. Renee patted it in passing. It was a delightful change from all of that crummy stone.

Beyond was a room reeking of the Middle Ages. Dark, oaken furniture, tapestries, and a gleaming, broadplanked bare floor. Correction, *pseudo* Middle Ages, Renee decided after a second look. The tapestry patterns were art deco. So were the carvings decorating the chairs and tables. They looked brand new, designed by a computer, not by cottage-industry craftsmen in a castle. Contrasting with the fake aura of past ages, a golden orb hovered in the room's center with no visible means of support. The object radiated light and warmth, and Renee was drawn toward it as if by a magnet. Reacting to its heat, what was left of her clothes steamed and her hair began to stink. She marveled, wondering what such a futuristic gadget was doing amid the quaint decor. What was *she* doing there, for that matter?

Fox Face shook himself like a wet dog and stuffed his shirttail back into his pants. He was a flashy dresser and had good taste, even if he also had a foul temper. His clothes were form-fitting, made of an iridescent red-and-black fabric.

Prince Chayo had gone to a blank spot on the wall and punched some invisible buttons. Instantly, a TV-size area lit up and the image of a beautiful brunette appeared. She and Chayo conversed for a few moments in a language incomprehensible to Renee, then the screen cleared and the wall returned. Chayo nodded, his expression bemused. The entire exchange had seemed to be a check-in with his answering service.

Now that there was adequate light, Renee could examine her unasked-for companions. Despite her first impressions, she now realized they weren't quite human—or certainly weren't from any racial or ethnic stock she'd ever encountered. Chayo's skin color was that of melted butterscotch ice cream. And his hands had only four fingers, lacking pinkies. Fox Face's complexion was so pale it was translucent, far beyond lacking a tan; but he had the normal complement of fingers. Tae was closer to the standards Renee was familiar with, except for his eyes, which were abnormally large and a startling, glittering bright blue.

Who *were* these three weirdos?

His voice icy with sarcasm, Fox Face said, "Is it all right *now*, Prince, if I—"

Chayo didn't let him finish. He lit into the skinny man, verbally chewing him out with a stream of gibberish. Tae waited mutely. He'd let go of Renee's hand as soon as they'd entered the room. Now he stood motionless, a slowly growing puddle accumulating under his enormous boots.

"All right. All *right*!" Fox Face exclaimed, sighing in resignation. "But I don't like it. Pushing the odds, and at a time when that's extremely dangerous." Chayo flipped back the hem of his cloak, tossed aside his floppy hat, and shook rain off his baggy jumpsuit. He folded his arms across his chest, determined to outlast his opponent. Fox Face assumed a braced-for-action pose. "*Very* risky, especially after what's happened," he muttered. "If they detect us again . . ."

Then he went rigid, staring into nothing. A long pause. And another feedback whine and pop.

Now Fox Face had *two* pendants. As his eyes refocused, he cringed, glancing all about warily. After a few minutes, when it was plain nothing further was going to occur, he straightened and came toward Renee. The second pendant, a mate to the ones he and Tae wore, dangled from his beringed fingers.

The pendant's jewel was fascinating. Renee compared it to the miniature tesseract model in the campus's math building. The little stone inside the metal wires positively seethed with shifting hues: gray, green, and gold.

Fox Face gestured for her to put it on. She considered that option too long for his patience, and he forced it over her head. The chain caught in her hair, and she yelped.

"Must you be so brutal, Martil?" Prince Chayo demanded.

She understood him! And now that he wasn't spouting all that gobbledygook, Renee discovered that he had a sexy voice to go with his cute face. He hadn't spoken English, though. In fact, his speech patterns really hadn't altered. Yet he suddenly had become comprehensible. The effect was that of being handed headphones in a language class or the UN, or of watching an expertly dubbed foreign film. She looked down at the pendant, the only new element in the affair, and touched it tentatively.

"I—I am sorry." Fox Face—Martil—was regarding her. He *did* look apologetic for pulling her hair. Then he shifted back to business. "Now you can understand Chayo as well as me, and he can understand you, I might add. You *do* understand?"

As she nodded, Prince Chayo took her elbow, steering

her closer to the warmth-giving golden orb. "Esteemed Lady, please avail yourself of the comfort of my Lith. We sincerely regret any distress we may have caused you . . ."

Martil cut off the niceties just as Renee was beginning to enjoy them. "Not now. We have more important matters to attend to first." His mop of black hair straggled over his forehead and around his ears, framing the intensity of his hazel eyes. "Lady Whoever, I will make this as clear as I can. Tae is going to contact your thoughts. We are going to learn who you are, what you are doing here, and why you almost killed us a short time ago."

That big, smiling hulk named Tae moved toward her, one paw reaching for Renee's head.

chapter
2

SHE parried, knocking his arm aside, bracing herself. "Just hold it right there, or I'll put a serious crimp in your sex life!" Renee wasn't sure she could actually deliver a kick hard enough to disable the blond, even though her self-defense skills were fairly tightly honed, and she'd been forced to use them a couple of times in the past to get out of sticky situations. Neither of those guys had been the size of Tae, however, or had looked nearly as tough. "You have a lot of nerve—blaming *me* for what happened," she yelled, working to sound fierce. "I've already had a hard day. I was driving along, minding my own business, when you bozos kidnapped me and yanked me here—wherever this is. You probably wrecked my car, doing that. You got me soaking wet, stole my clothes, bruised my foot, and pulled my hair. I'm the one who's got explanations coming, not you!" she finished, glowering up what she hoped was a threatening storm.

Tae's fingers were arrested in that reaching-out pose, and his grin was widening, which Renee hadn't thought possible. Still, her threat had worked; he wasn't making any further moves toward her.

"The Esteemed Lady is correct," Chayo said, looking worried.

Martil grimaced. "You are obliged to say so, of course,

14

from your cultural point of view. Oh, very well. I will rephrase.'' He bowed mockingly to Renee. "There is a problem in communications here. It can be resolved if Tae serves as a medium of interchange. He will not infringe upon your privacy without your permission. He will merely make it possible for the Ka-Eens to operate at full translational efficiency. There are terminologies they will not be able to render well, since they are non-anthropomorphic.''

Renee gulped and limited herself to one query. "Ka-Eens?''

"The pendants. They are Ka-Een entities. Yours is a loan, as it were, though apparently you have no need of one for . . . ah! No matter. More of that later. Understand that while the Ka-Een has tremendous powers, it also has its shortcomings. Permit Tae to bypass one of those. I promise you will not be harmed.''

Had she read too many of the wrong kind of novels? They must have rotted her brain! How else to explain this screwy dream? But . . . it was going on far too long for a dream, and it didn't *feel* like a dream. Her emotions were a jumble of astonishment, fear, and curiosity.

"Telepathy, huh? Well, okay. Go on.'' She closed her eyes as Tae's fingers touched her forehead. There was no shock or pain. Not even the alleged esper tactic of someone rummaging through her head. Disappointing. She opened her eyes. Martil was smirking at her. Chayo seemed faintly embarrassed.

"Convinced?'' Martil asked scornfully. "May we begin? Your name might be the appropriate first courtesy, since I gather that you've already learned ours.''

"Renee Amos.''

"This will go much faster if Tae guides your tongue. Don't try to speak for yourself. Simply begin thinking about what was happening shortly before you . . . joined us. Omit *nothing*.''

With effort, she attempted to re-create the moment on the expressway when it all had come unraveled. She even reproduced her mental ramblings. Words tumbled out, without any conscious work on her part. Odd phrases she wouldn't have used ordinarily—as if these circumstances were ordinary. "Expressway'' became "vehicular path.''

"Car" became a complicated description starting with "four-wheeled, internal-combustion-powered engine . . ." A *few* terms sounded like her. For one, "cultural minority" to pinpoint a woman's status in the U.S. in the late twentieth century. Feeling as though she were interrupting herself, she protested, "You're changing some stuff."

"No. Tae is converting them for our benefit. That is necessary, Renee Amos." Martil's tone had softened a bit. "Your normal phraseology will be meaningless to us unless the Ka-Een's translations are interpreted by Tae. Continue."

Renee did so, or rather Renee-Tae did. She suppressed the flood of questions she wanted to ask, because those tended to interfere with the flow of words. When that occurred, Chayo and Martil seemed annoyed at having the thread of her account broken even for a second.

It all sounded so . . . uninspired. Her growing up on the edge of the city. The humdrum lives her parents and she had led, and her predictable grief at their deaths. Scrimping through university on her bare-bones scholarship and making up the difference as best she could with hamburger-flipping night jobs. Lucking into a grad assistantship while she tried to find a more permanent position, without success. Seriously considering going back into study and switching her major to get a degree in clinical counseling or a similar set of credentials. With those, maybe she could move up to an *important* slot with Social Outreach Sisterhood or another service organization, and really contribute to the world. Until she did, she was going to remain a tiny, insignificant cog in a massive, slow-moving instrument for change . . .

And so on.

When she spoke through Tae, Chayo and Martil had noticeably different reactions. Prince Chayo was utterly bewildered by what she was saying. Martil nodded smugly, and once he murmured, "How quaint. How typical of that level of a patriarchal humanoid culture."

Finally, it was all there. Her little nothing of a life, spread out for dissection. She'd brought herself and events up to date, including her fierce resentment at being yanked out of her own milieu, ordered around, dragged along unwillingly and thoroughly scared into the bargain. The words stopped, but Tae didn't remove his fingers from her forehead.

Martil sat down in one of the oak chairs, sprawling there. "Oh, they will rejoice, back at HQ, over this exhibition of the unforeseen range and strength of the Ka-Een. Indeed. 'A minor inconvenience,' as they will call you, Renee Amos."

"But what has happened?" Chayo wanted to know. Hadn't he been listening? "She should not have come here. Only you two were to arrive. The Esteemed Lady Renamos deserves both apology and full explanation of how this outrage has occurred. Most rudely taken from her sphere, and without her permission—"

"I am aware of that, Prince." Martil rubbed tiredly at a mole on his chin. Renee smothered a maternal urge to slap his hand and tell him to quit that. He went on. "In terms you and she can comprehend—she was caught in the Ka-Eens' transference line. She made this journey completely unknown to Tae and me, and definitely unplanned by us. Riding our coattails, as it were. Or, rather, our lead beam, since she preceded us. Presumably unique conditions existed on her world at precisely the right—or the wrong—time. Those allowed her to become trapped in the Ka-Eens' essence at the moment of transposition. It is not supposed to be possible. To the contrary. You are fortunate to be alive, Renee Amos. I do not know how you accomplished that without a Ka-Een controlling your essence."

"This?" She touched the pendant she wore. "I thought it was a translator gizmo."

Martil's eyes sparkled appreciatively. "It is that as well. Ka-Eens are most versatile. But a Ka-Een also enables the one it possesses to travel across great distances."

It made a kind of wacky sense, if she granted this was real and not merely a dream induced by shock and blood loss. She'd know better than to tell any of this to Evy or Susan or the others, however, once she got back to the SOS offices tomorrow morning—or whenever. Babbling this sort of stuff could get her classified with the loonies. Worse, it'd make Evy laugh at her.

"Well, then?" Renee asked.

Martil looked confused. That surprised her. Wasn't he Mister Know-All-the-Answers? It seemed peculiar that he hadn't already thought of the obvious solution.

"Look, whatever you've got going here—and I hope you know now that *I* didn't try to take the top of your head off, back there in that stone alley—I don't need to be mixed up in it any longer. Put me back to where the Ka-Een picked me up. I won't even complain if my car's wrecked. You'd better pray, though, that it didn't run into anyone else after you snatched me from under the steering wheel . . ."

For the first time, Tae's idiotic grin vanished. Briefly, his fingers broke contact with her brow. When he touched her again, he was trembling. His broad chest, visible through the V neck of his tunic, rose and fell rapidly.

As for Martil, his expression was a study in chagrin.

Renee didn't like seeing either reaction.

"It is reasonable, Martil," Chayo said. "You must agree. The Esteemed Lady Renamos is most patently an innocent bystander."

"Innocent, yes," Martil conceded. "Nevertheless, her inadvertent hitchhiking in the Ka-Een transference *did*, indirectly, cause my pain, and nearly got all of us killed. That unexpected leak in the Ka-Eens' essence beam made it possible for the local Gevari rebels to detect our arrival point. It defeated your best efforts to avoid that very problem by selecting isolated and inconspicuous entry coordinates. Let us hope the Gevari were deceived by our ruse and think we're dead."

"Oh. You faked them out with that exploding rag?" Renee asked.

Martil nodded, smiling weakly. "However, you are no longer a bystander, Renee Amos. Because it is impossible for us to return you to your own world."

Something in his gaze made the queasiness in Renee's gut turn to an icy lump. "You *have* to!" she cried. "I have work to do. My ongoing cases with abused children and counseling battered women . . ." Martil continued to shake his head, looking distraught. Renee's outrage became shivering dread. She pleaded. "Just—just send me back. Turn the Ka-Eens around. Twiddle their dials. Tell them to drop me off on their way home . . .''

"Ka-Eens are not vehicles. And you are dealing in matters far larger than you have yet grasped. Where, exactly, would they 'drop' you, for example?''

Startled out of her terror, she admitted he had a point. Where *would* she land? On top of Everest? The bottom of the Atlantic?

"W-well, just . . . on Earth. Preferably on dry land, at sea level. I'll take it from there. It'd be nice if they park me someplace that's close to . . .''

Chayo was gaping at her. He said in a pained tone, "Esteemed Lady, do not taunt us. Please give them the name of your sphere.''

"Her word *is* 'Earth,' Prince,'' Martil said sharply. "Just as yours is, and mine, and Tae's. She knows it by no other name. In her dialect, the sounds would be distinctive. But its meaning is the same in every humanoid language.'' He stopped scolding the younger man and returned his attention to Renee. "Have you a study of the universe in your knowledge?''

"Y-yes. I've always been interested in astronomy, and I've read a lot of books that . . .''

"Good. Tae.''

She heard herself saying, "My solar system contains one sun and nine known planets and numerous planetoids. My world possesses one large, natural satellite. There are several terrene planets and several gas giants circled by ice-crystal ring formations. Familiar stellar arrangements visible from my system are designated as The Big Dipper, Orion, Leo, Scorpion . . .'' Martil groaned, and Renee-Tae finished lamely, "I have little further useful information in this regard and am unable to furnish adequate astronomical coordinates of my solar system's relationship to other systems classified by your culture or Chayo's.''

For a long while, Martil slumped, shaking his head dejectedly. When he looked up, he dodged Renee's gaze. "It is impossible,'' he said.

"Put me back. Please!''

"Impossible,'' Martil repeated. "We moved, from our point of departure to this, Chayo's world, a distance incalculable, perhaps inconceivable by you. Somewhere along that route, you joined us, without warning, and without the help of a Ka-Een. I still cannot fully absorb *that*. Along that route are many, many solar systems. And among thousands of planets is the one you call your 'Earth.' There are also literally thousands of others there which would not support humanoid life for a fraction of a second. The Ka-Een have no way of determining when you, as it were, 'came aboard.' From their viewpoint, you simply winked into existence. They cannot return you to your home because they do not know where it is. If they attempted to retrace the pattern, the odds are overwhelming they would jump wrong, and you would arrive on a world not your own—entering an environment instantly fatal to you.''

He spoke slowly and carefully. Renee guessed that Tae's contact made the words even more potent. They seemed to strike her like missiles.

Until now, she had assumed this experience—assuming it was real—would be brief. It would end, like a quickie vacation, when Martil pushed some fancy buttons on the Ka-Een pendant and reversed things. Apparently, that wasn't the case. Not at all.

More and more, with a sick, sinking feeling, she was accepting that the situation wasn't a dream. There had been no time telescoping, no blurred scene shifts, none of the regular aspects of a sleeping fantasy. This was going on far too long, far too vividly, and in a straightforward, steady sequence.

And if this wasn't a dream, she was trapped. Utterly and irretrievably trapped.

No way out. No way back home to friends and co-workers and the only world she had ever known.

Renee felt as if she were riding in an out-of-control elevator car, its cable severed, as it plunged from the top of the World Trade Center. She swallowed hard, fighting an internal tidal wave of tears, and lost.

This couldn't be happening! She was blubbering. She, the clinic's toughest probationer, the former tomboy, proud of her resilience and her ability to bear up under the onslaught of the clients' relayed pain.

Their pain. Never before had she had to cope with an avalanche of personal terror like this!

She swayed, dizzy and nauseated, and Tae's fingers jerked away from her forehead. Martil and Chayo grabbed a furry blanket off a bench and wrapped the coverlet around her, gently leading her to a corner of the room and easing her into a comfortable chair. For a time, the men hovered, solicitous, fetching Renee a tumblerful of water, putting her feet up on another chair to counteract shock. She didn't respond, too lost in that awful funk, and eventually they withdrew, their manner awkward. Plainly, Tae, Martil, and Chayo were concerned, but uncertain what more they could do to help her.

Dimly, watching the scene from a seeming distance, Renee acknowledged that she knew their feeling. Every day, men, women, and kids who had suffered devastating emotional and physical blows sought help at SOS's clinic. Sometimes, medical treatment and tender loving care weren't enough. The victims had to be left alone to weep and sort through their agony. All compassionate onlookers could do in such cases was be there for those people when they were ready to rejoin the wider world.

I'm not going to participate in that process any more, she thought. It's gone. No, I am. I'm light-years away from the clinic. Stranded here. I'll never see Evy or my other friends again. Maybe they'll wonder what happened to me. Maybe I'll even get written up in the sensation rags and occult books: "The Woman Who Disappeared on the Freeway."

But eventually, people would begin to forget her. Her life up till the moment she'd been kidnapped out of her car had been one of massive insignificance. No major contributions to Earth's cosmic scheme of things. Looking at it that way, she wouldn't really be missed. Another probationer would replace her at the clinic and on the Sisterhood's staff. Her car would be towed away for junk. When she didn't return, her landlady would have Renee's small batch of furniture and books hauled into storage in the apartment's basement and lease the rooms to a new renter.

Gone. As if she had been erased.

Martil was right. She couldn't go back. And she knew,

now, she wasn't lying on the expressway, delirious with shock.

Was there any other possible explanation for all of this? Well, maybe she was dead. A chilling idea, that.

Okay. If I'm dead, where's the so-called "blinding white light," "the tunnel to the afterlife," and all the dead relatives and friends awaiting me on the "other side"?

The sole light was Prince Chayo's magically glowing Lith. The only tunnel she'd gone through had been those damned gray stone walls, and a hell of a lot of rain. The voices "from beyond death's door" weren't; they were those of Martil and Chayo, right here in this very present-worldly room with her.

Besides, her throat hurt and her eyes stung from all that bawling. And her instep throbbed from where she'd stepped on the pebble. Pain? Not even the lurid, sensationalistic rags mentioned pain in their breathless reports of what it was like to be dead—and miraculously return to life.

"It could not have been prepared for, Prince," Martil was saying, "though I do feel compelled to offer my apologies. You took such great care to elude detection. It seems a pity this has thrown your plans into confusion."

Chayo nodded absently. "As you have stated, it could not be helped. Your quick actions made the attackers think you are slain. Given that, maybe we can continue successfully. There *must* be an end to this crisis. Arbiters, your presence is crucial. But—" He looked anxiously at Renee. "—what will this do to your mission?"

Martil, too, turned to stare at her. Tae was already gazing in her direction, as he had been all along. Renee got to her feet, still clutching the furry blanket, and shuffled toward the men. She still felt somewhat rocky, but at least she was no longer blubbering.

"I don't know," Martil said unhappily, shaking his black mop. "I've received a faint suggestion from the Ka-Eens that she might be incorporated into the team. An apprentice. But that can't be. She has no training. No advance preparation regarding your species' customs and the problems we're facing . . ."

"It would be wonderful if she joined you!" Chayo exclaimed. "My royal mother was not pleased that the Arbiters were sending two males. The addition of my Lady Renamos . . ."

"Out of the question!" Martil snapped. He rubbed at his temples, and the crease between his eyebrows deepened as Prince Chayo went on arguing in favor of Renee's joining the team.

What team? Nobody had asked her opinion or filled her in, and she was getting damned irked about that. The nerve! Discussing her future like she was a lab animal or something, as if she weren't even in the room!

"You must accept the Esteemed Lady Renamos," Chayo insisted. By now she was getting used to the way he slurred her name, making it into "Renamos." Was he doing it, or were the Ka-Een pendants using translational shorthand? "It is fair. And if you do not, the Gevari may use her presence as an excuse to misunderstand . . ."

There was an earsplitting roar, the Lith globe flickered, and a section of the ceiling caved in with a dusty *crunch*.

Renee quailed and once more flung her hands over her head, letting the furry blanket fall where it might. When she dared to peep between her fingers, she saw she was surrounded by male bodies. They, too, were crouching and covering their heads. Martil was the first among them to regain his voice. "Oh, they haven't misunderstood and their detection methods are working beautifully! How did they find us again so quickly?"

"Watch out!" Chayo shouted. "Resonance! The Lith will react! Turn your backs!" He shoved Renee against the wall and shielded her with his own body.

There was a sharp cracking noise, and glassy shards began ricocheting around the room. Illumination dimmed to a twilight glow supplied by a few gleaming panels above the tapestries.

Then a whining screech made Renee wince. Oh, no! Not another of those incoming feedback howls! Those were followed by explosions. And *this* time Tae couldn't throw a fake-out rag away into the great outdoors.

"I hope you have an escape hatch in here!" Martil yelled, somehow making himself heard above the din.

Surely "escape hatch" wasn't what he said, but that was the way Renee's Ka-Een interpreted the phrase; she was getting used to that instant-conversion-into-familiar-terms effect.

Chayo quit trying to push her through the wall and squirmed to one side. He ducked caroming debris, groping at a panel. Renee sensed he was seeking that "escape hatch." She yearned to help him, but she didn't know what the thing looked like. As the prince prodded a particular spot, a narrow door opened.

A secret passage! Just like in a horror movie!

Well, isn't that what this is? she thought. A crazy, futuristic horror movie. And I'm caught in the middle of it. A woman could get killed this way.

At Chayo's urging, she, Martil, and Tae scrambled through the opening. The prince was the last to leave. Beyond the door, there was a tunnel lit by an eerie radiance. Renee glanced back and saw Chayo tugging at a handle on the inner side of the door.

Suddenly, a muscular arm seized her about the waist. She was hoisted off the ground, tucked under Tae's arm like a bag of dirty laundry. The blond was running, not even breathing hard, loping down a ramp.

Renee's ribs ached where she was being jounced on the big man's hipbone. She struggled to get loose, with no success whatsoever. Tae only slowed his pace a trifle to avoid running over Martil, who was leading the exodus.

A tremendous, echoing *boom* rang along the tunnel. Renee's ears closed up shop for a few seconds. The sound was so loud it hurt, vibrating her skull and breastbone. She grabbed at her aching head, and was immediately thrown off balance, tipping face downward in the crook of Tae's arm. Hastily, she put out her hands, skipping her fingertips on the floor until she could push herself back into a more stable position.

Eventually, the tunnel began to level out. Tae powered down to a trot, then to a walk, then halted and set her back on her feet. She tugged what remained of her skirt and blouse into some semblance of decency. "I can walk, you know," she said aggrievedly. "Even run, when the occasion warrants."

"Not fast enough," Martil said. "You're too short."

True, but did he have to be so blunt in pointing out her flaws? She'd wanted to grow up to be a statuesque Amazon, like Evy, but her genes hadn't cooperated. Was it her fault her ancestors had been people of average height or less?

"Which way now, Prince?"

In response to Martil's question, Chayo took Renee's elbow and steered her to the right. The tunnel connected with a cave there. Small, floating globes—baby Liths?—clustered against the ceiling, casting a harsh, mercury-vapor-style light over the underground scene. At several locations, flashing orange lamps marked other entrances to the cave. Renee turned and saw a similar flasher over the tunnel they'd just left. Was there an entire suburb of pseudo-medieval apartments like Chayo's, each one with a tunnel access to here? Whatever here was.

"Where are we?" she asked.

"In the lower level of Niand's transportation complex," Martil said, looking to Chayo for confirmation of his guess.

The prince nodded, his expression petulant. "They wrecked my quarters. Those Gevari! Those motherless . . ."

"I'm sure a man of your rank has numerous accommodations," the fox-faced man retorted. "We've already discussed the fact that this can be dangerous. Better a wrecked room than wrecked people."

Renee certainly agreed with *that*.

Martil felt gingerly at the crown of his head, and Tae peered at his scalp, frowning worriedly. "Oh, are you hurt?" Renee said, ashamed that she'd been so self-centered. "All that glass flying around back here . . . we'd better do some first aid."

Annoyed by the attention, Martil said impatiently, "It wasn't glass. And we haven't got time to waste on such minor matters. It isn't wise to hang around there."

No argument!

A large, egg-shaped thing zipped by a curve in the cave's wall and whispered to a stop a few yards away from the quartet. Renee gawked at the object. All she could think of was a pale blue hosiery container with a thyroid condition; the thing was bigger than her apartment's bathroom.

Chayo bowed to her, ushering her toward the "egg." It developed a purse-lipped bulge on the side facing her. Martil and Tae were hurrying toward the oversize whatsis, but Chayo insisted that this time "Esteemed Lady Renamos" should enter first. Without enthusiasm, she allowed herself to be hustled inside.

Once she was there, Prince Chayo invited her to sit, though she saw nothing to sit on. Martil yanked at her arm. Her middle ears jangling, Renee toppled, readying herself to break her fall. However, she didn't fall. Instead, the "egg" produced a cushiony seat. It blossomed beneath her, soft and balloony, almost obscenely comfortable. Other seats appeared to accommodate the men.

"Er . . . thank you," Renee said lamely. Who was she thanking? Chayo? The "egg"?

They were moving. There had been no start-up jolt, no sensation of acceleration. Just an instantaneous shift from standing still to frictionless velocity. From the outside, the "egg" had been opaque. From within, its walls were totally transparent. Renee watched a near-blur of underground scenery as the vehicle swept along invisible tracks. She caught glimpses of more tunnel exits marked by orange flashers, and people emerging from the ramps. Most of them were getting aboard other "eggs" and riding off to who knew where. Obviously, the cave was a sort of subway, equipped with lots of these egg-shaped private cars rather than trains.

Chayo noticed her stupefaction and misread it. "Do not be frightened, Lady Renamos."

"I'm not." Renee leaned back. The egg vehicle created extensions of the balloony chair cushions, cradling her head and shoulders. How convenient! She said, "At this stage of the game, I'm ready for damned near anything."

"Not quite," Martil warned her. "Prince, can your Gevari rebels trace us here?"

The prince studied his well-manicured nails—on his six fingers and his thumbs. "I do not see how they could. These accesses number in the thousands, and they are quite busy, as you see. Our matter-relay units, however, are much more easily interfered with.''

''Then we must remember not to use those.''

Chayo raised his head. His features were taut with rage. ''Martil, they struck at me. At *me*. I had accepted this incredible threat, in my thoughts, but I had not fully believed they would reach so high. At the queen's son! They would never have dared, ordinarily. Nor would I ever have been a target. I am of small importance,'' the prince said with self-contempt. ''They do so in order to destroy you, Arbiters. Are they mad? I knew they were vicious, but *this*! Can they not realize what is at stake?''

''You knew you were dealing with death when you volunteered to serve as your mother's intermediary to the Arbiters.'' Martil was the soul of fatalistic reason. He acted as though he were used to being shot at. ''Millions have died in this war of yours. And billions more may die, if we are not successful. Don't you understand that, even now?''

''It . . . the resisters' stance is almost beyond grasping.''

''Not to us,'' Martil said, sighing. ''It is difficult for humanoids at your level of development to comprehend fully the deaths of more than a few entities at a time. And those are generally the lives of those physically close to them. That is a gap in sensitivity we hope to correct, especially for your military leaders and your opponents' military leaders. We must. The alternative is too terrible to consider.''

Renee was galloping, mentally, to try to keep up with the conversation and fill in the blanks with speculations. A war. A *big* war. Prince Chayo's people and their enemies. It sounded like Chayo's mother was trying to get peace negotiations rolling, but hard-core elements of her society weren't about to stop the killing. All too familiar. Chayo referred to Martil and Tae as ''Arbiters.'' Ah, ha! Neutral imports, apparently. From somewhere offworld.

Far offworld, judging by Martil's explanation of why it was impossible for the Ka-Eens to return Renee to her home.

Remembering that grim reality, she was plunged again into depression. She had been a resister, too, resisting the truth of her situation. But the longer this experience went on, the more she gave in. No denying any of it. She was stuck. Thrown headlong into murderous political infighting among aliens and the visit of a pair of referees.

Tae had seated himself beside Martil and was picking lith fragments out of the smaller man's hair and scalp—like a huge blond ape grooming a dark one. Martil cooperated by cocking his head to one side so that Tae could work quicker. The fox-faced man stared intently at Renee and said, ''Before we can proceed with our mission, one critical problem must be settled: What are we going to do with you?''

chapter
3

A chill chased away Renee's depression. She countered her fear with a bluff. "What do you mean? You weirdos and your Ka-Eens kidnapped me, and you made it very clear that you're unable to put me back where you found me. That makes you responsible. If you think you're going to get rid of me by dumping me off somewhere like so much garbage, think again!" In the back of her mind, though, were images from TV news. Clumsy kidnappers and hostage-takers who in effect had done exactly that; burdened by innocent excess human baggage, they'd taken the easy way out and simply killed those unlucky enough to be swept up in their affairs.

Some of her apprehension must have shown in her eyes. Martil grinned reassuringly. "No, we have no plans to dump you, as you put it." He sobered and went on, "But you will be in danger no matter what is done. Do you understand?"

Renee nibbled her lip and nodded. "I'm a stranger in a strange land." She glanced at Prince Chayo and said, "If he's representative of the local humanoids, I'd stand out like a sore thumb anywhere I went on this planet. These Gevari rebels seem to have pegged me as part of your team already. If you dropped me off, even politely, even in someplace supposedly safe, I wouldn't have any guarantee that they wouldn't zero in on me. And without your know-how—and that trick of detecting incoming strikes with your headaches—I'd be a dead duck in no time.''

Martil's jaw dropped. It did Renee good to see that. She'd flabbergasted him, left him momentarily speechless. A *brief* moment. ''That's . . . excellent. Superb summation of the problem. I begin to grasp why you have this unprecedented affinity with the Ka-Een; such quick adaptation to alien details is amazing, particularly since you have no training.''

''Training. That's the real sticking point, isn't it?'' she said. Chayo's head swiveled comically as he listened to first one of them, then the other, struggling to follow the discussion. Renee nodded again. ''I'm a liability to you. This lump you didn't ask for, who can't contribute anything to your peace mission, and can't be parked somewhere on the sidelines until you wrap up your business.'' After a pause, she added, ''I'm grateful for the fact that you *don't* want to park me like that. I'd get eliminated fast, if you did.''

''Perhaps not. You have proved yourself remarkably resourceful, given the circumstances.'' She started to bask in the compliment, and Martil shot her down. ''Hardly an accomplished team member, however. Your naivete and noncomprehension of details present a most serious dilemma. What *are* we going to do with you?''

Tae had finished picking through Martil's hair. Now he reached across the ''egg''—no strain for someone of his size—and touched Renee's hands firmly. A froggy grin brightened his heavy face. Nothing was said, and he didn't put his fingers on her brow as he had earlier, yet Renee received a strong impression of encouragement. More than that—acceptance.

''I doubt it can work,'' Martil said, scowling. ''Too much for her to learn, too fast.''

The blond shifted his focus to his partner, his grin widening.

Martil's exasperation was an aura, filling the egg vehicle. ''After all the precautions we and the prince took, it . . . oh, all right. All right! I see no other course, either. But I'm not nearly as sanguine as you are. Go ahead.'' Tae hesitated, and the smaller man rolled his eyes, his exasperation reaching the boiling point. He heaved another heartfelt sigh and said, "Renamos, Tae wants to give you basic information regarding our mission here and this species and their crisis. It is a stressful procedure, but it will not harm you."

"More acting as interpreter for the Ka-Een?" Renee asked anxiously.

"A different operation."

Apparently, he wasn't going to tell her any more than that. Maybe he couldn't. She suspected he wasn't *Homo sapiens*, and Tae probably wasn't. Prince Chayo definitely wasn't. It might be impossible to supply all the data she needed to survive and fit in—or try to—by normal means. Renee steeled herself, squinching her eyes nearly shut, saying, "Okay. I don't like being so ignorant, and if this is the only way to jump, I guess I'll have to."

Tae shifted his grip from her hands to her head, and a tsunami picked her up, carrying her along at a breathtaking, terrifying speed.

Illusion. She hadn't moved. But she *seemed* to be hurtling along, being pelted painlessly, tumbled over and over. With great difficulty, she drew herself back, within her mind, examining the process. She wasn't being engulfed by water but information, and it was happening so rapidly it was impossible to get a grasp on any of it.

As abruptly as it had started, the contact ended. Renee sagged, feeling drained. She blinked, assessing. No pain. Not even a lingering trace of a headache, as she'd half expected there would be. Just the same, the sensations weren't pleasant. She rubbed her cheekbones and muttered, "I—I've been stuffed with computer tapes."

Yes! That was what it was like—watching Evy scroll SOS's stat files at a speed too fast to read, until the computer found the requested area, where it would finally slow and stop.

Except that the data buzzing inside Renee's head refused to slow down.

"Don't fight it," Martil advised. "You will absorb it gradually—hopefully in time for it to be useful in these circumstances. This is the best that can be done, on short notice."

"If you say so," Renee grumbled, unconvinced.

"Thank you, Martil, Tae," Prince Chayo said. "This eliminates a concern. Now it is feasible for Esteemed Lady Renamos to attend the interview with my mother." He turned to Renee and suddenly reddened. "But you should have reminded me of your needs, my Lady. This will never do. I should be severely chastised for being so remiss. Sector Fifteen," he ordered, and she felt a subtle shift in the direction the egg vehicle was taking. She wondered what had caused Chayo's embarrassment. Then he explained. "You must have fresh raiment before you are presented to the Most High and my sister, her Eminence."

Martil grunted unhappily. "I ought to protest, but she's already in too deep. You don't mind accompanying us to the interview with the queen?" he asked Renee.

"Why not?" she said, shrugging. "Sure. After all that's happened, what's an interview with the matriarch of the entire Niand culture?"

Now how had she known that Prince Chayo's mother held that rank? A vision of multiple solar systems—Niand's home world and widely scattered colony planets—danced in her brain. Bits and pieces of background, bubbling to the surface.

"You will absorb it gradually . . ."

Hey! This was a great way to master a course in a hurry! She could patent this and make a fortune—if Tae would rent himself out as an instant-learning device.

Except there was no one to sell such things to, here. Chayo and the Arbiters knew far more than she ever could. No doubt everyone on this planet, in this civilization did. She was likely to come off as a total dunce, even if she did succeed in absorbing the needed info. It was going to take much more than the basics to be useful to a team of peace negotiators, wasn't it?

She focused on another, comparatively minor topic, one of personal interest. "Since I'm going to get a new wardrobe, thanks to the prince, would you mind telling me what happened to my old one? Half of what I was wearing evaporated en route to the Ka-Eens' landing point."

"The landing point is the administrative center of the

Niand Federation,'' Martil said. ''But, to answer your question, Ka-Eens only transport selected organic materials. I presume you were wearing some nonorganics. Those would have been lost in transit.''

''Oh.'' Plastics, and all that other synthetic stuff. Renee eyed Martil's and Tae's clothes curiously. The materials didn't look organic, particularly not Martil's glittery shirt, but obviously they must be, or they'd be half-naked, too, as she was. At least now she knew why she was sitting in this ''egg'' barefoot and wearing what amounted to skirt- and blouse-shaped doilies.

Martil rubbed absently at his scalp. She felt obliged to inquire, ''How's your head? Were you cut much?''

''Only a little,'' he said. ''I can be repaired while Chayo's people are garbing you properly to meet the queen.''

Queen. And Chayo was a prince. She'd heard the terms several times now, but still was having difficulty connecting them to real people. Princes were supposed to be figures in Hollywood productions. Cardboard actors in white uniforms and gold braid, not cute men with butterscotchy complexions wearing floppy hats, baggy jumpsuits, and capes.

The ''egg'' stopped with no deceleration that she could detect. All at once, they had arrived. The reappearing oval door looked even less appetizing from the inside looking out. Chayo led the way and turned to take Renee's hand. But Martil exited ahead of her, earning a glower from Chayo. As Renee stepped over the vehicle's threshold, she wondered if all the spongy seats disappeared when the riders left them. She refused to look back and find out if they did. Naive, was she? Well, she'd do her best to avoid acting like she'd just dropped out of a tree.

Though, in a sense, I sort of did, didn't I? she thought.

Chayo took her elbow, guiding her to an orange-lit archway and up a ramp. Martil and Tae tagged along in their wake. Renee heard their wet boots squishing. At the top of the ramp, a perfectly ordinary-looking door opened automatically. The thing was a positive relief after encounters with Liths and traveling eggs.

There were guards posted in the corridors beyond.

Some, like Chayo, had butterscotch-colored complexions. Others were darker, with shiny skins resembling burnt caramel.

Why do I keep thinking of food-oriented colors? she wondered. Because I'm hungry, that's why. About now, I should be sitting down to a late supper, not trotting around in the bowels of a palace.

This was a palace, she recognized with a start. She was getting another dribble of info from Tae's instant-education process. A *big* palace. They walked along corridors for minutes, took an open-sided elevator up to a higher level, and walked some more. They rode an airport-style moving platform for a while, got off, walked further, rode another elevator. Renee couldn't keep track of all the twists and turns and she had no idea where they were in relationship to the place where they'd climbed out of the "egg," let alone how far they were from Prince Chayo's wrecked apartment—or in what direction. She rather doubted Martil or Tae knew. Little wonder that the Arbiters had needed a native guide.

Then a disquieting thought struck her. What if the original attack, there in the street, and the destruction of Chayo's apartments were staged events? What if he was actually a traitor? He could be leading them into some sort of trap. But if he wanted to dispose of them, that could have been done earlier.

It didn't make sense.

Did she expect it to? Well, she'd sort of hoped things would start making sense. If they didn't, she was in even deeper trouble than she'd imagined.

Finally, they reached their destination, a suite staffed by a half-dozen matronly women. Their leader nodded to Chayo and muttered a ritual greeting. She didn't bow or otherwise kowtow to him, Renee noticed.

Chayo hadn't been shamming modesty when he'd said he was of small importance in the Niandian government. Technically, he wasn't. This was a sort of parliamentary matriarchy, a peculiar mix of antique, hereditary families and elected authorities. And the queen's son couldn't inherit, though a woman Chayo married might. There were further details, simmering in a mental pot just beneath the surface of Renee's conscious thoughts. More of Tae's cram course info. But she couldn't quite peg what *else* was different about Niandians, from her way of looking at a culture. Well, maybe it would come to her, in time.

"The Esteemed Lady Renamos was attacked by the Dolian renegades on her journey here," Chayo was telling the matrons. "She cannot be presented to my mother in such damaged clothes. Please attire her as befits her station."

"Of course! Oh, poor ravaged dear!" Renee smothered an urge to glance behind her for a suitably disheveled female matching that description. Then she eyed Chayo admiringly. What a liar!

The matrons' leader gestured offhandedly. "Prince, you will find clothes for my Lady's servants in the anteroom."

Servants? Martil and Tae? Oh, sure!

Chayo and the Arbiters retreated and walls materialized, seemingly out of nothing, isolating Renee with the Niandian matrons. She had no time to panic at being separated from the men. The women swarmed around her, solicitous, positively toadying. It was a startling experience, one that made her vaguely uncomfortable, being the recipient of such treatment. That simmering subliminal pot gave her another glimpse of Niand's rigid internal pecking order. Chayo's introduction had placed "Esteemed Lady Renamos" very high on that status ladder, and the palace wardrobe mistresses were reacting accordingly.

The women helped her undress, dumping the pitiful remnants of Renee's skirt and blouse into what she assumed was an incinerator chute. They ushered her into a luxurious "comfort station," a touch she appreciated greatly. Then there was a cubicle full of "instant shower"; it smelled wonderful, left her skin silky soft, and took the stink out of her rain-soaked hair and fluff dried it. Slowly, Renee began to relax, wallowing in this sybaritic experience. Now and then there was a faint twinge of guilt, but only a faint one. Evy would have sniffed at the routine, dismissing it as the trappings of sex objectivism. It felt marvelous, though, being fussed over like a movie star.

The oldest wardrobe mistress ran a small measuring

device around Renee's body and rattled off a stream of gibberish numbers. Those weren't *her* dimensions, she was sure. Not in base ten. But the Niandians had eight fingers, not ten, and that must have made a difference, centuries ago, when they were inventing their number system. Following orders, the subordinates scurried to select the clothes the boss lady decided on. Renee hoped they had her size in stock.

"Oh, my Lady's poor hair!" Poor hair! Thirty-five bucks for that set and comb-out. Not good enough. The lead matron began attaching wigs and falls to the Earthwoman's mane.

Wasn't this makeover and refitting taking rather long? By now, Martil was probably chewing the furniture with impatience. Renee had always been disdainful of clotheshorse women. The type who tried on fifteen outfits and primped endlessly while their dates and friends had to wait. That wasn't the Sisterhood's style, at all. They were *new* women: practical, businesslike, no behaving like a sitcom caricature of a bubbleheaded female whose main interest in life was marching to the fashion moguls' tune. Huh-uh!

Just the same . . .

The matrons helped her into a cleverly designed body stocking with convenient Velcro closures at strategic locations. Her hair was expertly styled. A dashiki top finished off the procedure. Then one part of a wall converted itself into a mirror, and the other walls disappeared as suddenly as they had appeared earlier. Martil's, Tae's, and Chayo's reflections flanked Renee's in the mirror. Tae was patting Martil's mop into place with a "there! that's that" air, so apparently they'd had time to do some first aid on the smaller man's scalp cuts. The chief wardrobe mistress sniffed at the men, annoyed that they, too, hadn't changed into "fresh raiment." By turning down the available services, they had cast a slur on this palace department's efficiency.

The matrons had certainly performed wonders in Renee's case. She was dressed in yellow, her makeup was lovely, and her hair had been brightened to auburn and enhanced with those falls and wiglets. These miracle workers had shaved ten pounds off a figure Renee considered dismayingly lumpy. And the V-neck dashiki did great things for her frontage. Well, that *was* her best feature, and when you got it, flaunt it. At this rate, Evy would read her out of the Sisterhood as a backslider.

No. Don't think about Evy. I'm not going back. Can't. Ever.

"Very good," Martil pronounced after surveying Renee. "Though it would be better if we were on our way to meet a patriarch, not a matriarch."

Chayo took her elbow and steered her out of the wardrobe suite and into a hallway. Renee discovered that the clothes "worked." They moved the way clothes ought to move. Brightening, she said, "I think I'll keep these."

Martil waved a hand, shushing her. They were twisting and turning through corridor after corridor. Secret passages? The back entrance to the queen's inner sanctum? This network of halls didn't match Niand's other futuristic aspects. Finally, after a lengthy walk, Chayo stopped at a well-guarded door and motioned for Renee to go ahead.

"If you don't mind, I'll pass on 'ladies first,' this time."

"Proceed," Martil snapped. "You're in this with us now, remember? Follow the local customs."

"If it wasn't for the honor of the thing . . ." Renee began, joking to hide her nervousness. "But what do I do? What do I say?"

"Smile, and stay close to Tae." The blond's huge hand planted itself in her back, propelling Renee through the open door. She had expected a Ruritanian boudoir. Instead there were Liths, utilitarian furnishings, just a few diaphanous draperies, and a wall lined with floor-to-ceiling electronic maps with winking lights.

All the room's occupants were female, and most of them wore the same dashiki-style clothes Renee had been dressed in. A bit of her nervousness eased when she saw that. One remarkably ugly woman appeared to be in charge of the inner sanctum's servant corps; she and they were fetching, carrying, and generally catering to the remaining two Niandians.

"Honored Mother . . ." The women who were the center of attention turned at Chayo's approach, and he knelt and kissed the hem of the elder's dashiki. Renee winced inwardly as the matriarch stroked Chayo's head absently, as she might have a pet's. There was something deeply unsettling about that scene. Ritual satisfied, Chayo rose and gave the younger woman a brotherly hug. She nodded condescendingly as he murmured, ''Did you get my message, Zia?''

''You may go, Beyeth,'' the matriarch ordered the ugly woman. The chief servant and her subordinates withdrew with ill grace, their curiosity radiating from them like perfume. Beyeth glared sternly at the Arbiters before she closed the outer door behind herself.

Niand's ruler and her daughter surveyed the offworlders narrowly. Renee returned the favor. Seeing the two women and Chayo together made their family relationship obvious. The matriarch was thinner than her adult children, and her complexion tended more toward a mellow ivory tone than Zia's golden, butterscotch-tinged skin or Chayo's somewhat darker version of the same hue, but all of their features came out of an identical gene pool—prominent cheekbones, turned-up noses, striking pale eyes. The matriarch's gaze was particularly piercing, but none of them was a slouch in the locked-gazes department. Zia reminded Renee of a silken tank. Ingenious makeup, and perhaps skillful cosmetic surgery, had honed and polished natural beauty to stunning near-perfection, but it didn't hide the steel beneath the princess's gorgeous facade. She looked a hell of a lot tougher than her brother did, in many ways. Hers was also a face Renee had seen earlier—on the answering-service TV in Chayo's wrecked apartment.

The matriarch's laser eyes bored intently at Martil and Tae for a long moment, then darted in Renee's direction, perturbing the Earthwoman.

Okay. Now what?

Tae's fingertips pressed lightly against Renee's back, and she bowed, though not so deep it could be called a kowtow. Enough, however, to make her hope that the chief dresser had pinned on those wigs and falls securely. The matriarch and Zia bowed slightly, acknowledging the newcomers' presence. ''Welcome, Lady, to you, and to your companions. We had prepared for but two Arbiters, and feared this delegation would not be to our liking,'' Niand's ruler said, speaking precisely, picking and choosing her words. "Yet . . . it is well.''

"You honor us, Most High, Eminence. It was solely to please your royal persons that the Arbiters so altered our representation and I was sent here.'' Renee blinked. Had *she* said that? No, Renee-Tae had.

"We are grateful that the Arbiters see fit to accommodate us in this way,'' the matriarch replied. "The message my son Chayo received told us of these . . . these male Arbiters.'' Her glance turned, for an instant, to Renee's companions, silently expressing distaste. Then the monarch went on, "It is—Chayo was informed that these males are known as Martil of the Bright Suns and Tae of—of the Green Union.'' She bit off those last two words, almost choking on them. Recovering, she asked, "How must we address you, Esteemed Lady? What is your title?''

Again, without consciously willing it, Renee-Tae spoke. "Most High, I am Renamos of the Sisterhood of the Nine Worlds.''

Given the stiff protocol in action here, Renee didn't dare swivel around and blurt out her annoyance at Tae— and punctuate that with a kick in the shins. So she hurled visual daggers at Martil. He didn't respond in the slightest, adding to her pique.

Then Zia was moving forward, approaching Renee. After a split second of oh-my-god apprehension, Renee realized that Tae wouldn't let her goof up. She held out her hands, taking Zia's, and the two young women brushed cheeks politely. It was a parody of celebrity guests on a talk show greeting one another, and no more sincere. Formality. The princess had to perform this particular one; Niandian culture insisted that the matriarch remain aloof from public physical contact. Only that hem-kissing ritual was permitted. Her daughter carried out any necessary kissy-face routines.

Up close, Chayo's sister seemed absolutely luscious. She made Renee feel like a cow, and she was relieved when the charade ended and Zia retreated a pace or two. "Which male is—'' Zia wrinkled her cute nose "—is of the Green Union?''

Martil gestured theatrically. "My companion is Tae of the Green Union." As soon as he'd said that, the matriarch and Zia lost all interest in him and stared at Tae with undisguised loathing. The room's figurative temperature plummeted. Renee longed to make a hasty getaway, but she couldn't; Tae was holding her in place.

So she heard Renee-Tae saying, "There must be truce, Most High, Eminence, or there can be no meaningful discussion."

Meaningful discussion. Oh, yeah! The diplomats' favorite mealymouthed phrase for "Knock it off, before we kill each other."

After a long, tense moment, the mood of hostility softened a bit. Zia murmured, "We must concede that his form is not overly offensive." She had a low-pitched, sexy voice to go with her gorgeous looks.

Renee wondered what in the hell the princess was talking about. But somehow she kept her mouth shut, or Tae did that for her. Her head was throbbing and her stomach aching. Lack of sleep and food was making her short-tempered. She had to watch it, or she might blurt out something tactless. Martil sensed that and took over the conversation. "We are pleased that you approve. The Arbiters so arranged Tae's appearance, the better to implement—"

"You may enter," the matriarch cut in, stomping on whatever else Martil had intended to say. The outer doors of the large room opened and a bunch of Niandians trooped in. Most were well-dressed middle-aged women. A few were men, a couple of them wearing what were obviously uniforms. The latter two, especially a hard-faced guy who looked like a local version of a Pentagon type, fumed visibly. The women bowed to the matriarch and her daughter; the men knelt and went through the ritual hem-kissing routine, adding a formal brush of the lips across the backs of the ruling females' hands. Even while that was going on, the matriarch was making introductions, a flood of alien names and titles. Renee nodded, trying to memorize designations and the faces that went with them. Apparently, the group was the matriarch's cabinet—her top ministers and generals. Two of the four generals, Renee noted, were men. So that much didn't change from one humanoid species to another. It seemed Niandian males were just as likely to be the war-game players here as they were among Earth peoples. Then another, bemusing thought struck her: Most of the matriarch's top rankers were women, which meant that the few men in her cabinet must be very good at what they did.

The cultural minority has to, in many cases, be even better at doing a job than the cultural majority, simply in order to reach a more or less equal status with their "superiors," Renee thought. The familiar patterns, thrown topsy-turvy: "He must be really good, to qualify for the matriarch's cabinet . . . !"

A lot of polite greetings had been traded absently, the ruler's cabinet officers going through the same knee-jerk initial responses to Tae's presence, then backing off verbally. But the hard-faced general didn't back down. "Treacherous Green Union monsters!" he exclaimed suddenly. The women cabinet members glowered at him, and Zia gasped in annoyance. "We were promised that an Arbiter peace mission would also be sent to the enemy to—"

"Control yourself," the matriarch interrupted him, her tone one she might have used toward a high-strung, likable teenager. "You always jump to conclusions, my dear Vunj. Calm down and explain yourself."

"Please, you must act with caution, Most High," Vunj begged. He punched at a panel on the wall with twinkling lights. Flanking walls lit up, dancing with insert star maps and rows of alien numbers and letters. The matriarch studied the display thoughtfully. "New attacks, launched less than three *iyas* ago. Our outposts besieged—"

"Yes, yes, I can see that," she said, again slicing rudely across his words.

He insisted on spitting out the rest of his accusations, earning an affronted glare from the matriarch and the women of her cabinet. "Betrayal by those slimy abominations, while your own son tries to traffic with one of the devils in an Arbiter's guise . . ."

"Do you want the slaughter to go on forever, Vunj?" Chayo demanded. In striking contrast to his usual deferential manner, he was downright belligerent toward the general.

"It is better than a shameful, cowardly—"

"Propaganda posturing, from a motherless—"

"Be still, both of you!" The quarrel choked off, though Chayo and General Vunj continued to clench their fists and scowl at one another. The matriarch turned to the Arbiters. "Your reply to our message assured us that you would seek a truce from the Green Union as well as from Niand. And yet they persist in these attacks and commit further atrocities upon our people. Is this to be the proof of your sincerity?"

"And is Niand blameless?" Renee-Tae countered. "Can you deny that your military forces have sometimes committed atrocities against the Green Union? Can you deny that even now certain units are preparing or actually conducting strikes deep into the Green Union's territories, despite your claims that you desire a truce?"

General Vunj spluttered, not convincing anyone. The guilty truth was in his eyes, and in the matriarch's and Zia's.

Vunj tried to divert the argument, aiming his hatred at Tae. "I plead with you, Most High, give that disguised shape-shifter to my intelligence people. We'll interrogate the monster and—"

The matriarch opened her mouth, but it was Martil who spoke, saying icily, "Tae is *not* a citizen of the Green Union." Stunned shock gripped the Niandians, both men and women. Plainly, tromping on their ruler's absolute command of a conversation simply was not done. Heedless, Martil went on, "You were promised a team of Arbiters representing both sides of this conflict. Species *types*, not members of your own interstellar communities. The team working, at this moment, in the Green Union, is composed of an Arbiter of their race and a humanoid in Green Union form, just as Tae has assumed *your* form. You have been favored by having two humanoid representatives on our team, in the persons of Renamos and myself. More will not be granted."

Renee-Tae pointed to the war map, a miniaturization of a battle raging across light-years. "It will take time to effect a truce. Attacks will not cease instantly. For a while, loyalties will be strained. We must not be rash with accusations of treason."

Chayo jumped into the debate. "I am no traitor, but there are traitors among us. Niandians! Mother, the Gevari destroyed my quarters only a short while ago. They knew the Arbiters were with me, and they tried to kill them!"

"What did you expect?" Vunj asked, sneering. "You volunteered to contact these mediators, to deliver us to our enemies—"

"Be still!" the matriarch exclaimed, and Zia and the general traded enigmatic glances. Renee couldn't read their expressions. Were they afraid? Contemptuous? The matriarch took Chayo's hand and said anxiously, "Were you hurt?"

"Not I, but the Arbiter Martil was, slightly . . ."

"Oh, all of this must stop!" The matriarch sank into a chair that appeared magically out of the floor. She no longer seemed the total autocrat but a sad, motherly woman mourning too much war and death. Her face could have come straight from a fighting-front journalist's photo album. "My children, my people, they must be spared any further grief or agony, before it is too late."

"Indeed," Martil said. "And it should begin with a conference of Niand's leaders. We were told such a conference would already be convened here in Niand's capital when we arrived."

"There have been . . . delays," Zia said, and Chayo regarded her with a puzzled frown.

"Yes, difficulties, many difficulties," the matriarch agreed. "Please be patient, Arbiters. The Gevari rebels refuse to break off their terrorist campaigns or end their subversions, and—"

"Then we may be helpless to aid you," Renee-Tae said.

"I beg of you!" Niand's monarch said, her voice shaking.

Martil dispensed entirely with the fiction that Renee was the group's spokesperson and said, "It is easier to begin a war than end one, as you are discovering. The situation has occurred often, among many species. When fanatics assume control, a war is likely to come to a horrible conclusion for both opponents in an interstellar conflict such as this. And innocent species, not at all involved in your disputes, will be at risk because of that. We Arbiters will not allow them to be slaughtered with impunity by you *or* the Green Union.''

General Vunj blustered, ''You threaten us, alien?''

''Only with the truth. It is because your war threatens to spread beyond the stellar territories where you and the Green Union are presently fighting that the Arbiters have agreed to step in. Our team was sent here to help negotiate a peace. You have realized your war is overwhelming your ability to handle it, else why did you send for us?'' That got Chayo a dirty look from the military men. Martil went on. ''You had to go to extreme effort to contact the Arbiters, but our welcome has been contradictory, to say the least. We are willing to assist you and your people, Most High. However, you must also help yourselves. Whether or not this particular Arbiter team remains on Niand or departs is immaterial. We are now watching your actions—and the Green Union's—very closely. We will be on guard to protect everyone. Use your ultimate weapons—and you know to which ones I refer—and we will use ours.''

chapter
4

Renee shivered. Martil had ditched his wry mannerisms. He had addressed the matriarch and her daughter and the cabinet with deadly seriousness. In a few words, he had painted them a picture of Armageddon on a scale that boggled the imagination—or that boggled Renee's imagination, at any rate. She wished his pronouncements would be interrupted by an inane TV commercial, but knew that wasn't going to happen. As he'd said, he was threatening the Niandians with reality. An entirely too grim reality.

"We—we have heard of your weapons, Arbiters," the matriarch said, her voice unsteady. "And we respect them. Yes. What do you wish of us?"

"The promised conference of your Federation's leaders, the assemblage necessary to achieve a truce."

"This will be done. Vunj?" The matriarch turned to the burly man and he nodded hastily. He was pale and considerably subdued. "We must consider how to arrange this," the matriarch went on, addressing her ministers. Like General Vunj, they'd been thoroughly scared by Martil's warning. As the Arbiters waited on the sidelines, the Niandians set about weighing methods. Every now and then, one of the group couldn't resist glancing at Tae and shuddering, and Vunj frequently interjected muttered comments about the Green Union's "slimy abominations'' into the verbal hash. That reaction continued to puzzle Renee. She knew their animosity wasn't reciprocated by Tae; the wavelengths she was getting via that big hand at her back were full of goodwill, not racial hatred.

Back and forth and up and down, the Niandians thrashed out possible tactics. How to circumvent the machinations of the pro-war Gevari rebels and gather that high-level assembly of Niand's widely scattered leaders.

To Renee's relief, she wasn't expected to contribute to the conversation. Nor was Martil. He had laid down the law; from the Arbiters' standpoint. Now it was up to the Niandians to produce.

The matriarch clearly ran the show. Her ministers offered opinions, often strong ones, and suggestions. But every decision was made by the queen, usually after she and her daughter had a brief, whispered conference. Throughout the process, Renee got the impression that her universe had been, if not stood on its head, tipped off balance. Body language, vocal clues, eye contact—a dozen subtle telltale nuances. The male participants and the two female generals followed a certain familiar pattern, one associated with so-called masculine virtues. A tendency to aggressive body movements, brusque speech. The military types, of both sexes, had a jut-jawed damn-the-torpedoes stance Renee had seen their counterparts on Earth take in countless TV interviews and movies. And yet none of the males was in charge. They didn't dare interrupt a Niandian woman in the way numerous studies had shown human men interrupted human women as a matter of course. Quite the reverse. Occasional smoldering expressions revealed that the Niandian males resented being stepped on like that, but they took it. In fact, they even resorted to wheedling as much as they did to the usual firm ''I know what I'm doing; trust me'' masculine inflection. Whenever that happened, the matriarch, Zia, and the women ministers would swap tolerant glances, tacitly forgiving the men's patently obvious little tricks.

The scene was upside down and skewed sideways from the social arrangements Renee had always known.

Eventually, the conversation had reached a point where

Vunj and the other military officials were being asked to come up with logistics plans, figures, and estimates of travel times and transport vehicles. Zia muffled a yawn, crooked an elegant finger at Renee, and moved to one side, outside the queen's debating circle. Renee hesitated, then received a mental nudge from either Tae or her Ka-Een: "Go ahead. We won't let you go splat."

As she and Zia edged out of the cabinet's earshot, Zia said softly, "We will meet the Arbiters' terms, rest assured." She looked directly into Renee's eyes, seeking approval. The alteration in her attitude was startling. Renee realized earlier objections had been a song and dance. The Niandians probably felt they had to put on a show of suspicion and self-interest. It must be a serious strain on their species' pride to admit they'd gotten themselves trapped in an endless war and were forced to appeal for outside arbitration to settle it. Face had been saved, and now Princess Zia was willing to put forward a friendly feeler.

"I am glad to hear that," Renee said. "I hope it won't be necessary for us to exercise the option Martil of the Bright Suns spoke of."

"Oh, no!" Zia said, aghast. "Definitely not."

Chayo sidled close to the women and chided his sister, "You should not monopolize the Arbiter."

With a nasty smile, the princess retorted, "What you mean is, you want to monopolize her. Don't intrude. This is woman's talk, of no interest to you." Chayo retreated reluctantly, his expression very sour. Zia laughed, nodding to Renee as though they were conspirators. "They go through such efforts to attract our attention, don't they? My brother is quite taken with you, ripe for the plucking, my dear. You do have your choices, don't you? Two males on your team, seeking your favor." She eyed Martil and Tae calculatingly. "The thin-faced one is too rude for my taste. But the large, fair one is attractive. And that form does hide his . . . his alien origins quite successfully, I must agree. Do you find him pleasing? The big males are so sweet, when they're attempting to win one's affections, aren't they?"

Nuggets of implanted information glittered in the back of Renee's mind, suddenly becoming available. "It isn't quite what you think," she said. "Among some humanoid species, females do not have the ability to deny intromission to their males nor the option of conceiving—or not— as they will."

Zia's perfectly shaped eyebrows rose. "Truly? Our creators of fantasy have speculated on such a . . . a perverse concept, imagining that it might exist elsewhere in the galaxy. But I had not . . ."

Renee forced a superior smile, playing the part of the experienced star traveler. "It is true. Such arrangements produce a very different interplay between the sexes than you have always known, Eminence."

The revelation shook the princess badly.

As that background data Tae planted in my head is shaking me! Renee realized. I don't dare admit to Zia how flabbergasted I am by this evolutionary flip-flop! Homo sapiens might have taken this reproductive strategy, millions of years ago, when we were still halfway between apes and hominids, but we didn't.

Unbidden, a stream of information welled up and flooded her mind.

The Niandians' evolution followed the path some species of birds and animals did on Earth. Niandian females couldn't be raped. Unless they voluntarily relaxed certain genital muscle groups, the male got nowhere. And they had considerable control over conception, as well. That probably developed in a stressful geologic age, so Niandian females could prevent birth and lactation when food was scarce. And as their species evolved and became an interstellar power, that biological fact has determined the entire course of Niandian culture . . .

Not a reversal of Homo sapiens. A strange, angling parallel track. The Niandian males still had a more than ample supply of testosterone—deeper voices, bigger and heavier structures, and secondary sexual characteristics like beards. But coming on strongly to a Niandian female didn't work. It wouldn't have when they were still prehominids, and it didn't now. If the Niandian male hoped to be reproductively successful and pass on his genes, he had to, quite literally, win the favor of a female, put on a display, perhaps—wheedle, coax, bring her presents, defer to her. Without her consent, the race died. No forc-

ible entry, here. A Niandian female wouldn't be receptive even while unconscious—except to mayhem. And even if she survived the "mayhem," she wouldn't conceive, and her rapist's genes would die with him.

So they had gone in another direction, and their whole society went with them. A matriarchy, with special overtones. Women here felt free to interrupt men, not the other way around, as was common in Earth's Western cultures. And that was just a tiny giveaway to biology-determined customs permeating Niandian habit and thought . . .

Zia seemed to be going through the same sort of inner upheaval Renee was. The princess had been remarkably silent for some time. Martil broke the awkward moment, butting in and saying, "My apologies, Eminence, but it is time for us to leave. We are going to survey an area stricken by your enemies. It is necessary to assess the war's effects, for our report."

The princess recoiled in dismay, and Martil's earlier announcement of this same plan was creating consternation among the matriarch and her cabinet.

"It is far too unsafe, Arbiters . . ."

"We cannot permit it . . ."

"Only if Vunj and an armed force accompany you will . . ."

"We are going!" Martil repeated loudly. The queen blinked, taken aback. Zia glanced at Renee, nodding as if to say, "I begin to see what you meant. This Martil of the Bright Suns does not have the personality of Niandian males. Not at all!" As if to underline his independence, the Arbiter added, "Do not worry that reprisals would be taken should anything untoward happen to us. I give you my word, that is not our way. Prince Chayo, you will act as our guide?"

"It is *my* duty to do that," Zia protested. "It is my place, as my mother's heir and chief minister . . ."

With a vulpine leer, Martil turned down her offer. "Ah! But Prince Chayo has been the intermediary in these truce discussions. It was he who first made contact with the Arbiters—"

"On *our* command," the matriarch said testily.

Martil shook his head, refusing to acknowledge that

nitpicking detail. "Chayo made the contact and therefore he will be our guide and no one else. That is part of the terms of our deal, Most High, Eminence, ladies, gentlemen." He bowed mockingly, then said sotto voce, "Renamos, lead off. Back the way we came."

She did, feeling boorish and ungracious every step of the way. Renee muttered out of the corner of her mouth, "Don't you think a politer good-bye was in order?"

It wasn't until the four of them were in the corridor outside the matriarch's boudoir–war room that Martil said, "Not really. Kowtowing past a reasonable limit is not on our agenda. Never forget, Renamos, now that you're on the team, who's in charge here."

She worried that Prince Chayo was going to lose brownie points for agreeing to leave the royal presence on such short notice. But Renee couldn't hang on to the thought. She muffled a yawn, trotting along with the men. Her stomach growled. Damn, she wanted a snack! About now, normally, she'd be watching the late news—which would be a hell of a lot less frightening and wild than what had been happening to her these past few hours.

Martil was talking to Chayo, softly, as if afraid of being overheard. "Not the matter-relay system. No. It's too dangerous."

Ah, yes, Renee mused. Let's avoid anything else dangerous. Please!

Up and down ramps. Riding in open-sided elevators. Turning right and left again and again. Renee hoped no one was expecting her to keep a log of this journey. She'd always been a lousy Girl Scout.

She had also never been an ant, and this whole screwy Niandian home world was composed of ant tunnels!

But apparently they weren't going to walk the whole way to wherever it was they were going. Prince Chayo led them out of a ramp exit, into the brightly lit cave. An "egg" whipped to a stop in front of them almost on cue. Had Chayo ordered it, special? The four of them climbed in, and the vehicle zipped silently off on its trackless course.

Renee sank back in the magically appearing cushions and tried to recapture visions of dull old reality—coming home from the Metro Council sessions; thinking about

Evy's words about taking it slow and diplomatically, that they'd get the job done, sooner or later; the expressway; plans for supper.

Giving those memories any solidity was almost impossible.

"Anything?"

She'd closed her eyes. Hearing that, she opened them, and saw Tae methodically examining the interior of the "egg," his long fingers splayed out and probing. He was terribly intent on the chore, and Renee giggled. Martil's mouth quirked in amused understanding. "Think of him as a living detector of potential nasty surprises. We've had quite enough of those, thank you. By the way, how is your headache?"

"Hmm? Oh, I guess it's still there, sort of," Renee said. "But I can ignore it." She eyed Martil with gratitude.

"My Lady Renamos is discomfited?" Chayo asked.

"She said her headache was bearable," Martil snapped. So much for sympathy! Tae quit prodding the wall of the "egg" and sat on the floor. Either the vehicle couldn't pick up his wavelengths and manufacture an instant seat to his specifications, or he didn't want to sit on one. "All right," his fox-faced partner said. "We have no listeners, and no tracking devices or destructive implants that Tae can find. So . . . Chayo, I appreciate your backing us up, there in the matriarch's war chamber. And for agreeing to accompany us on this survey trip. We desperately need a friendly communicant while we're on Niand."

"How did you know that I would—"

"That's why I've been appointed an Arbiter to humanoid worlds," Martil said, flashing a knowing, slightly evil smile.

"If I'm not butting in," Renee said, "why do you want to look at the planet's surface? It's nothing but caves, gray stone walls, and a steady downpour. And exactly where are we going?"

Martil's smile turned into a sneer. "Not half a hemisphere away from the capital, that's where we're going, isn't it, Chayo?" The prince nodded, and the darker man's expression sobered. "Tae says Vunj may have connections with the Gevari rebels, your idiotic fight-to-the-death faction.''

Renee hadn't heard Tae say anything of the sort. As a matter of fact, she hadn't heard Tae say anything period. She felt left out. Of what? Did she really want to be in on every awful tidbit of info regarding what was shaping up to be the Last Trump for this world? Did she want to know right when the bomb would land, to the second? No.

Chayo's eyes were pained. ''It is possible, though I pray he is not.''

''There was a definite flash of guilt in his mind when you mentioned that the Gevari had wrecked your quarters.''

''Guilty?'' Renee said with a derisive snort. ''He acted like he'd have been a whole lot happier if we'd all been blown up, particularly Chayo.''

''It is possible,'' the prince repeated. He slid down in his cushiony chair. ''I hope he is only a sympathizer, not an activist. He is director of Niand's defenses, and undoubtedly it disturbs him to contemplate peace without achieving a military victory first. But if he is secretly a Gevari . . . ! How ironic! That *I* should be the one to contact you, Arbiters. I've always suspected Vunj was my father and Zia's. Of course, that's not the sort of thing you can ever be sure of.''

''Your mouth is open, Renamos,'' Martil needled.

''You bet it is!''

''A true member of the Sisterhood of the Nine Worlds would not have been so shocked by the logical result of Niand's sexual patterns,'' he added, jabbing in another needle.

''Oh, shut up! And I want to have a talk with you, later, about that corny title you laid on me.'' Renee turned to Chayo and asked, ''Isn't there some way you can find out if this Generalissimo Vunj is your father or not?'' The prince stared at her blankly.

''Niand is a matriarchy for good reasons,'' Martil said, his tone impatient. ''Sexual domination among this species is biologically determined. Those basics have been relayed to you, Renamos. Don't tell me you haven't grasped them yet.''

"Intellectually, I have," she said, shaking her head. "Emotionally, it's another case. This is an inversion of the age-old setup my Sisterhood, among other groups, has been fighting. But Niand's system is as bad in another way. That hem-kissing ritual. It's disgusting! And Chayo's mother patting him on the head. Like she was saying, 'don't worry your handsome, empty little head about it, boy.' What kind of mother behaves like that?"

"My Lady, please don't," the prince pleaded.

Martil warned, "Doesn't your species have any proverbs about adapting to your host's customs, Renamos?"

"Yes, but . . ."

From his seat on the floor, Tae reached out with a gorilla-length arm and plonked his big fingertips against Renee's elaborate new coiffure. The info he'd already fed her was underlined by a torrent of further data.

Skewed. That was what the Niandians' biology had done to their civilization and their species' attitudes. Renee once had thought it would be a treat to see the cultural majority, white males in particular, getting a dose of what it was like to change places with women, blacks, Hispanics, Asians, and other cultural minorities. However, that wasn't exactly what was going on in Chayo's world. Images flowed through her mind's eye, a confusing mélange of the familiar and the bizarre. This was no feminist utopia, despite the power wielded by Niandian females. Some humanoid instincts for domination seemed constant, no matter which sex ended up ruling the culture. And wars, too, were universal, unfortunately. The Niandians had practiced slavery, though they'd never had certain aspects of that loathsome system. Property inheritance, tribal decision making, allocating resources—all had been drastically affected by Niandian biology. There had been no harems, in the usual sense. But there had been often cruel power wielding by successful breeding females over the women of conquered tribes. Niandian women had sometimes been as vindictive and bloodthirsty as the worst of Earth's male warlords of previous centuries. In the end, though, survival of the race had demanded the best from the Niandian female's urge to give birth to the next generation and to nurture. Indeed, the matriarch served as a living symbol of Niand's ancient deity, the Great Nurturer. And the mothers had eventually prevailed on the home world, for the sake of the children, Niand's future. Their technology had grown faster and faster, to lengthen and improve life and make things better for each subsequent generation of Niandian kids.

But the deep-seated humanoid instinct to defend the "nest" had arisen again when Niand, now an interstellar federation, had run into an alien civilization. Defend the Motherland! Kill the Green Union monsters! Protect Niand! Protect the children!

Maybe humanoids never did outgrow that drive, a relic from their pre-hominid days, when they had to fight to the death against other predators encroaching on their caves—their territories.

Tae removed his hand from her head and Renee muttered, "I see. That's the way it is. Different. No better, no worse."

"Very good," Martil said.

"Chayo, I—I'm sorry. I shouldn't have said that about your mother. It was narrow-minded and ungracious of me."

The prince accepted her apology absently. "You are kind, my Lady. But it doesn't matter. I think the Gevari are going to win. They and Vunj are going to get their continuation of the war to its bloody conclusion, whether or not he and they are working together."

"That would menace a hundred billion others, innocent beings," Martil said. "We will not permit them to die with your combatants."

"Over our dead bodies," Renee said, without thinking.

"If it comes to that, yes: Over our dead bodies."

She winced. "Martil, I wish you wouldn't use expressions like that."

"It was your expression, and it happens to be true."

"I didn't know I was volunteering for a suicide mission . . ."

Martil sighed. "I explained the alternatives." A smile teased at his mouth. "I am glad you did volunteer, though. You're turning out to be surprisingly useful.

Dealing with a matriarchy is always tricky. We're never sure where the control lies.''

"The control lies here, with my mother," Chayo said testily.

The black-haired man grunted. "Control. *Mmph!* Your communication to us indicated that your Federation encompassed approximately twenty-five colony worlds throughout ten solar systems—"

"Eleven!"

"Eleven," Martil amended, waving a hand as if shooing flies. "And we are to believe one word from your mother produces instant compliance everywhere in this far-flung civilization?"

"She is the Most High." Chayo hunched forward in his seat, his posture rigid.

Tae eyed Martil thoughtfully, but didn't try to break things up. Renee wondered if *she* should step in. No, let it go. They're both big boys.

Martil crossed his arms over his chest and said, "Ah, yes! The Most High Matriarch—of one planet."

"Of all Niand! You fail to understand. This is the home world, the mother world, the birthing of Niand. Her roots! When the Most High of the home world orders, everyone obeys."

"Of course! And that's why your mother has to request extra time to convene your Federation's leaders and discuss a truce. She's known the Arbiters demanded such a meeting for some time. She knew when we were coming; the conference should already be assembling."

"If you had responded when we first begged for arbitration, it would have been otherwise," Chayo retorted. "How long ago, by your time reckoning, was our plea received? In the interim, the war has worsened. Many have died who need not have, if you had responded with alacrity! So much for the Arbiters' claims of altruism!"

Tae cradled his chin in his hand and looked morose. Martil squirmed and said bitterly, "We responded as fast as we could. Your message was not received as promptly as you seem to think. Niand's primitive subspace communications methods take forever to traverse—"

"Primitive!" Chayo half stood, breathing fire, and Renee decided she'd better get into this after all.

"Hey! Aren't you supposed to be on the same side?"

Chayo immediately sat down. "My Lady Renamos, a thousand apologies for my crude words and behavior. If I have offended—"

"Only my ears. Knock it off, will you? You, too, Martil."

The fox-faced man took that with a toothy grin, his shoulders heaving in silent laughter. "Ah! The tempering female peacemaker! Indeed, you are correct. We should concentrate on more important—and less personal—matters. Prince, when did the last major surface attack take place?"

Chayo was happy to recite dates and locations, and he and Martil soon settled in for a heavy shoptalk session. Renee listened with half an ear, relaxing now that the two men had stopped hitting on each other verbally. She stared at the passing scenery. Somewhere along the line, the egg vehicle had emerged from the underground subway. Now it was tooling along through miles and miles of city skylines alternating with rural horizons, a night scene illuminated by Liths and the glow of three small moons. Seeing those moons flattened any remaining doubts Renee had about the alienness of where she'd landed.

The scenery and the conversation started to blur. She felt her head tipping sideways—and the vehicle's cushiony seats instantly created a pillow for her to rest on.

Her thoughts drifted. Useful. So that's what she was. Not a bad compliment, actually. But how was she useful? By serving as a voice for Tae, who didn't seem to need a voice? Telepaths bypassed mere talk.

A matriarchy. Evy and the other SOS staffers would have loved this situation on Niand. Susan had a degree in history; she'd have been enthralled. When the mood was on her, Susan dripped quotations from Mill and Friedan and tossed around terms like "matrist" and "patrist eras." They might have enjoyed this whole weird trip. But if it had been Evy or Susan caught in the Ka-Eens' transfer beam, it wouldn't have been Renee, and . . .

Her throat thickened with unshed tears. Evy, Susan, the Social Outreach Sisterhood, her past life—none of it mattered anymore because she would never share her experiences with her friends. That city, that world, that life was gone. Slipping through the fingers of her memories.

A falling sensation made her sit bolt upright with a start. Wide awake now, Renee realized the sinking feeling had been sleep-induced. She was sitting right where she was before she'd dozed off. They were still cruising along in the egg vehicle. But now there was bright sunlight outdoors, sparkling off snow.

Martil smiled at her. "Better?"

Muffling a yawn, she said, "Uh-huh, though I'm still hungry. How long has it been?"

"Since you've eaten, or since you went to sleep?" She made a scowling grin at him, and Martil said, "Chayo, you have food dispensers? Please order us something to eat. And I can't tell you how long you've been asleep, Renamos, because I don't know what time-measuring method you normally employ. It was a short while by my standards, an excessively long time by Tae's. You do feel better, in general?"

"Yes and no." Renee stood up and stretched. She had no trouble maintaining her balance. The ride was so smooth that she felt as if they weren't moving at all. She sat down again next to Martil. "Actually, I don't feel too bad, for somebody who's had less than eight hours' sleep in the past four days or so."

The wall beside her bulged inward. Renee stared apprehensively at the spot. There was another egg vehicle, rolling alongside theirs.

"What would you care to eat, my Lady?" Chayo asked deferentially. "I do not know your tastes."

Tae unfolded himself from the floor and stepped over to the connecting link between the "eggs." His head almost brushed the ceiling. After a moment's contemplation, he poked the bulge and a shelf appeared. It held steaming trays of food. Tae handed one to Renee, then passed out the others to Chayo, Martil, and himself.

Renee studied her selection carefully. The stuff smelled like a cheeseburger with all the trimmings, but it looked like chocolate pudding. No gourmet, she. Shrugging, she dug in. There was no crunch, and no catsup, but the meal was delicious and filling. The men were finishing at about the same time she scooped up the last of her food, and she started to thank Chayo for his hospitality. As she did, she felt a definite change in motion. The lunch-wagon egg vehicle slowed and separated from the egg the four were riding in and left an oval opening in the wall. A moment later, the egg stopped completely, and the purse-lipped door gaped still wider, tacitly inviting them to exit.

Martil brushed crumbs from his fingers and rings and dropped his now-empty tray on the floor. Renee readied a scolding. What a litterbug! Then the tray vanished, sucked out of sight. Tae's food tray and Chayo's did the same, when they chucked them, so she imitated them. When in Rome, and so on.

The travelers climbed out onto a gleaming metal platform. A half dome arched above them, cutting the wind and providing some warmth. Although the landscape around them was dotted with snow, it was not cold beneath the transparent partial shelter. Sunlight reflected blindingly from the snow. Renee raised her hands to shield her eyes. "You'd think a civilization that can put people in super egg trains could control the weather a bit better. Rain. Snow. Don't the Niandians have any eighty-degree bask-on-the-beach days?"

Amused, Chayo chuckled and said, "That might have been arranged, my Lady, if the disaster here had not ruptured the climate-moderating equipment."

"Very thorough penetration, and despite what I am sure were powerful protective screens," Martil said. He leaned on the railing lining the domed platform and surveyed the area.

Renee did a small survey of her own and whispered, "It—it's really been bombed out, hasn't it?"

"Bombed?" Chayo stared ruefully at her Ka-Een pendant, plainly longing for a translation easier for him to comprehend.

"Not bombs, Renamos," Martil corrected. "The weapons involved were far nastier. Contained charges, perhaps, or particle-beam devices. Lobbed in here from a considerable distance, I'd estimate."

"Why didn't they mash the egg railroad line, while they were at it?"

This time, Chayo didn't look so puzzled. He must have

heard word equivalents that were within his frame of knowledge. "Our surface transportation is not limited to any particular paths, my Lady. The egg vehicles can be directed to go anywhere, even here."

She gazed out over miles and miles of broken shards and lumps, coated with snow. The scene was haunted, the debris occasionally lashed by a snow devil eddying in the moaning wind. Architectural rubble extended to the horizon. Anyone who had seen footage from war zones would recognize a massive bombardment's aftermath. The strange peacefulness of the view troubled Renee. "It's . . . pretty."

"The bodies were vaporized, or otherwise tidied up, I suppose," Martil said. "That's the usual system. The planet's natural climate—or what passes for natural in these circumstances—is doing its best to reduce the remains to the soil. But there's not much hope of that for centuries to come, or at least until peace intervenes and the Niandians can hasten the process with technology. We mustn't stay at this site too long. It's undoubtedly hot."

Wind fluffed Renee's hair and tugged at her clothes. She should have felt cold, but she didn't. Like a Pavlovian dog, she was reacting to what Martil had said, illusionary nettles of lingering radioactivity burning her skin. "Why did you want to see this place?" she asked.

"Indeed," Chayo chimed in. He turned his back on the ruined landscape. "You obviously knew what you would find here, amid what was once one of our home world's greatest cities. I'm sure you've seen the same thing elsewhere."

Martil, too, turned from the appalling scene. "Yes, I have. Tae and I are far too familiar with the results of humanoids' war games. We've seen this sort of thing too many times, on too many planets. That's why we're Arbiters." He rubbed at the mole on his chin, his expression sad. "Protocol. Ignore what I said earlier. We do appreciate the difficulties your mother is working against, the time-lapse factor, and resistance from within her own government and among her people. She needs time to assemble her Federation's council, a group leadership with the authority to put an end to this stupid war. And

Tae, Renamos, and I need time as well—time to fully absorb the currents of your culture. We can use any further information you can give us, Chayo. Speed is of the—''

He broke off, his mouth open. Martil quit picking at his mole and his hand darted to the top of his head. He squinted, frowning. Renee had never seen the arrival of a splitting headache so graphically portrayed.

''How . . . how *could* they? *Here!* I thought we had thrown them off our track!'' His pale face twisted with pain.

Tae stirred from his normal, hands-hanging-down posture. One big paw closed around Renee's hand, jerking her forward. Martil, still clutching his head, used his free hand to push Chayo along, following Tae's lead.

They were running. At least the men were running. Renee was staggering, dragged in Tae's wake. She was doing her best, but halfway wished he'd pick her up and tuck her under his arm again, as he had in the tunnel below Chayo's escape hatch. Her legs were too short for her to match the men's strides.

Why were they running?

Because Martil had a headache—and he seemed to be a living detector for incoming artillery shells, or the Niandian counterpart of that.

But why were they running down toward the ruined city? Martil had said it was ''hot.'' Radioactive. A place to stay far away from.

''Over there!'' Martil pointed to a large, mounded lump of snow, the wreckage of a building. The spot was perhaps a hundred yards to their left. Tae veered in that direction immediately.

Now he tried to carry Renee, putting an arm around her waist, but not quite lifting her off the uneven ground. Apparently he didn't dare stop long enough to get a solid purchase. She was hauled along in an awkward, ridiculous position, her feet on and then off and then on the snow-covered dirt and debris again and again.

There was a tremendous roar, and they were all being thrown ass over teakettle.

She put out her hands, landing in the snow, sliding, digging in the toes of her new boots in a frantic attempt to stop. Something large and heavy fell on top of her, mashing her deeper into the cold and wet and knocking the breath out of her.

For a panicky few seconds, Renee struggled desperately to free her face from the white, fluffy crystals, on the verge of suffocating. When she was finally able to raise her head, she blinked through snow-crusted eyelashes at a rain of lumps of baby blue garbage. The stuff was pattering to earth all about her. Several pieces plopped onto her hair, and she shook them off.

The thing squashing her flat removed itself, and hands were under her armpits, helping her to her feet. Martil and Chayo were on either side of her, both looking anxious. They were rumpled and completely plastered with snow and dirt.

"Are you all right, my Lady Renamos?"

Clutching her aching midriff, Renee gasped, "I think so. What fell on me?"

"Tae," Martil replied.

The tall blond seemed unhurt. He was looking back the way they'd come, and Renee traced his stare. The domed platform, the ramp, and their egg vehicle—and the lunch-wagon egg that had accompanied them for a while—had disappeared. A laze of smoke curled up from that spot, drifting in the cold breeze.

"Don't tell me. The Gevari hit at us again, right?"

Martil brushed at his clothes. "Oh, yes. Conventional armaments, fortunately, and definitely launched from this planet. Which should mean the Gevari are confining their attack to . . ." His sharp face contorted into another blossoming headache, and Tae lumbered toward Renee again.

She looked around for someplace to run to. In the next moment she was swept off her feet and saved the decision. In contrast to their first wild scramble, Tae got her securely under his arm before he went loping off. Renee wished the blond hulk could think of a more dignified way to carry her.

Martil and Chayo galloped ahead, ducking into the shadow of the wrecked building. Then Tae and Renee were in the shadow too, and she blinked, trying to adjust her vision. The two smaller men were crawling through a cramped opening close to the ground. Tae dropped Renee there, next to what remained of a collapsed doorway, and pushed at her. She got on her hands and knees, heading for cover, half-outraged and half-hysterical with laughter as Tae planted a hand on her rump to hurry her along. She tumbled down a slope of loose earth, landing in a tangle of arms and legs—Martil's and Chayo's. Tae entered right behind, sprawling across the three of them.

There was another deafening roar, closer this time.

The noise was so loud Renee feared the top of her skull would crack and come off. She gulped, swallowing hard, relieving the painful pressure in her ears. It—the bomb or particle-beam weapon or whatever—continued to growl and moan for quite some time. Dust, shaken loose from wrecked beams and the flattened building's former upper stories, flaked down on the cowering foursome.

When the sound eased a trifle, Renee sat up, batting pieces of what looked like rotten wallpaper out of her hair. She disentangled her legs from Chayo's and Martil's. "About now, I wish your beauty salon experts had rigged me in white. If they had, I could play possum out there in the snow."

"You'd be dead, in that case," Martil said tonelessly.

"Is anyone hurt?" Chayo was counting noses.

"Not yet." Martil was still holding his head and wincing. "It can't be from a Ka-Een essence-transfer beam this time. I wonder how they're locating us? Chayo, alternate transportation from this site?"

"Matter-relay units were destroyed in the original enemy attack. And anyway, the Gevari can interfere with matter relay. They'd send us where they wanted and kill us instantly." Chayo tugged at his sideburns a moment, then brightened. He fumbled at a pocket and drew out an object resembling an ironed ballpoint pen. After a bit of dial twiddling, he began talking, identifying himself and yelling for the chief of palace communications. A burst of static spat out of the radio-pen.

"Somehow, I suspect there's interference with that, too," Renee said worriedly.

Chayo dial-twiddled some more, producing a lot of squalling and scratching noises, and a blur of incoherent humanoid sounds. Amid the hash, one familiar contact cheered him considerably. He held the communicator close to his lips and shouted, "Zia? Zia! Gevari, attacking us at Hell-All! Send help! Notify defense—"

The princess's static-broken words walked over his. Chayo's face fell, and he slowly lowered the device, punching a control to kill the audio. "She didn't receive my message. Didn't hear me."

Renee wrapped her arms protectively around herself. "Martil, they're going to kill us." She wished Tae had been putting words into her mouth when she said that. Then she'd have someone else to blame for the horror gripping her.

Martil scrambled up the dirt slope and peered out the collapsed doorway. Tae tugged at his boot. The smaller man batted him away. "They're certainly trying hard enough to kill us. I'd hoped that once we had arrived on Niand's home world, they would realize that the Arbiters mean business . . ."

Tae grabbed his belt and dragged him back down the slope, all but throwing him into Chayo's and Renee's arms. Then Tae's weight buried the three of them.

Another thunderous explosion shook the ground. Chunks of stone fell out of what remained of the room's ceiling, crashing on either side of their huddle. Renee bit her knuckles and lectured herself sternly to forestall a total funk.

Cautiously, the four of them raised their heads. A gory cut dribbled blood down one of Martil's cheeks. Chayo had an ugly lump over an eye. Renee examined her palms. They were scraped and oozing—from being battered against this stony floor, rammed into walls, butted into the remains of a building, and fallen on. She cursed softly, fighting tears. "Martil . . ."

He was peering up the dirt slope. His expression was twisted with agony. "Closer yet. How are they homing in on us . . . ?"

Tae flipped out a long arm and hooked his fingers around the smaller man's pendant. Comprehension dawned, and it was no comfort to either of them. "More sophisticated methods than we'd expected, eh?" Martil said. "They detect a Ka-Een and start throwing."

Renee stroked her own pendant. The Ka-Een had trans-

lated this world and these people for her and allowed her
to fit into this incredible adventure. And because of the
Ka-Een Martil had loaned her, she was going to be killed.

Martil sat down heavily, gritting his teeth. He swiped
the back of his hand irritably at his bleeding cheek.
"Damn! Chayo, make a run for it. It's us they want. No
pinpoint accuracy, so far, but they're bound to hit us by
default, sooner or later. Get out of here while you can."

"No." Chayo seemed grimly amused. "That's useless. They won't let me escape. I know their techniques.
I learned them from Vunj. If they're still receiving information that you exist, and they will since you're still
alive, they'll saturate this entire area. There's nowhere
for me to run. No, I can't escape."

"But we can!" Martil said, talking rapidly. He seized
Chayo's arms and shook the prince bodily. "*We* can. Not
you. So get away!"

"No time. Don't you understand? I know how they
think."

A fresh series of crumping *boom*s reverberated near
their cubbyhole. Through the slit of daylight above, where
they'd entered this trap, Renee saw gouts of earth and
rubble being thrown high into the air. She wanted to dig
a deeper hole and crawl into it.

"No time," Chayo said again, utterly fatalistic. "If
you can escape, Martil, please do so. I must not be responsible for your deaths."

"No time, indeed." Martil nodded to Tae. "All right.
All *right*! We'll have to attempt it. It worked once, so
presumably Renamos has a special affinity with the Ka-
Eens' essence. Perhaps just enough. Here, you two, join
hands."

Chayo recoiled, yelling to be heard over the roar of
explosions walking around and toward them. "I will not
imperil my Lady Renamos!"

With a cry of exasperation, Martil manhandled the
young prince, thrusting him at Renee, throwing them into
each other's arms. Under other circumstances, she might
have enjoyed that. In one of those frozen-in-time, irra-
tional observations, she noted that Chayo's eyes were a
lavender color. Very nice.

Then Tae and Martil were making contact with the two

of them, forming a sort of seance circle. A very small, tight one. "She's in considerably less danger than you are, Chayo," Martil screamed, practically in the Niandian's ear. "Brace yourselves!"

The bomb noise was overwhelming, rattling the brains within Renee's skull. The earth heaved like a maddened animal. It didn't take any additional instructions from Martil to make her embrace Chayo for dear life. She was cold, shivering with terror.

She saw Martil's lips moving, and his eyes weren't quite tracking. It was the same routine he'd gone through when he'd produced Renee's pendant out of nowhere.

Explosions were everywhere, beating on her, an immense fist of sound, stunning her to everything but the gut knowledge that this had to be it.

Then the world disintegrated, dissolving into a parade of descending colors: gold, green, gray . . . and black.

chapter
5

"R_{ENAMOS}, let go!"

Dim impressions of a world outside the blackness. That had sounded like . . . like Martil. Slowly, her mind climbed toward the surface of an impossibly deep lake. Something heavy was pushing against her, and as she rose toward full consciousness she found that she hurt, ached all over. The light hurt, too, when she opened her eyes. She groaned and flinched and reopened her eyelids, more carefully and gingerly this time.

Normal, soft white, interior light. No snow. No deadly, blooming clouds caused by bombs.

Martil's face swam into view in front of her. His features were taut with concern. He tugged gently at her arms. Renee glanced down. Chayo was slumped against her, and her hands were clasped tightly across his back. A near death grip. She let Martil pry her fingers apart, and Chayo fell away from her, his head cradled by the black-haired man. The young prince slid back onto the floor, sprawling across Renee's knees, because she, too, was sitting on the floor.

A floor! A nice, firm, ordinary floor! It looked and felt like fancy linoleum. And it was a wonderful relief, after so much bomb-blasted rubble and dirt.

Renee turned from relishing that reality to anxiety for Chayo. He was ghostly pale. And the bruises and cuts

66

he'd suffered during the bombardment didn't help his appearance, either. Well, at least he was breathing; she could see his chest rise and fall.

Tae moved into the picture from Renee's right. He knelt beside Chayo and gathered the prince into his arms without effort, lifting him. Numbly, Renee watched the blond carry the smaller man to an oversize hassock. He laid Chayo down there, straightening his arms and legs, pulling off his shredded cloak. More than bombardment damage had taken its toll on Prince Chayo's clothes; they were as tattered as Renee's had been, when she'd first arrived on Niand. She wasn't surprised to find that the marvelous garments supplied her by the matronly dressers in the palace had since evaporated.

"Can you hear me now?" Martil squatted by her side, one arm around her shoulders.

Renee shuddered and snuffled a few times, trying to bring up a tension-shattering laugh. She didn't make it. "A few more like that, and none of us would have passed 'Go.' "

"I don't know the exact reference, but I take your meaning. Relax. It's all right now."

"Is Chayo . . . ?"

"Unconscious," Martil said, a bit too quickly. "We don't know much else, yet."

"Then you shouldn't have moved him! He might have broken bones or internal injuries!"

"No. Ka-Een essence transfer does not harm physically. Not in the way you fear. The damage, if it occurs, strikes deeper. Maybe there *is* no damage, this time." Renee wiped away the blood trickling down Martil's cheek from the cut on his face. He smiled at her encouragingly. "Chayo is most likely suffering from a form of psychic shock."

She got to her feet, groaning, grateful for Martil's support, and walked to the hassock where Chayo lay. Tae was fussing over the prince like a mother hen, very solicitous.

Then a gang of ten or so oddly assorted persons bustled up around the four. The newcomers were fat, thin, short, tall, and none of them precisely human-looking. For Renee, it was like watching an out-of-synch film, or a TV image badly distorted by "ghosts." The strangers clustered near Chayo, and she, Martil, and Tae were forced to step back.

"This—this transfer didn't hurt me," Renee said. "I don't see why it hurt Chayo."

"It's a highly individual thing," Martil explained. He put his arm about her shoulders again and steered her to an adjacent hassock. He refused to let her focus all her attention on Chayo and the consultation of alien physicians. At least she hoped that's what the out-of-synch people were. They certainly acted like it. Martil said, "You have a most unusual affinity with the Ka-Een, remember?"

"Where are we?" she asked tiredly.

"This world's name wouldn't mean anything to you. But it's where we came from, most recently—Tae and I."

"Oh. The Arbiters' world."

An eyebrow arched out of sight beneath Martil's shaggy black bangs. He nodded. "Good approximation." He added bitterly, "So we're right back where we began."

Tae had followed them from Chayo's hassock. Now he put out a big hand, gently touching Martil's head. The blond's close-set eyes were open wide, and he shook his mane vigorously, lending emphasis to the thoughts he was winging his partner's way. It wasn't tough to understand the silent conversation. Not tough at all. That fact surprised and pleased Renee. She'd come a long way in a big hurry from believing everything was a shock-induced illusion or a nightmare. Now she was even able to pick up telepathic overflow from Tae. "You—you're going to use your super stop-the-whole-thing weapon you warned Vunj about?"

Martil's translucent skin paled still further. "No! No. Not yet. We haven't *begun* to exhaust the options for working out the problems between Niand and the Green Union."

Renee was much comforted by that reassurance. "I'm glad. I don't know what you guys have up your sleeves, but after hearing you psych out the general and those others, I don't think I want to know."

"It's—the weapon—our last resort. We never use it unless . . ."

A couple of the out-of-synch people rustled to a halt in front of the trio. The intruders made noisy *tsk tsk* sounds. From their physical shapes, Renee made a guess that this pair were females. Both carried big tote bags, and the markings on those pouches were probably the Arbiters' equivalent of Red Crosses; the fuzzy people looked *that* medical.

One of them made a beeline for Tae. That puzzled Renee. Martil had this mess all over his face, and she was scraped up, and instead they wanted to treat good old strongman Tae. Then the big man obeyed a gesture from the female doctors and turned around. Renee gasped. Tae's back was a wreck. His tunic was slashed and torn and seeping blood in a dozen places—a slightly foaming, pinkish blood. Suddenly, Renee remembered how many times the blond had shielded the others with his body, out there in the snow-covered rubble when the bombs were falling. It was only his stoic lack of reaction that had made her think he was indestructible.

The second doctor moved toward Martil. She shimmered a bit as she shifted position. It hurt Renee's eyes to watch these out-of-synch people. The doctor took an instrument resembling a miniature football out of her tote bag and rolled it down Martil's cheek. Blood and the cut vanished.

"They'll take care of you next," Martil told Renee. "In minor injuries, it goes by rank, severity of wounds."

"Mmm. Sort of a noncritical triage?"

"Very good!" Martil squirmed, not appreciating the efficient repairs being carried out on his flesh. He looked resignedly annoyed, like a small boy submitting to having his ears washed.

The medico—medica?—finished with Tae and began swabbing a tiny football over Renee's abraded hands. Instantly, the oozing places were whole, though still slightly reddened. Before Renee could thank the alien woman, the little football was being applied to her foot, removing the beginnings of a nasty bruise there, caused when she'd stepped on that rock in those gray stone alleys.

How long ago had that been?

Actually, probably not very long. Four or five hours in the past? Things had happened with astonishing speed—

an entire lifetime's worth of dizzying and terrifying events, crammed into a minute space.

"No! Not right now! We have too much to do!" Martil argued. Renee didn't grasp what was bothering him. The out-of-synch doctor who'd been patching him up had pressed a sequin-decorated flashlight against his neck. Martil's hazel eyes began to get glassy. He slumped. "Damn! I was afraid of this. Concentrate on the scratches while a galactic sector is in danger of annihilation." Then he yawned hugely.

Renee jerked away at the touch of something cold. The doctor going over her with a fine-toothed stethoscope had goosed her with one of those sequined flashlights, too. A dreamy lethargy swept over Renee. "Mmm, they're knocking us out, huh? A sleeping pill in a flashlight. Neat." She also broke off into an enormous yawn. Her words distorted, she complained, " 's not fair. Don' even know if Chayo's awright yet. Not fair . . ."

"It never is," Martil said, and Renee sank into what felt like tons of cotton batting.

Visions danced in her head. A mixture of happily ridiculous and stark panic, compounded of recent experiences. Unseen enemies bombing her. Faceless unknowns out to get her. Martil, his face sly, making acid comments on every new situation. Chayo alternating flowery compliments with equally glib straight-faced lies. Tae grinning, a beefy, blond humanoid frog. Caricature villains, swarming in at the four of them and intoning viciously, "You know what we mean, and you must be eliminated!" More faceless enemies threatening to torture Renee to extract information, to kill her, to do things too fierce to mention.

After a very long time, the mists of the nightmares and dreams started to drift off. She hovered in a not-quite-awake stage where she could analyze the sleeping fantasies from a figurative distance. The nightmares had lost their effect. They lingered, but were balanced by the good portions of her drugged dreaming. In the latter, the unexpected occurred constantly, and it all seemed completely logical.

Just like the reality she'd lived through with Martil and Tae.

Faint, distant voices prodded their verbal snouts through the remnants of her sleep.

Well, I have to wake up sometime, came the thought to her sleep-shrouded mind.

Renee opened her eyes a crack and found the light outside was quite bearable. Slowly, she sat up. She was on one of those big hassocks. Someone had covered her with an exquisitely lightweight blanket and put a velvety pillow under her head.

An animal sat on the hassock, too. A big animal, like a Siamese cat the size of a well-fed Saint Bernard. When she sat up, the cat sat up, too, and stared at her intently. It didn't have normal, slitted cat eyes but many-faceted insectlike eyes. It wasn't merely looking at her, either. She got the same sort of telepathic slopover she was learning to know well from being around Tae. The cat was checking her for damage, silently asking if she was all right. Silently, Renee replied that she was quite well. Satisfied, the immense cat slithered off the hassock and disappeared through a door that hadn't been there a moment before and wasn't there a moment later.

Watch cat? Making sure the patient was in good shape? Interesting.

And how *did* she feel, really? She felt great. Great! Top of the class and ready to take on anything.

Renee stretched tentatively and discovered that she didn't ache or hurt anywhere; not even a twinge. Marvelous. And astonishing, for somebody who normally woke up feeling like a soft-boiled egg that had been stepped on.

She threw back the gossamer blanket. It was peculiar that she wasn't cold after having done that, because she didn't have a stitch on. Sleeping raw, even in a northern climate, could become popular if all rooms were as cozy-warm as this one.

Her clothes were draped neatly over a nearby valet-rack. They were freshly cleaned and pressed—and reconstituted. When she had arrived . . . here . . . the stuff had been cheesecloth, just like her original clothes had been when she'd arrived on Niand. Now the body stocking and dashiki were together again, good as new. Or better. They felt different, silkier. She suspected the garments were clever organic copies of the clothes supplied by the palace's dresser corps. Renee assembled herself and went looking for the distant voices.

She traced them to a drapery at the end of a long corridor and timidly twitched the curtain aside to peek beyond. The curtain was good insulation; once she got her ears past it, the voices were normal to loud. One was Martil's. He and Tae were sitting on a giant hassock, surrounded by other hassocks containing an assortment of the out-of-synch people. An argument was in progress. Very little of it made any sense to Renee. She touched her Ka-Een pendant chidingly. That was the only thing she'd been wearing when she woke up. But despite the fact that the words she was hearing were in English, Martil and the rest were referring to too many things that had no adequate translations.

The argument was taking place in an enormous room— not the one she'd arrived in. This one was so large she expected the voices to echo, though they didn't. Like most of the people in it, the room was out-of-synch. Were the walls and ceiling swathed in moving gauze? Or were they merely made out of several sheets of shifting, badly made glass? Or was the appearance distorted by something high-tech? Holograms? No way of telling, not from her limited background regarding such phenomena.

One of the out-of-synchs pointed, and half the room's walls went blank, then lighted, various spots twinkling. A gargantuan version of the matriarch's war-room wall display.

"Come in, Renamos," Martil invited. Then he addressed the out-of-synchs. "Tae and the Ka-Een have informed you concerning Renamos and her unique adaptability and courage."

Did a red face go well with a yellow dashiki and body stocking? Renee hurried across the room and sat beside Martil. She was pleasantly embarrassed, and extremely grateful to see two friendly faces in this alien setting.

Several unfamiliar faces crowded close, too. But apparently they weren't interested in her. Tae was the focus of their attention. All of these pushy out-of-synchs circling the hassock were about Tae's height, which Renee had estimated conservatively at a good six-four. As Tae stood up to confront them, he . . . flickered. For a split second he also went out-of-synch. Renee drew back, and found her retreat blocked by Martil's arm.

Very slowly, Tae turned and looked down at her. Yes, it was Tae. Same wide, froggy mouth and close-set blue eyes and butchered blond hair. But it wasn't Tae. Something else glimmered behind those eyes. They were still blue, but beneath the surface they became brilliantly shiny and immense, much larger than any human pair of eyes ever had been.

The pressure of Martil's arm against her back reminded Renee of all the three of them had been through together. She could cope with a little anomaly like this new one, surely! Gulping, she sat up straight, telling herself to behave in a civilized fashion.

Tae came back into full synch. He grinned, a dazzling display of teeth. Tae. The big guy she knew and rather liked.

"All right?" Martil asked gently. As she nodded, he said, "You are being honored. Tae rarely reveals his original form to humanoids who have come to know him in this one. Generally, they become violently upset. He doesn't want to alarm them."

"I'm not upset. Not any more. It—it was just a bit of a surprise, on top of a hell of a lot of surprises, as I hope you weirdos realize."

An utterly-without-reservations smile split Martil's vulpine face. He rubbed noses with her and hugged her and said with a laugh, "Oh, yes! We weirdos realize that. Thoroughly!"

"If I'm the joke, let me know what I'm doing wrong, huh?"

Calming, Martil said, "No antagonism now. Your adaptability *should* enable you to overcome such touchiness. I blame some of your problems on cultural traumatization; your feminist affiliations have led to overcompensations. However, one must take the quirks, as it were, with the talents. No joke. Merely relief. You brought Prince Chayo through the essence transfer intact."

Renee felt guilty. "I'd completely forgotten about him. I'm terrible! How is he?"

"Didn't you hear me? He is well. Recuperating, as you were."

"Great! He's not hurt?"

One of the out-of-synchs was trying to butt into the conversation. Martil ignored him. "He was quite stunned, of course, but he's very much alive. Your affinity with the Ka-Een protected him from fatal psychic shock. Without that, I doubt we'd still have an effective means of operation in the Niand–Green Union conflict. Chayo is our royal peacemaker and intermediary. If he had died, I don't . . ." Finally acknowledging the buttinsky, Martil snapped, "All right. All *right*! We continue to have the authority you gave us, and we intend to exercise it."

"That could be revoked."

Renee understood those words. Sort of. The sound was that of many voices in action all at once, more or less on the same pitch, and with tons of vibrato. Totally inhuman, though it definitely wasn't a mere machine talking. She assumed it was the out-of-synchs speaking in unison. Without moving their mouths, she'd noticed. Were she and Martil the only true speakers here? The buttinsky seemed to be a particular extension of the telepathic Many-Voice.

"*Do* you revoke it?" Martil demanded. When there was no immediate answer, he gestured to the twinkling wall. "Consider. We have two subsectors affecting fourteen separate galactic units. And a no-person's-land ten units wide between the main combatants. Numerous planets, hundreds of intelligent species. Innocents. Directly in the war's path. This cannot go on, especially now that Niand and the Green Union both have the Bender Principle weapon. Their civilizations have displayed much potential for eventual mature and peaceful development. They must not be allowed to waste that potential, or destroy it, in a conflict that means extinction for both their races."

He was talking mass destruction—again. Renee shuddered. She remembered crouching in a concrete hidey-hole, bombs falling all around her. Bad enough. But they'd escaped. What if people died by the millions? Billions! In the dark ages of her own life, on one world, in rather small wars, comparatively, thousands of innocent people had been killed. Now Martil was discussing megagenocide, wiping out entire species, including small children and countless helpless animals who'd never have a chance even to express an opinion on the interstellar clash that was vaporizing them.

"The Green Union." That was the Many-Voice. "It must not be permitted, true. That is our duty."

"I know!" Martil flapped his hands in consternation. "Tae knows. Renamos knows."

"She is not a representative of the Arbiters . . ."

"She is now." Martil's eyes narrowed challengingly. "Can you deny it? She has affinity with the Ka-Een no Arbiter has ever enjoyed. And her planet is intimately connected with this Niand–Green Union crisis."

"W-what?" Renee stammered.

Martil waved again at the wall. A large area brightened to an ugly red. "That section, Renamos, is the one which was traversed by the Ka-Eens' transfer beam . . ."

"You must not divulge the coordinates of the Arbiter worlds," Many-Voice protested.

"Oh, shut up! Go on, Martil. You know I'm too stupid to be able to finger you for a bombing attack, assuming Earth was advanced enough to contemplate such a thing."

Martil's grin was radiant. "You are not stupid," he reassured her. "Far from it." Then he went on, "The lead beam Tae and I rode to Niand."

"The same one I rode."

"Indeed. And without a Ka-Een to possess you. Incomprehensible! Now, somewhere in that red area, many light-years wide, is your home world, your Earth," Martil said.

Renee nodded. "I see. Backlash. If Niand and the Green Union that they're fighting decide to drop the other shoe and use their super weapons, this—this Bender Principle you're talking about—Earth gets caught in the fallout."

"I *said* you were not stupid." There was a gloating tone to Martil's comment. He glared at the out-of-synchs.

"And the super weapon wipes us out," Renee finished. "Us and everyone else in that red zone."

"On a scale beyond your imagining. Beyond mine," Martil said grimly, "if I had not already witnessed such destruction elsewhere in the galaxy. That is why we have to—"

"Martil!"

Chayo was running toward them. One of the giant Siamese cats panted in his wake. The prince looked tremendously healthy and bright-eyed. He also looked totally freaked out. Driven wild by delusions. Renee had dealt with druggies wearing the same frenzied expression—not tracking at all, madly intent on getting revenge on someone, on strangling them with their bare hands.

"You will not have them! They are my responsibility! I will protect them with my life!" Chayo roared, and he bowled into a couple of the out-of-synch people. A dozen others immediately jumped to their aid, trying to restrain the prince. However, Chayo hadn't taken time to dress when he'd wakened in a frenzy, and unclothed skin made him slippery. He wriggled out of the aliens' grasp easily. Kicking, flailing, and punching, he shouted, "Run! Run! Escape them!"

More out-of-synch physician females were advancing on him purposefully. Martil held out an arm, halting them. "No. Let us try, first."

He didn't bother asking Renee and Tae to help. They waded in with him, eager to assist. Renee once had a roommate who went berserk if anyone woke her too suddenly. Remembrance of those incidents warned her this wasn't going to be a picnic.

They had to shove aside a mass of aliens blocking the way. Renee wasn't sure whether they would feel like caterpillars or some other ughish creatures, but contact was nicely solid. She muttered, "Excuse me," and bulled on through.

Chayo was in the middle of the tangle. He was still fighting unseen demons or enemies, screaming threats and an occasional mea culpa.

"My fault! My fault! My responsibility! You will not have them! Never!"

Tae got behind him and closed an arm across Chayo's chest. Martil seized the prince's calves and the two of them picked him up bodily. It was quite a struggle, especially for Martil, as Chayo continued to thrash wildly. Renee caught the Niandian's hands and yelled, "Chayo! Chayo! Hey, it's us! Come out of it!"

Martil was yelling at him as well, with no results.

"Should I slap him or something?" Renee wondered aloud.

"And you were the one worried about broken bones if we moved him while he was unconscious." Martil combined a friendly sneer with his grunting effort to control the prince's murderous kicking. "No, don't hit him. Not yet."

Tae managed to get one hand free and clapped it against Chayo's skull, mashing flat the light, curly brown hair. Almost at once, the smaller man's frenzy lessened. The glitter faded from his eyes. Tae knelt, easing the prince down to the floor. Renee and Martil cooperated, but they maintained their grip on Chayo's hands and legs.

"Martil?" Chayo whispered, blinking. "My Lady?" Renee felt him stiffen, the muscles in his wrists knotting as he exclaimed, "Where is Vunj, that motherless . . . !"

"Chayo, you're not where you think you are," Martil said. He nodded to Tae. More information went through those big fingertips. Gradually, comprehension dawned on the prince's regular features. He wrinkled his nose, looking chagrined, and Martil smiled. "All right now?"

"I—I believe so." They let him go, and he sat up slowly. With their help, he got to his feet and gazed around suspiciously at the out-of-synch people. One of the insect-eyed cats trotted toward them. It was towing a valet rack with its prehensile tail. Chayo's reconstituted jumpsuit was draped over the rods.

"Put it on," Martil said in a big-brother tone. "Some of the cultures comprising the Arbiters have strong reservations about public nudity. You have offended them greatly." As Chayo obeyed, Martil went on, "Do you remember our transfer from Niand at all?"

The prince Velcroed shut his jumpsuit's collar and cuffs. He winced and rubbed the back of his neck. That surprised Renee. Hadn't the out-of-synch physicians repaired him fully? Martil had said the Niandian was fine. Well, maybe Chayo had thrown something out anew, during all that thrashing around moments ago. "I—I'm not sure that I do remember,'' Chayo said. ''There was a terrible pain in my head and my throat. And I remember being more afraid—and angry—than I had ever been in my life. I saw Vunj's face, looming over me, larger and larger. And the three of you . . . dying. It was quite vivid.''

''I wish you wouldn't make it so vivid on the recap,'' Renee said. ''Nothing like that happened to *me*. In fact, I felt pretty calm, considering. I mean, the *first* time I went through one of these transfers.''

''That's intriguing,'' Martil commented. ''Chayo's re-action was far more understandable. Save that generally there's no reaction at all to an attempted transference when one is not possessed by a Ka-Een. In the few such cases on the Arbiters' records, the transferees died of psychic shock.''

''But it wasn't non–Ka-Een transfer,'' Renee said. ''He was piggybacking with me.''

Martil raised an eyebrow. ''I told you that you were unique. If one is not possessed by a Ka-Een, any attempt at transference is in effect a non-essence transfer. Our previous experience made us think that was impossible. And Chayo most definitely was not possessed.''

Renee was taken aback by the vehemence in Martil's statement. Not surprising, in retrospect, that he'd been so wary of her at first. If instant death was the usual lot of hitchhikers on a Ka-Een essence-transference signal, no doubt it had astonished seasoned star-hoppers that she'd lived through it with no damage. Not only lived through it, but found it no more hectic than a bumpy bus ride.

''Chayo, are you in control of yourself now?'' Martil asked. ''Good. Then, to orient you, you are on, well, let us say one of the Arbiters' worlds. It was necessary to remove here in order to flee the bombing. You can thank Renamos that you're alive.''

''Truly, I do!'' Chayo went down on his knees and took Renee's hand, showering it with kisses. ''My Lady, my life is forever in your debt, my soul is at your feet, my being yours to command.''

With difficulty, she extracted her fingers and hid her

hand behind her back lest he start the routine over again.
"I wish you wouldn't do that," she said.

He stared up at her, stupefied. "But, wh-why, my
Lady?"

"Do you *know* why?" Martil's expression was sly.

Renee glowered at him. "Because it makes me uncomfortable. It's—it's too much."

"An excess of compliments, perhaps. Nevertheless,
Chayo's polite lies are appropriate, are they not?" The
prince agreed instantly with Martil's question. Martil
went on, "He *is* grateful to you. His manner of expressing that, of course, is determined by his biological status.
Among Niandians, males are the applicants, not the
granters of favors. Surely you can see his position. Is it
not the reverse of an arrangement you and your organization sought to overturn, Renee?"

"Niand's culture is a hell of a long way from equality," she said with heat. "And I *don't* want a reversal of
domination; I want choice and balance. Even-steven.
Common courtesy extended to all, without regard for
whether they're male or female. And extra respect de-
pendent solely upon hard work and/or talents."

"Ah! Spoken like a true member of your Sisterhood."

"One of these days, I'm going to hit you, Martil. I'll
take that as part of my share of equality," Renee retorted.

"Shall I hit him for you, my Lady?" Chayo offered.

She giggled and shook her head. "N-no, thank you.
But please don't gush over me, either."

Before he could reply, a musical tone resounded
throughout the hassock-littered auditorium. The Many-
Voices trembled with excitement, making them even more
out of synch than normal. There was a whine and a pop
and two additional figures stood among them. Both were
tall and dressed in full, black robes. Their heads were
huge shimmering blobs and seemed to be all eyes: immense, bright blue eyes, like Tae's, in that glimpse of his
inner self he'd permitted to Renee. The newcomers'
forms shifted visually, never quite still. It was impossible
to make out any details. The image Renee could hang on
to the longest was one of rangy bipeds with a few ex-

posed patches of shiny greenish-gray fur. The major effect was that of watching upright, humanoid seals.

Someone touched her arm lightly. Martil. Renee was proud she hadn't jumped and had no urge to shrink away from the newcomers. Martil gave her a lopsided grin. "*Very* good!"

"Okay," Renee said. "Now tell me—who are they?"

"The Arbiters from the Green Union. Our counterparts."

Renee studied the aliens. "Offhand, I would have said they *were* the Green Union, with that funny-looking fur of theirs."

Martil was busy keeping an eye on Chayo. The prince was watching the newcomers with undisguised loathing. Martil had a brief argument with some of the Many-Voices. Reluctantly, it seemed, they yielded to whatever he demanded. Tae put his fingers against Chayo's head again. The Niandian tried to pull out of the intruding grasp. Tae didn't let him.

Martil held up a hand, requesting patience. "A moment. This will be of considerable importance to you, Prince. Ah!" A three-wheeled cart caromed through the crowd and came to a stop in front of the men. Atop the driverless little vehicle, a Ka-Een pendant lay nestled in a fluffy white cushion. Martil picked it up and held it out to Chayo. "This is tuned to your requirements. It will enable you to better comprehend what is about to happen."

"You didn't go to that kind of trouble for my Ka-Een," Renee grumbled, then added dubiously, "did you?"

"We were desperate, then," Martil said, very arch. "We had to take the only available Ka-Een willing to possess a peculiar alien female who didn't really need a Ka-Een."

"Now look! If you—"

"Shh!" Martil gestured emphatically at Chayo. Looking wary, the prince put on the pendant.

"You'll be one of the possessed, too," Renee said.

Herded by Tae and Martil, she and Chayo walked to a front-row hassock and sat down. Martil sat between the Niandian and Renee, and Tae sprawled on the floor at their feet. "Chayo," Martil began, "I want you to listen. And think before you allow your emotions to respond."

The Many-Voice was babbling. Distracted by the noise, Prince Chayo glared, reserving most of his smothered rage for the two new arrivals in the middle of the room. However, he ducked his head in grudging agreement with Martil's plea. "I will listen."

"Good! Those two who have just arrived here—one is genuinely of the Green Union species, though not of the Green Union; the other is humanoid, like you, me, and Renamos. She has been altered. Converted to match the Green Union somatotype."

"Converted," Renee said, shocked. She conjured visions of Frankensteinian labs. "Permanently?"

"Yes." As she glanced at Tae, Martil continued, "Yes, Tae has been converted to humanoid form. I once considered making the change in his direction, but for various reasons that wasn't feasible."

Tae craned his neck and grinned up at Renee. Her opinions were in a sudden jumble. All her assumptions thrown for a loop.

How would it be, to give up one's own body forever and take on the form of a total alien? Could she voluntarily accept becoming one of those green-furred seal people? Really?

"But—but Tae showed me what he looked like."

"A form he no longer has." Martil patted Tae's shoulder affectionately. "It was a tremendous sacrifice. It is for any Arbiter who must choose so. Our work requires it, though. Renamos, Chayo, the Arbiters deal in concerns far greater than you can imagine. We maintain many such teams as Tae and myself. Teams composed of the dominant species of this quadrant of the galaxy."

"For other such wars as ours?" Chayo asked. He was getting interested in the situation despite his hatred of the Green Union representatives. There was even some sympathy in the look he directed toward Tae.

"Only two such species need be mentioned here, in this particular war. It can be treated locally."

"Locally?" Renee's tone was dazed.

The Many-Voice was becoming louder, and Martil hurried with his explanations before the others drowned him out. "One of the new arrivals is a humanoid placed permanently in the body of a Haukiet: a member of the Green Union, as Chayo thinks of it."

"And now the real Haukiet and the converted Haukiet are back from their mission?" Renee speculated. "Did they have any better luck than we did?"

"Let us learn."

New shapes appeared in the space between the wall-size war map and the cluster of hassocks. There was no whine or pop; they simply burst onto the scene. All of them were glistening, green-furred beings. They were moving and talking, oblivious to the mixed assortment of onlookers. A conference of some type was in progress. Green-furred mucky-mucks debating, questioning, listening to a couple of Haukiets in the middle of their confab. Two oddly familiar Haukiets. They were dressed a bit differently from the others, for one thing.

Renee squinted, making comparisons. She wasn't wrong. The two Haukiets in the confab were the same two aliens who'd popped out of nowhere minutes earlier. In fact, that pair was watching the scene—and themselves—along with everyone else here. Renee leaned toward Martil and whispered, "Holograms?"

He grinned and rubbed noses with her. "I said you weren't stupid. And your species' technology must be more advanced than I realized if you spotted that detail so quickly. Now be quiet and listen."

Caught between a smile and a pout, Renee obeyed. And for a while, she was bored stiff.

"Whereas . . . in consideration of the awesome duties of our noble leaders . . . re-dedication of the principles of . . . under these perilous conditions . . ."

Politicians. A Haukiet version of a smoke-filled room. The Green Union's top-level wheelers and dealers, discussing a crisis. If Renee's Ka-Een was translating the exchange correctly, the basic patterns of an intelligent species' high rankers didn't vary overmuch, whether they were humanoids or shape-shifting green-furred bipedal seals.

One of the figures—one of the holograms, to be precise—interrupted the officialese and said menacingly, "There has been more than sufficient time for argument.

A decision must be made. You will observe.'' The speaker reminded Renee of Martil laying down the law to Vunj.

A miniature tableau winked into existence, enlarging until it blotted out the scene at the politicians' confab. It even hid the duplicates of the Haukiet Arbiter team. A three-dimensional scan of appalling recent events. Slaughter and destruction, in the gory, hideous, stomach-turning process. The people shown being killed were Haukiets. Their enormous blue eyes gazed out appealingly at the audience. Aliens, yes, but . . .

Males, military types and peaceful healers and protectors alike, mowed down. Females, some clutching their infants and kids, dying. Wave after wave of them, trapped, trying to flee, making pitiful cooing cries as they were murdered en masse.

Renee moaned and buried her face in her hands. Martil forced her to look up, and to keep on watching the ''show.'' She did, and wondered if Chayo was watching as well. Could this holographic newsreel cancel out the prejudices his civilization had drilled into him, perhaps since his childhood? He hated the entire race of Haukiet, saw them as the vicious enemies of the Niandians. Could he be reached by these visions of aliens suffering and dying, as his own people had suffered and died?

The holographic scene blinked, and now it *was* Niandians dying. The same thing. Equally gut-wrenching. Overwhelming. And somehow it was impossible to persuade oneself that these were mere pictures. The images were too real, swarming into the brain. They bore an additional whammy, light-years beyond mere projections. The sensation was that of being sucked into the heart of these awful events, evoking an empathy one hadn't known was there. It kept dinning at the onlookers, making them believe.

This is real, Renee thought. This happened. Intelligent beings with hopes and fears and desires, just like me. They, with their dreams and pain—dying. In numbers beyond counting. Dying horribly. Each death new, fresh suffering, ripping me open, as they are being ripped open.

It went on and on. Shattering.

Renee fancied herself a sophisticated movie buff.

Surely she would soon reach a saturation point, when these sickening sights no longer had the power to flatten her like this. She'd be able to watch these as mere visions and shut off the emotional impact.

That moment never came.

The torture continued. The scenes shifting ever more rapidly. Niandians dying in hideous ways. Then Haukiets dying. All dying. Guilty and innocent alike.

And then, there were two images, dominating the rest. A faceless Niandian and an equally unidentifiable Haukiet. They were different, and yet the same, both the quintessence of "die-hard." The kind who refused to back down, even though their acts would condemn billions of innocents as well as their enemies to death. The pair bent over powerful control devices, ignoring their associates' frantic appeals to stop. The die-hards were doing something terrible, irrevocable . . .

A blinding light spread, and Renee saw—while knowing, intellectually, that such a thing was impossible—countless beings on dozens of worlds being bathed in that light. The light killed, agonizingly. And it went on, reaching wider and wider, destroying even the planets those beings stood upon.

And when it was done, there was utter emptiness.

"Look!" Martil said urgently. Renee wiped her eyes with the backs of her hands, and she looked.

The images of total destruction were gone. The hologram of the Arbiters and the Haukiet top dogs was the only illusion remaining in the auditorium. The scene showed the confab in shock. What the returning Arbiter team had depicted with that "hologram within a hologram" scenario of interstellar slaughter was a replay. How much more impact must it have had when viewed close up and personally by those Haukiet leaders! The Haukiets' shape shifted erratically, making distressed cooing sounds. In human terms, they were reeling emotionally.

The Arbiters had a peacemaker's dream come true. They could grab the warmongers by the brain and the soul and hurl them right into the middle of things. No more distancing from their high-level decisions. No more abstracts of nameless casualties and body counts. No more lofty blathering about the ''necessity of deep strikes into enemy territory'' to protect the home world's ''sacred honor.'' No more casual slaughter on a wide scale for the sake of victory—and to maintain the top dogs' status quo. These holograms brought the combatants' leaders face-to-face with their victims, and with their victims' agony. The impact was enormous.

Renee's Ka-Een was translating the hasty exchange that had taken place at the Haukiet Union HQ. Agitation. Remorse. A total state of being appalled. ''It—it must end . . .''

''Immediately,'' the Arbiters were saying—or thinking. ''You must suppress your Yoff rebels as well as your military commanders.''

''This will be done. At once. No more killing. It all will stop, now.''

It did. The last of the holograms winked out.

Renee fought nausea, a leftover from what she'd experienced during the presentation. ''That—that was a hell of a lot more than just an illusion, Martil.''

He looked a trifle shaky, too, though surely he had witnessed similar graphic reports by previous Arbiter peace missions. ''Yes. It has to be. The beings controlling an interstellar conflict must be made to understand exactly what they are doing—and that their enemies are not faceless entities but people. People who can suffer, and whose suffering becomes the leaders' suffering, through these holograms.'' Martil turned and asked tentatively, ''Chayo?''

The Niandian sat in a slumped position, shuddering. ''It—it cannot be allowed to happen. That last . . .''

''The bright light that kills? The Bender Principle weapon. Your General Vunj would have identified it at once.''

''As did I!'' Chayo cried. ''A recent development by our scientists, held in careful reserve. A weapon that kills everything in its path and requires no space fleet to deliver. But the risk . . .''

Martil nodded somberly. ''Desolation is the result. Light-years wide. The deaths of numberless living creatures, many of them quite unknown to Niand or Haukiet. A holocaust spreading across entire star systems . . .''

Chayo grabbed Martil's biceps, shouting, "No! It must not be! It must be stopped!"

"So we hope. With the cooperation of Niand's leaders and the Haukiets'. Both sides have to rein in their hatred of their alien opponents. And both have to control their more fanatical elements, Niand its Gevari, the Haukiets their Yoff rebels. We are Arbiters. We have no desire to take an active part in this interstellar war. But we may be forced to do so, should either faction decide to use the Bender Principle weapon. Those holograms of mutual destruction were for instructive purposes, but they were not merely symbolic." Martil's voice was icy. "Know this. The Bender Principle device is a bludgeon. The Arbiters command a scalpel. And if we must, we will use it to protect those innocent populaces. Or to avenge their deaths, if we are unable to prevent them."

The prince stared at Martil, shaken. Renee, too, felt as if she were suspended over a chasm. She envisioned that scalpel, that incomprehensibly advanced weapon the Arbiters controlled. Something the Niandians and Haukiets had heard about, and dreaded. Something even more terrifying than those awful Bender Principle weapons both interstellar civilizations had developed for possible use against their enemies. There was no anger in Martil. Instead, Renee sensed distress, mingled with adamant resolve.

The Arbiters didn't want to step in that way. They wanted to arbitrate, help the opposing species come to terms with each other, before they went past the point of no return.

But if push came to shove . . .

"To protect the wider universe," Martil said, his manner remote and withdrawn, "the dealer of such a death will be dealt death."

chapter
6

"**T**RY it again. Outside yourself."

Renee eyed the training weapon held in Soh's small, dark hand. The very sight of that stinger was irritating. The Earthwoman was tired of being bitten by that low-voltage gnat.

Outside herself.

After three days, and a hell of a lot of sleep-time force-fed supplementary education, she was finally getting a solid grasp on the concept. Renee darted forward, zig-zagging in her best touch football goal-drive form. She reacted beyond normally processed thought, her focus simultaneously on the training weapon and on Soh. At the last possible instant, Renee leapt, sliding beneath Soh's arm, bypassing the stinger.

The Earthwoman caught Soh under the breasts. Thumbs dug in. Renee used momentum smoothly. No wildly out-of-control, bowling-over reaction this time! She was right on top of it, in command, the tackle executed to perfection. This wasn't a useless tumble that benefited the trainer more than herself. It was a concentrated attack.

She flattened Soh. As they went down, Renee let her hands jolt upward until she had a tight grip on the trainer's throat. Guarding against tricks, she planted a knee in Soh's gut and pinned the smaller woman's legs with her weight.

"Very good," Martil commented from the sidelines.

Renee didn't relax, though, until Soh assured her that the contest was truly over. Over the past couple of days, Renee had made the mistake several times of letting down too soon—and had been jabbed in some tender spots and thrown for a loop as a result. Now she got to her feet and held out a hand to help Soh up.

"You have improved rapidly," the trainer said. Renee's Ka-Een pendant throbbed beneath the Earthwoman's workout suit, translating. Soh's voice was ultra-feminine, with a rich, low timbre. "I might almost trust you with my life. You have learned the true victory—to disarm without unnecessary damage."

"If only we could always have that choice," Martil muttered, and Renee glanced at him unhappily.

Soh bowed, fingers touching her forehead in a gesture of respect. "There is nothing more I can teach you, Renamos, in the time which is allotted to us. If you survive your mission, return, and we will continue these lessons." A depressingly fatalistic remark, that, implying that survival wasn't guaranteed.

Her pleasure in her athletic achievement somewhat dampened, Renee imitated Soh's graceful farewell gesture. What a gem the trainer was! An exquisite, petite humanoid with Oriental features and skin the color of brown velvet. Fragile-looking, but dangerously tough. Soh didn't need that stinger; she could defend herself quite nicely with nothing but her bare hands, as Renee had learned the hard way. The stinger was simply a simulator, to give the student something to aim at.

How would Evy react to Soh? Renee wondered. With envy and pride, I'll bet. This is a black sister par excellence. Capable of going anywhere, anytime, and taking no lip from anyone. She'd sure teach some super-macho jerks I've bumped into a lesson . . .

Depression descended over Renee like a cloud. Evy. All the people and places left forever behind. No going home again.

She had to force a smile when she waved as Soh climbed aboard a skimmer. The teardrop-shaped vehicle hovered, then soared away across rolling grasslands and copses of fuzzy trees.

Martil didn't intrude on Renee's bleak mood, allowing her to work it out at her own pace. Eventually, she took a deep breath and shook off depression. Martil gestured toward the bottom of the hill they stood on. Chayo and his trainer were exercising there while Tae looked on. Renee started down the trail toward them, Martil falling into step at her side. "You have made much progress."

"Yeah, well . . ." She shrugged deprecatingly. "I wasn't a full-fledged couch potato, even in the world I came from. But I sure wasn't a black belt, either. It'll take more than a few days of Soh's training techniques to turn me into a total muscle machine."

"That is not the intention."

Eyeing him sidelong, Renee said, "I know. You're trying to bring me to an acceptable physical peak fast. All those cram courses I'm absorbing when I sleep . . ."

"Plus certain accelerated stimulations of physical potentials. Standard form."

"For Arbiters." Renee grimaced. "I can't complain. Your high-tech gadgets even cancel out the usual aches and pains. I ought to feel like I've plunged into a marathon with inadequate preparation. But I don't. I don't even have headaches after being stuffed full of info during every sleeping session. However, do you really think all of this can convert me into an instant grad-level Arbiter?"

"No." She started to snap at him and Martil grinned. "Much of the required training was already accomplished before you rode the Ka-Eens' transference beam. You were physically fit. And your ability to adapt and accept your unique affinity with the Ka-Een further stands you in excellent stead."

"I'm a regular superwoman," Renee said sarcastically.

"Hardly that! Unusual, though. Else the Ka-Eens would not have clasped onto your essence so readily."

Renee wriggled her shoulders, loosening up after the tension of her workout with Soh. "Whatever. Okay. I understand that the out-of-synch physicians decided Chayo wasn't quite back up to par yet; he needed a few days of ultra-enhanced reconditioning before you could send him home to Niand. So I get the fallout, tuning up my bod, practicing mayhem with Soh.'' She waved a hand, indicating acres of blue-green grasslands with their spangling of alien flowers. ''I still don't see why we travel here to get in shape. It's so beautiful!''

''Why should an attractive location hinder recuperation and a stretching of your athletic skills?'' Martil asked ingenuously.

''Because the scenery makes it difficult to concentrate on chopping your trainer's jugular, for one thing. I suppose that's the idea: teaching me, if not Chayo, to avoid distractions. It hasn't been easy doing that, after you gave us the grand tour of your Arbiter worlds these past couple of days. Believe me, we're impressed. Even if I suspect this 'grass' is really Astroturf.''

Martil was regarding her with his patented sham-evil leer. She was becoming very familiar with that expression, and rather liked it. It made him appear hammily villainous. All he lacked was a handlebar mustache to twirl. He gestured dramatically, his rings flashing in the light of the planet's twin suns. ''Ah! We Arbiters are indeed the ultimate magicians . . .''

Renee smacked his hand. ''Quit bragging. I know all this is standard stuff, to you. Entire planets devoted to research. To linguistics. To physical training and leisure. To studying more advanced symbiotic relationships between the Arbiters and Ka-Eens. Cultural-cataloguing worlds. Worlds dedicated to picking up incoming messages from Out There, messages from light-years away, pleading for your help, like the Niandians and Haukiets have. You've put together a utopia.''

Martil's eyebrows arched out of sight beneath his bangs. ''The Arbiter worlds are hardly that.''

''You've reached the millennium, then.''

''It took considerably longer than a thousand years to . . .''

''Oh, shut up!'' Renee exclaimed. ''You know what I mean. This is a true rainbow coalition on a galactic scale. Perfection.''

''No, we are not perfect. There is always room for improvement,'' Martil protested.

"Close enough to perfection as makes no difference, from the point of view of us less-advanced beings." Renee's depression was returning, dragging at her. "You've showed Chayo and me what the future could be like for our worlds—if they don't fritter away their potentials hating their neighbors. Speaking of his world, isn't it about time you sent him back to Niand? And returned yourselves, to finish the job? Not that these fun and games haven't been enjoyable, but . . ."

"Not merely fun. Necessary, given the ordeal the four of us went through. Tae and I have been working out as well," Martil said, nodding.

Renee heaved a sigh. "I'd like to think these sessions with Soh would eventually help me peel off some pounds. But the Arbiter physicians said they wouldn't, no matter how long I trained."

Martil swatted her rump playfully, and she threw him a mock glare. He said, "It is simply a matter of redistribution, no more. You already carry the correct weight for your skeletal and muscular structure. Your Earth obviously is more massive than my home planet. It is true that you weigh more than I do, but that is of no consequence. It is quite natural, as is Tae's greater strength in relation to either of us."

"Go with what we've got," Renee muttered. She felt her ears getting warm, telling her that she was blushing. Now why should she do that? Nothing he had said ought to embarrass her, pleasantly or otherwise.

He was right on the mark when he noted that she outweighed him. By now, Renee had learned to take for granted a number of facts that would have startled her out of her shoes not much over a week ago, reckoned by Earth's calendar. Martil was humanoid, but he wasn't human. He was taller than she, and a great deal thinner, and lighter. One of the cram courses she'd been force-fed while she slept informed her that his race's bones were spongier than *Homo sapiens*'. In a pinch, she could no doubt pick him up and carry him. Not that she'd need to. With his Ka-Een working symbiotically with him, Martil could travel anywhere he wished in the proverbial blink of an eye.

The Ka-Eens. Info on *them* had been considerably more

vague than the general nuts-and-bolts stuff about the non–Ka-Een Arbiters, their work, and their interstellar complex. Often, Renee speculated that the Arbiters themselves weren't entirely sure about some of the details on the Ka-Eens. Those entities were definitely alive. But according to the Arbiters' own record banks, Ka-Eens didn't correspond to any other life-form encountered in the galactic quadrant. And contact between them and other species had to be initiated by the Ka-Eens rather than by the humanoids or other beings wishing to be "possessed" by one of the near-omnipotent entities. Puzzles. Like a lot of what Renee had been exposed to on this complex of widely separated Arbiter worlds. There were gaps in her condensed education; she hoped those gaps would be filled, gradually, as some of the force-fed data seeped into her conscious mind.

"Listen," she said, "there's something that's been bothering me ever since we arrived here. And you keep dodging my questions about it. If the Arbiters knew they were going to be dealing with a biologically determined matriarchy on Niand, why didn't they send female Arbiters instead of you and Tae? Chayo's mother and sister didn't appreciate that at all. In fact, it was almost an insult to them."

Martil hesitated, reluctant to reply. Finally he said, "I am afraid hearing the reasons behind the makeup of our Arbiter team may wound your ego. Your species ego, as it were."

Baffled and trying not to show it, Renee said, "Try me."

"Very well. The Niand-Haukiet war isn't considered important enough to pull female Arbiters off their more critical assignments elsewhere. Warring races must accept Arbiters *as* Arbiters, not as caterers to their special local biases. Tae and I happened to be the first available Haukiet-humanoid team when Prince Chayo's appeal for aid reached us. To be blunt, it's surprising that we had *any* teams free on such short notice . . ."

Renee halted. Agreeably, Martil halted, too. She stammered, "N-not important!"

"Not really. No. I said it might wound your ego."

"Ego, hell! That's not what's bugging me. It's the innocent species—like humanity—that are going to get squashed if the Niand-Haukiet war doesn't stop.''

''Indeed. They will, if the combatants do not come to their senses.'' She recoiled, outraged, but Martil caught her hand, holding her fast. ''That doesn't mean that the Arbiters wouldn't care if that occurred—and care deeply. Sometimes, though, such tragedies do occur. Often, we never learn of the disaster, not even after the event. The galaxy is so vast, and belligerent contacts among the star-roving species are, unfortunately, all too common. There simply are not enough Arbiter teams to go around. We constantly send out our message, offering our services to help negotiate peace. But some degree of technological sophistication is needed by the client races in order to translate our signal; we are unable to anticipate every single language out there. And when a communication reaches us, as Prince Chayo's did, it sometimes arrives too late. The destruction has taken place before we have even a chance to intervene. You must consider the larger picture, Renamos. The galactic picture.''

Dismayed, she nibbled a fingernail. ''I—I'm trying to. But it's so damned much to cope with all at once.'' Crosscut drawings of the Milky Way swam through her mind's eye. ''How far are we from, say, Chayo's home world? Right now. At this very moment.''

''How shall I describe that? In what terms?''

''Light-years.''

''Those mean nothing to a Ka-Een,'' Martil said. ''And Ka Ecn are our sole measurement of actual travel distances. If they could operate alone, there would still be a need for us ordinary Arbiters. The Ka-Een are unique entities, and their very uniqueness prevents them from fully understanding the motivations and actions of lesser species. The Ka-Eens' possessed partners, like Tae and me, must assess the situation presented by a mission from the viewpoint of the particular client races involved. Only then, and with strict neutrality, can we make our mutual judgments.'' He took a long, deep breath. ''But, to address your basic query: As light travels and is computed in what I comprehend of that measurement, we are approximately ten thousand light-years from Niand.''

"Approximately." Renee's voice cracked a trifle.

"A rough estimate, only, muddled by the fact that we are a very broad-based collective. We represent many species from many widely scattered stellar regions, and our missions operate throughout a quarter of the galaxy."

"That's . . . a hell of a big chunk of real estate."

Martil looked weary. "Then can you see why we might easily lose track of a war involving merely two species, comprising less than fifty square light-years in their combined spheres of influence?"

"But Earth's somewhere in the middle of their 'spheres of influence'!" Renee argued. "Earth and plenty of other planets that may be home to intelligent life-forms. I don't want us getting crunched while the Niandians and the Haukiets are debating who got to which godforsaken lump of orbiting rock first!"

"And we very much want to protect your planet, and every neighboring planet endangered by that war," Martil said, very earnest.

"Then hadn't you better head on out to Niand? I don't know why you've wasted so much time baby-sitting me. You need Chayo, sure. But I can wait however long it takes. You and Tae and the Ka-Eens take Chayo home, fast. If the truce the other Arbiter team worked out with the Haukiets holds, it could give some Niandian die-hards a chance to strike while their enemy is vulnerable. And keep the whole damned mess going on and on until they wipe out everything . . ."

Martil was amused, shaking his head. "It will take the Niandians some time to learn of that truce and confirm it. We knew, of course, immediately after the Haukiet Council's decision. The Ka-Eens could provide instant transportation for our team back to our central world to tell us of the fact. But both the Niandians and Haukiets are limited by time, space, and their rather crude communication and travel technologies. Further, they have not been able to conduct effective espionage behind their enemies' lines; their somatotypes are far too different to permit convincing disguises for their spies. No, it is extremely unlikely that the Haukiets' agreement to abort those hostilities is yet obvious to Niand. That is beyond their capabilities, though not beyond ours."

That final statement made Renee perk up her ears. Her position remained ambiguous, and for the past few days she'd been waiting tensely for any sort of clue concerning her future. "Ours? Does that mean I qualify as a permanent addition to the team?" She felt as though she were sitting in a personnel manager's hot seat, applying for an opening.

Wanted: Beings willing to abandon their entire past lives and be "possessed" by all-powerful non-anthropomorphic entities. Job entails considerable risk-taking in exotic locales. Join the Arbiters and see the Universe!

. . . If you live long enough.

He refused to meet Renee's questioning stare. "I can't tell you that—yet. In a way, you will know the answer before I do," he said, refusing to elaborate on those cryptic words.

They had reached the bottom of the hill. Tae and his and Martil's trainers were watching Chayo's exercise session. The prince's instructor was an older, stockily built man, and he didn't make things easy for his pupil. Eventually, though, Chayo succeeded in throwing the teacher. Both of them were grinning as they got to their feet. They slapped hands enthusiastically, reminding Renee of black Earthmen celebrating a victory.

No, she said to herself. Don't think of that. I'm never going to see Earth or any of my friends in the Sisterhood again.

Tae walked toward her and reached out, caressing her hair. And all at once, putting away her past was somehow less painful. The intense pang of loss softened. Mementoes were being tucked into a mental attic. When the anguish had faded to a bearable level, she'd be able to take those mementoes out of their figurative wrappings of tissue paper and hold them fondly. By then, they would be lovely souvenirs, but no longer her entire life. Tae's mouth curved in a froggy smile, and he drew back his hand.

Awed, she gazed up at him.

What is it like in your prison of a body, Tae? she wondered. What were you yourself like, before you agreed to let them lock you into humanoid form? I'm sure you were kind and gentle, as you are now, sensitive to others' feelings. Do you ever long to return to what you were?

The big blond Arbiter grinned. And Renee knew that he didn't yearn for the past. He was advising her to do the same. No spoken words were needed. In the past days, she had become increasingly aware of the silent current flowing between Tae and Martil and between Tae and her. She still wasn't nearly as adept at detecting and reading those signals as Martil was. How could she be? But she no longer assumed she was merely guessing at what Tae was trying to tell her.

There was another growing element in that network, one far more difficult to decipher: the Ka-Eens. Hers, Martil's, and Tae's, and, to a very tiny degree, Chayo's. Chayo's presence didn't really enter the picture; he remained strictly an outsider, never joining that subtle thread linking the rest of them.

Ka-Een entities. That was as useful a description of those caged, glowing members of the team as any other. Renee received fleeting impressions, now and then, of formless personalities, darting like cosmic silverfish, able to be in several places at once, and as intangible as gray-green-gold smoke. Yet real. Very, very real. As were their seemingly omnipotent talents for translation and fast transportation, among other tricks.

The men—except for Tae—had been trading friendly insults and arm punches. Finally, the gathering was breaking up, the trainers heading for their individual skimmers. Chayo and the Arbiters waved the others off, and the tiny vehicles wafted away above the rustic scenery. Trainers, Renee had learned, were fresh-air fiends, wanting to feel the wind in their faces. Soh and her counterparts resided on this planet, and could have used their Ka-Een pendants to carry them back to their homes in the blink of an eye. They preferred slower methods, probably for the same perverse reasons humanoids throughout the galaxy maintained craftsmanship hobbies and enjoyed collecting objects their technology had long since made obsolete.

Martil turned to Chayo. "A good session. You should be ready now."

The prince had just finished pulling on the Arbiters' version of a sweatshirt. He fished his Ka-Een pendant free of its neckline and stared blankly at the Arbiter. "What do you mean?"

"Don't you want to return to Niand?"

Renee suppressed a start of surprise. That was exactly what she'd nudged Martil about, minutes ago. Sly dog! He'd been meaning to set up Chayo's homeward-bound trip today, all along! Annoyed, she said tauntingly, "Maybe he's not eager to go back to being a target for assassins."

"Perhaps that problem can be avoided, this time," Martil retorted. "Chayo?"

The Niandian prince didn't look as callow as he had when Renee had first seen him there in the rain-drenched stone alley. And he was considerably slower to pounce on a suggestion. "Of course I would like to go home. And you? Do you dare to return to Niand, after the abominable treatment accorded you there?"

Martil nodded. "We have shown you much during your stay among the Arbiters. Our medicine, technology, leisure activities, and most of all, our peace. Benefits the Niand Federation may one day enjoy, if you survive your present crisis."

"That is why you have displayed these things, is it not?" Chayo said, a wan smile brightening his face. "To educate a savage."

"Hardly a savage! But we hope the experience will better enable you to convince the matriarch, your mother, of our good intentions—and of our power."

"Makes sense," Renee put in. "Your colonies regard the mother world, and the mother world's matriarch, with total reverence. And you *are* her son."

"You exaggerate my influence," Chayo said.

"No, I don't. She cares for you, more, I imagine, than she's supposed to in Niandian society. She was worried that you might have been hurt in the explosion at your apartment, and she broke up that fight between you and Vunj."

A glimmer of hope shone in Chayo's pale eyes. "Do you really think . . . ?"

"Yes! At least try. Aren't billions of your people worth it to you? They would be to me. They *are*, to me."

He drew himself up straight, some of his former puppy-dog enthusiasm in his manner. "I will do my best to earn your trust, my Lady Renamos."

"No! Not to please me. To please yourself. To do the right thing by Niand, and by the Green Union, too."

Martil nodded his approval and said, "The two of you need to change to other clothes." Chayo picked up the boots and cloak he'd worn when they arrived on this planet. Renee involuntarily stiffened. She wasn't used to this procedure, even yet.

The grass and the parklike scenery vanished. There was a fraction of a second when Renee seemed to feel her heart stop its beating. Total blackness. Total . . . nothing.

And then they were in a room with polished white walls. A section of Arbiter Central, as Renee was learning to think of it. They had just leaped—via the Ka-Eens—across a distance that made NASA's and JPL's longest journeys resemble flea hops.

"A skimmer is more fun," she muttered, glancing down to make sure that all of her, and her clothes, had come through intact. That was another reflex she hadn't been able to shake, an emotional defense against what her intellect was accepting. "I must admit, though, that a Ka-Een certainly provides some wonderful bonuses."

Chayo sniffed disdainfully. "Niand has had matter-relay units for several generations."

"Those are a trifle more limited in range than the Ka-Een," Martil said dryly. "Perhaps someday, when conditions are more settled and peaceful, you can demonstrate your civilization's so-called matter-relay units to Renamos. For now, however . . ."

They fanned out to their respective quarters. Standard pattern, when returning from one of these daily excursions. It was almost down to a routine now for Renee. She was actually beginning to enjoy being yanked hither and yon all over the Arbiters' interstellar complex. These few days had been a dazzling sequence of sights, sounds, and discoveries.

Her motel room, as she thought of it, was an all-purpose circular area fifteen feet in diameter. One of the giant hassocks served as both bed and chairs, and if she needed one, a table always appeared out of one of the wall panels, whichever one was closest to her at that time.

She shucked out of her sweaty exercise suit and the room became a sonic shower. It left her feeling invigorated, clean down to her toenails, and the recipient of a complete sauna and a massage.

Renee sat on the hassock. It molded itself to her behind a lot better than those egg vehicle's seats had on Niand. Gradually, as the euphoria generated by the shower abated, Renee grew thoughtful. She cupped her Ka-Een pendant in both hands. It had remained suspended on its chain, nestled between her breasts, throughout the shower, of course; she never took it off. No one possessed by a Ka-Een could. Once—and only once—Renee had tried to remove the chain and the glowing, caged jewel. The stomach-churning despair that gripped her then terrified her now, even in retrospect. It had been an all-enveloping panic, totally unlike anything else she'd ever experienced.

A gray-green-gold entity, encased in a cage that resembled gold, but wasn't. What *was* a Ka-Een? Alive? Definitely. But not an animal. Pulsing, though not with a heartbeat.

"Do you like waterless showers, too?" Renee asked softly. She gazed intently into the gray-green-gold fire. In private, one could talk to a piece of living jewelry and not feel quite like an utter idiot. "Do you have a name?"

"Haven't you asked yours that before now?"

Renee choked down an urge to scream something very unladylike. Martil was leaning against a nearby wall. She cursed the silent efficiency of the room's doors; he'd managed to enter without making a sound.

The Arbiter had changed clothes, even though he hadn't worked up a sweat on the Health and Fitness world. He'd donned a fairly plain outfit, for him: silver-flecked black pants and shirt and serviceable boots. Comparatively businesslike.

Sighing, Renee rose and headed for a wall her instincts, or her Ka-Een, told her contained a wardrobe. The closure slid open and she began to dress, knowing the closet would hand out to her whatever she should wear for the next activity on her schedule. "Look," she said sourly, "don't charge in here without knocking, huh?"

"A member of the Sisterhood of the Nine Worlds, a victim of primitive modesty?"

"Drop the body-pride propaganda. Just say I'm part of a species culture with reservations about nudity, to paraphrase the lecture you gave Chayo under somewhat different circumstances."

"What *is* its name?" Martil wondered.

Renee had wriggled into a brown body stocking and put on the orange dashiki-style tunic the closet had placed in her hands. Niandian fashions, those clothes. Was that a clue to what was coming next? She finished tidying up and growled, "Will you quit making fun of me?"

He looked surprised. "I'm not. Be sure to do the hair, as well." Renee moved to the other side of the room and let a gadget in the ceiling do quick, arcane, and flattering things to her now squeaky-clean mop. Martil went on. "Renamos, I was not being amused at your expense. If anyone has the rapport necessary to learn a Ka-Een's personal term of address, it is you." He stroked his own pendant fondly, his finger rings twinkling around the gray-green-gold within the nonmetal cage. "It is a great privilege to be possessed by one of them. A privilege, and an enormous responsibility. They are most particular about a joining of their essence."

There was a time—seemingly ages ago—when "essence" had suggested perfume to Renee, and very little more. Lately, she'd been reminded often that there were other definitions of the word, in use long before the perfumers and Mad Avenue people had moved in on it. "Essence" was the fundamental nature of something. That was an intriguing way to describe the Ka-Eens. They didn't appear to have physical substance of the sort Renee was familiar with. The Ka-Een could translate—language and solid forms, to employ both definitions of that word. And they communicated, after a fashion, on wavelengths so deep and subtle Renee couldn't always be sure an idea was her own or something insinuated into her brain by her pendant.

Martil continued to stroke his Ka-Een and said, "I have worn one so long, I cannot imagine life without it. No one truly possessed by a Ka-Een can."

Goosebumps raised on Renee's arms and spine. "They—they do sort of grow on one, don't they?"

"Indeed. And your quick, total affinity with a Ka-Een which was literally forced upon you is unheard of." Martil stared intently at her. "Such has never happened among us. And the Arbiters' Ka-Een and non–Ka-Een relationships have endured for a considerable time."

"I won't ask you to tell me how long in Earth's terms," Renee said, trying to make a joke of the conversation. The effort fell flat. "Sometimes . . . it scares me. It's like suddenly developing a twin. More than a twin. A second part of me. The sensations are so constant, I feel I could touch them. But there's nothing to touch. Not physically."

"No. I suspect Chayo does not feel these things nearly so acutely as you and I and Tae do."

"He still has a home to go back to," Renee said, yielding to self-pity. "I don't. So I adopted the Ka-Een wholeheartedly." She studied Martil curiously. "Do you and Tae have homes? I mean, besides the Arbiter worlds."

"Not in the sense Prince Chayo does. You are correct in that summation, and in a remarkable number of others." There was a heavy silence for fifteen seconds or so. Then Martil said, "Your affinity and adaptability are why your activities, these past few days, have differed substantially from Chayo's."

Renee regarded him with suspicion. "We've both been given the grand tour and had daily workouts, haven't we?"

"Yes. But Chayo's sleep has been unaltered. He has not been instructed during his non-waking periods. Nor has he been absorbing a steady diet, as it were, of sub-liminal information and viewpoint-shifting from his Ka-Een." Martil let his words have their full impact.

"He's a guest. I'm a—what? An adoptee?"

"Undetermined," Martil said, looking uneasy. Renee got the impression he'd plunged into these explanations with misgivings. Was he breaking the Arbiters' rules in doing so? It *had* spelled out things she'd wondered about—like why Chayo hadn't grasped some of the implications of the places they'd visited and the Arbiters and staffers they'd met. The tours had been much more than mere sightseeing, to Renee. Apparently all of it was just marking time for the prince. He'd enjoyed, for example, his physical-fitness training sessions, but they'd lacked the cram-course accelerated-learning quality Renee had been aware of. She'd known intuitively, or through her Ka-Een, that she was acquiring in days abilities that would have taken her months to master, back on Earth. Without the Ka-Een—and whatever the Arbiters were injecting into her mind and her physical processes while she slept—none of that would have been possible.

The whatsis in the ceiling had long since finished giving Renee a hundred-buck trim, set, and comb-out. Martil offered her a hand, and she moved closer to him, slipping her fingers into the curve of his palm.

And for a moment, there was a strong, unmistakable electricity flowing between them. The power of the unexpected reaction rocked Renee back on her heels. From Martil's widened eyes and startled expression, she guessed that he had been taken equally off guard.

Renee jerked her hand away, unprepared to deal with such a response on short notice.

The Arbiter didn't move. He was staring at her, and she sensed that he was trying to survey—calmly and dispassionately—their mutual confusion. "Uh . . . this was not planned for," he muttered.

"No, I don't suppose it was." Renee digested what he'd said and added, "So you can't predict every little twist and turn that's likely to come down the pike, huh?"

Martil's smile was shaky, lacking its normal confidence. "It was never claimed that we did." He cleared his throat and patted his Ka-Een pendant, as if seeking reassurance. "This physical interaction was . . . well, perhaps a pair of humanoids, male and female, thrown together, as it were."

Was he having serious second thoughts about what had happened? Overriding the basics with intellectual dissection? Renee sympathized; she, too, was attempting to distance herself from that completely unanticipated surge of sexuality.

Sure, she wasn't oblivious. She'd found herself eyeing Martil as well as Tae and Chayo ever since she'd met them. Perfectly natural. The same way she would have checked out an interesting and/or physically attractive man on campus or one doing business with SOS. The sort of automatic assessment that occurred constantly in ordinary human contact. Ninety-nine times out of a hundred, that's all it ever amounted to: an admiring looking-over. Shopping around.

Rarely had Renee known the type of instant—though short-lived—electricity she'd felt with Martil, moments before. But . . . she *had* gone through this, previously, a couple of times. With painfully mixed results. Those experiences nagged at her now, increasing her rush to caution.

It probably didn't mean anything, she thought. Except that I've been feeling down in the dumps a lot recently. Why shouldn't I? Kidnapped, by accident, admittedly, from the only world I've ever known. And being forced to learn in a hurry that I'm permanently stuck out here. Severed from my place and time. No sure indications of what's going to become of me. Thrown into a whole series of astonishing encounters and hair-raising adventures, without any advance warning. Having to make constant adjustments and swallow a hell of a lot of stuff I used to think was sheer fiction . . .

No wonder I'm at loose ends, all down the line. Vulnerable. Isn't that one of the shrinks' favorite terms? And vulnerable can mean "pushover." Lonely can easily shift into wanting physical comfort, and for physical, read sexual.

But . . . with a man who isn't even a *Homo sapiens*-type human? A man who responded mostly because he feels sorry for me? No!

She was relieved—and also a trifle ego-dented—that Martil seemed as willing to let the matter die a quick death as she was. It would have been more flattering if he'd put up a protest, or at least expressed disappointment. Instead, he cleared his throat again and said, "We must not read too much into this incident. I am certain you comprehend the subconscious causes. Neither of us is to blame for the unprecedented events which brought us into this proximity."

"Yeah, proximity," Renee said, mildly annoyed. "That old devil proximity. I suppose that would explain things . . ."

"Not that I find you unattractive."

She bristled. "Just a minute, buster. If anyone's going to pick up the options, here, it's going to be me. Who says I can overlook *your* drawbacks, momentary attractiveness to me or not?"

A sly smile brightened Martil's vulpine features. "Ah! Of course. I forgot. I must not trample upon your rights of selection. Forgive my presumption." Renee gritted her teeth, her temper roiling, near a bubbling seethe. The Arbiter's smile broadened to a grin. "Shall we put this topic aside, for the time being? There are other matters to attend to."

Despite his cheery tone, the words were a splash of icy water over the last remnants of Renee's mingled irritation and interest. Other matters. Like a war. She nodded, chastened.

Martil didn't offer her his hand, this time. He simply waved at a wall, and the two of them stepped through a door which formed itself for them, probably on the Ka-Eens' cue.

A few dozen yards along the corridor beyond, they were joined by Tae and Chayo. The prince tagged readily at the big blond's heels. Seeing that, Martil and Renee exchanged knowing glances. During the layover on the Arbiter worlds, Prince Chayo's attitudes had undergone a noticeable alteration. His bias had been softened, a lot. He no longer saw a cleverly disguised mortal enemy when he looked at Tae. In fact, he'd learned to like the tall Arbiter and often actively sought Tae's company.

If Chayo could bend that far, maybe there was still hope that all of the Niandians—or at least their leaders—could be made to concede the right of existence to the Haukiets.

The corridor led the four directly to the room with the oversize hassocks. It was busy, as usual. Hordes of the Many-Voiced out-of-synch people hurried through this area or huddled in groups, conversing in their odd, multitrack way.

Renee accepted their presence absently, as she'd come to accept a great many peculiar things these past days. Martil had filled in some of the informational gaps for her. She knew, now, that the out-of-synchs were actually several different distinct exterior forms. Some Arbiters and staffers deliberately hid their true appearances in that fashion, either to avoid upsetting other Arbiters who might be instinctively put off by their physical shells, or to protect their privacy. Some out-of-synchs weren't even in the big room; they were holograms, participating in Arbiter affairs via remote links. Some simply were aliens who reflected light rays oddly. Whatever their species, shape, color, or sex, they were all participants in high-level Arbiter decisions. This room was one of the key points in the interstellar peacemaking operation.

Nevertheless, none of the out-of-synchs paid much attention to the four new arrivals. The Many-Voice rarely did, unless Martil and Tae were bringing something up for a vote or otherwise requesting a group opinion.

The figures bustled about, eddying into shimmering clusters, the multitrack voices jabbering too fast even for Renee's Ka-Een to handle. The scene reminded her of an alien stock market. Everyone here was terribly intent upon her, his, or its business. Understandable. They were trying to plug holes in thousands of dams being broken by clashing civilizations, scattered throughout a quarter of the Milky Way galaxy.

Martil stopped at an empty area ringed by hassocks. Tae and the others arranged themselves in a small circle, with Martil anchoring one side of the ring. "We are ready to depart?" the fox-faced Arbiter asked.

"It might be wisest for you to send me to Niand alone," Chayo said. "I do not wish you to endanger your lives again."

"Ah! Tae and I have a mission to complete. We will accompany you, and this time we will make sure to stay close to those who can provide firm protection."

Chayo shook his head. "I cannot do that, as was amply proved when we were bombed at Hell-All."

Renee broke in. "Martil means protection provided by your mother and sister. They certainly have enough clout to fend off whoever bombed your quarters and us. If the team sticks close to the matriarch and her Eminence, the Gevari won't dare attack. And if your mother went ahead and convened the Federation's colony leaders, the diehards would have to be out of their skulls to strike; they'd lose whatever support they had with Niand's remaining fire-eaters." Martil was grinning rakishly. On the defensive, Renee finished, "Well, you advised me to learn all I could about Chayo's culture as well as the Arbiters'."

"And you have spent your time well," he said. "I take it, then, that you intend to return with us?"

"You— I have a choice?"

"Of course. Wasn't that what your feminist organization, your Sisterhood, was about? Free choices? Isn't that what you insist upon as your philosophy of life?"

Flustered, Renee said, "Yes, it is, but I didn't know you were going to leave the whole thing up to me."

"Why not? The Arbiters have trained you to defend yourself."

"And brainwashed me thoroughly."

"If you prefer that terminology. We prefer to think of it as rapid subconscious education," Martil said amiably. "The critical detail is—you are in the possession of a Ka-Een which chooses to remain with you. The Ka-Eens' judgment is that you are capable of selecting your future course. You may live here, as you have done in recent days. Or you may be transported to a world whose civilization is somewhat similar to that of your home planet and take up residence there . . ."

"Get dumped again, you mean," Renee said, her tone sharp. "No thanks!"

"Or you may choose to accompany us back to Niand. The option is yours. You cannot be forced to become an apprentice Arbiter. That is the way you view your present situation, is it not?" Martil waited until Renee gave a grudging nod, then went on. "You must decide of your own free will whether to accept the very real dangers involved in our work."

A nervous chuckle rattled in her throat. "You won't turn me down if I decide to say yes?"

"For reasons you will understand eventually, I hope, no, we won't reject you."

Renee took a deep breath. "Then I think I'd like to tag along."

Martil turned to the others. "Very well. We go together."

"Perhaps they have missed me," Chayo said longingly. "And Niand is my mother world. If I am to die, I prefer to die there, striving to preserve my people—and prevent the slaughter of the Green Union and the innocents on my Lady Renamos's world."

Martil's body became rigid, his eyes unfocused. Renee felt him moving into total rapport with his Ka-Een. With all four of their Ka-Eens.

And the room with the big hassocks disappeared.

chapter
7

Renee had grimaced when the transference started. Now she unscrewed her face and peered ruefully at Martil. "I'd like that more if I knew how to turn my own pendant on, instead of depending on you to zip us all over the universe."

"No doubt you will do exactly that soon enough, given your affinity for our partner entities," Martil said, grinning.

They had landed in the palace in Niand's capital. Glancing around, Renee saw that they were in an anteroom adjacent to the matriarch's boudoir/HQ; visible through a half-open door were that floor-to-ceiling lighted war map and a wisp of diaphanous curtain, blocking off a corner and some furniture. Chayo moved in that direction, intending to make contact, when an ugly woman exited from there. She was carrying clothes and humming absentmindedly. But when she saw the prince and the Arbiters, chores were forgotten. She instantly dropped the clothes, shrieked, and fled back into the boudoir/HQ.

Chayo rolled his eyes. "Beyeth has never taken out-of-the-ordinary things well," he said. "However, she is an expert carrier of gossip. The news of our return will be transmitted to everyone in the palace in short order."

In the next room, vocal pandemonium was in progress.

Renee heard the servant, Beyeth, shrieking and babbling excitedly and the matriarch's stern, disbelieving tones as she attempted to calm the other woman. As Chayo led the way across the threshold, Beyeth shrieked anew and ran out, apparently rushing to carry the news, as the prince had predicted.

"Ch-Chayo . . . ?" The Matriarch's expression was a chaos of incredulity and tearful anguish. "Oh, if this is a trick, a cruel image used by the Gevari . . ."

Her son knelt, quickly going through the hem-kissing ritual. The matriarch didn't let him finish. She gripped his arms, urging him to stand. Touch convinced her of the reality of his existence. "You— you're alive! Alive!" And the two of them embraced, both weeping.

Renee, Martil, and Tae waited on the sidelines. There were thundering footsteps approaching. Then Princess Zia, Beyeth, and a handful of Niandian soldiers burst into the boudoir. Zia froze momentarily, gawking at her mother and brother. Beyeth chattered frantically, too fast for Renee's pendant to translate smoothly. But it was plain the faithful servant of the royal family was crowing in triumph. "See! See? I told you he was back!"

Her shock absorbed a trifle, Zia raced forward to join the embracing matriarch and Prince Chayo. Beyeth grinned fondly, making an observer forget, briefly, her spectacular ugliness. Even the soldiers seemed delighted at this astonishing turn of events. Their chatter hung in the air, hovering around the reunited royal trio.

"I knew those Gevari hadn't got him with that bomb assault on the old ruined city . . ."

"But how did the Prince escape 'em? According to the general's investigation, they had the place zeroed in . . ."

"Them Arbiters musta done it! I heard they had thousands of tricks up their sleeves . . ."

"Yeah! Look at the Lady Renamos. She pulled it off, she and those assistants of hers . . ."

Renee swallowed a guffaw. She and her assistants? Right! Martil, too, had the grace not to laugh. He and Tae waited with reasonable patience for Chayo and his female relatives to finish their emotional display. It had been a shock for Chayo's mother and sister, undoubtedly, and they had a lot of grief-turned-to-joy to pour out. Renee glanced at the big blond Arbiter, wondering if his species would have reacted the same way. Tae smiled knowingly, answering her question without words: *Yes.* The Haukiets might not embrace in the same manner, and they probably had no need to speak. But the feelings wouldn't be much different in a similar traumatic situation.

A wall panel, not the war zone one, was lighting up. Beyeth gestured imperiously to the ranking soldier. "Transfer those calls of inquiry out to the communications staff. Inform each of the Most High's loyal subordinates and the people of Prince Chayo's safe return."

Zia had managed to pull herself out of the tearful three-way hugging session, and as the soldiers marched toward the exit she added an order: "Be certain to notify General Vunj. He will be exceedingly surprised. Correct, Mother?"

The matriarch held Chayo's face in her hands, gazing at him like a woman wakening from a nightmare. "What? Oh, yes. Vunj will be surprised, to say the least. As are we! But he will be grateful as well. Oh, my son! How wonderful it is to see you again!" She groped for a chair, blinded by a new rush of tears, and her children and the servant hurried to aid her; for once, the automatic chair the floor produced wasn't quite in synch with the matriarch's thoughts, and she needed help to settle herself into it firmly.

Other servants were peeking in all of the doors by now, muttering among themselves. A few of them tried to catch Chayo's eye, and when they did, waved at him eagerly: "Welcome home!" He was visibly gratified, and somewhat amused, by the storm of attention his return had brought.

Zia comforted her mother until the older woman's tears dried. Then the matriarch lifted her head, staring at Chayo. "We . . . oh, we thought you were dead! Vunj's top recovery units searched and searched the ruins of Hell-All, after your garbled message to your sister was finally deciphered. But there was nothing! Only newly created wreckage. We could not even find your body . . . or the bodies of the Arbiters."

A muscle twitched on Chayo's jaw. "The Gevari rebels

did their best to destroy us. Were it not for the talents and technology of my Esteemed Lady Renamos and Martil and Tae, I *would* be dead. And so would they.''

''I—I thank you, Lady Renamos . . . Arbiters Martil and . . . and Tae.'' The matriarch held out her hand to Renee, wanting to touch her son's rescuers. Responding, Renee took the woman's bony fingers in her own. The ruler smiled, blinking away a few tears clinging to her lashes, and said, ''Please. You must call me by my personal name, my dear Renamos. I am Onedu.''

''I am honored for the privilege, Onedu,'' Renee said, returning the matriarch's warm smile. Contact! And progress! And she hadn't even needed Tae's big hand sending vibes through her back to establish such a solid Arbiter-Niandian link!

Matriarch Onedu sat up straighter, her eyes flashing with a surge of anger. ''Be assured, my son, that when the Gevari's foul treachery was discovered, there was vengeance taken. A most severe vengeance. It reached far out into our Federation, to a number of key colonies where the Gevari had been most active of late. You should be pleased to hear that you have a most loyal following, Chayo.''

''Fiercely loyal,'' Princess Zia confirmed. ''And large.''

''When the news spread of the outrage committed against you and the Arbiters, your faction rose and was in the forefront of the retributive strikes. Not even Vunj could temper their anger. You must immediately go on the Niandian communications link,'' Onedu said, ''and show our subjects that you live. Oh, how relieved they will be!''

Martil broke in, asking bluntly, ''Are we to take it, from your account, that the Gevari rebels have been eliminated?''

Onedu labored to drag her attention from Chayo. She looked blankly at Renee for a moment, then at Martil, and said slowly, ''No, I would that were true. But their power has been drastically diminished.''

''Their numbers have been slashed,'' Zia added. Her tone was somber. ''It was . . . a very bloodthirsty business, that vengeance of Chayo's faction.''

The matriarch nodded. "The Gevari who remain have gone very far underground, politically. It is ironic. By their murderous assassination attempt, they turned much of Niand's opinion toward peace efforts—the thing the Gevari have most opposed. It is no longer popular to be known as one of them, or even to share their sympathies." Her features brightened as she looked up at Chayo once more, and again she patted his face lovingly. "This son of mine has ever been cherished by the majority of the Niandian people . . ."

"That's good to hear," Renee said. "But as long as there are *any* Gevari rebels still running around out there, we'll have our peace negotiations cut out for us. All too frequently, beleaguered fanatics react to official suppression by even more violent last-ditch tactics to keep the war going."

Martil leaned toward her and whispered, "Didn't I assure you that you were properly prepared for this mission?"

"You did nothing of the sort," Renee lied, sotto voce.

Inwardly, she was replaying what she'd just told the matriarch, and finding it all too true. Fanatics. Do or die. An attitude that if they weren't going to be allowed to play their war games anymore, they'd blow up the whole damned place, and everyone in it.

"The Gevari will not succeed," the matriarch was saying sternly. "After what they have done, they—and their cause—are no longer an issue. However, much remains to be settled before there is any hope of peace. Hostilities have not ceased."

"Have there been any wide-scale attacks by the Green Union of late, Most High?" Renee wanted to know.

"Not wide-scale, no. But numerous brutal forays in isolated stellar systems."

Martil said, "Remember what the Arbiter Renamos explained to you, when last we spoke. That this war encompasses a great deal of distance, and communications are necessarily slow." He didn't mention his disdain of the primitive technologies of Niand and the Green Union, which showed tact and considerable restraint on his part. "Keep that in mind when you deal with lingering warfare in your various colonies. As we trust the Green Union will do in their regions of space, when still-belligerent units of Niand's forces have not yet received word to lay down their arms.''

''Has the Green Union agreed to the truce the Arbiters have proposed?'' Zia wanted to know. Her face was very open, and distrust flared in her pale eyes.

Chayo didn't let the Arbiters reply to his sister's query. He said glibly, ''As I observed, from the vantage of the Arbiters' own worlds, such a truce is indeed being seriously discussed.''

Discussed. Being weighed and considered.

A lie. Or at least a distortion of the facts. Chayo had witnessed the successful Arbiters' mission to the Haukiet leaders. Why was he determined to sit on that info, for the time being? Was he concerned about premature leaks of that news? That made sense to Renee. The Gevari rebels were down, but not yet out. They could seize on this nugget and make one final ''kill all the Green Union monsters!''-style strike at the Haukiets' nerve centers.

And the peace would fall apart before it could be confirmed.

In this case, a fast lie might well be the best move.

But . . . did Chayo fear a leak *here*? In his own mother's HQ? Who was he guarding against? Perhaps someone in that small army of servants and soldiers, peeking at the scene from the boudoir's various doorways.

A phrase out of Renee's past studies popped into her mind: A ruler is rarely, truly alone.

And plainly Chayo intended to make dead sure that only his mother and sister would hear about the truce. He wasn't going to spit it all out right now, when there were so many other ears—some of them possibly belonging to spies—waiting for any scrap of info he might drop.

''Then that is where you have been in this absence?'' Matriarch Onedu wondered. ''On the Arbiters' worlds? How was this done? There was no evidence of a spacecraft. I do not understand how these journeys are made. How the Arbiters travel here and there so freely.''

Chayo pursed his lips. ''Nor do I understand the technology, Mother. It is far above our present state of science, as are the Arbiters' powers.''

That reminder of the outsiders' presence—and the earlier mentioned threat of their superweapon—crushed Onedu's remaining curiosity on that particular score. But she couldn't resist scolding her son a bit. "I do think you should have notified us, Chayo, that you were alive. Zia and I were devastated, thinking you slain. And you could have warned us when you were returning."

Renee stepped in, wanting to spare Chayo the necessity of telling any more lies. "There were reasons. Arbiters' reasons, Onedu." She paused, glancing at Martil, waiting to see if he wanted to take over. He didn't. His sly expression as much as announced that he thought she was doing fine. So far. He might have tons more experience in Arbiter affairs and tons more knowledge in general. But on Niand, he was at a disadvantage, just as Tae was; they had the misfortune to be male. Renee said, "In light of the Gevari's nearly successful assassination attempts, the Arbiters felt it best to keep strict secrecy concerning our travels. Now that we are back on Niand, we can entrust our safety to you and her Eminence . . ."

"Call me Zia, please!" the princess interrupted. Her smile was a lovely veneer. Maybe she felt friendly toward the female Arbiter who'd rescued her brother, but Zia hadn't warmed up nearly as much as the matriarch had. Still on her guard, and it showed in her face. Unlike Evy, the Niandian princess had no background in putting on what was called a "ghetto face," the unrevealing mask that told a potential opponent nothing about the emotions within. Why should Zia learn that trick? She'd never been in a subordinate position. Quite the contrary.

"Zia," Renee responded politely, nodding.

"And of course you can depend on our protection," Onedu added. She and her daughter both extended their hands to the Arbiters. It was an all-embracing gesture, and the older woman spoke for them. "You shall not beg for our shelter in vain. The Mother and the Mother-Sister will shield you from all who might wish you harm." The matriarch continued in a less formal tone, "And rest assured we will also purge the Gevari from our nest."

"Most High, Eminence," Martil said, "my Lady Renamos must speak to this matter of espionage. Please attend her words."

He had rolled out a red carpet, and if she wanted to

be treated as a full-fledged member of the team, Renee had to step onto that mat. She felt Tae's guidance, subtle but strong, and some of her apprehension abated. He and Martil were simply letting her carry the ball right now to underline what they wanted said. It would have more impact, coming from a woman. Renee addressed Onedu and Zia carefully. "Consider: How many persons knew of our journey to the city of Hell-All? It was discussed, if I recall, only within this room, in your presence, and that of certain Niand soldiers."

"Vunj and his cohorts!" Zia gasped. The matriarch gaped at her daughter, and Zia went on. "You know intelligence has had its doubts about his willingness to seek a truce. We must insist upon a thorough investigation. Without letting him realize it, naturally."

A chill chased up Renee's spine. She hadn't formed any love for the general the time she'd met him. But she couldn't ignore Chayo's later comments—that General Vunj might well be his father, and Zia's. Presumably Zia also had her suspicions on that score. And the matriarch's reaction tended to confirm her children's guesses about their father's identity.

"That will be done, on my command," Onedu said with obvious reluctance. "We must neglect no avenue in our search for all traitors. Still . . . it is difficult to accept."

"Perhaps there is treason in the general's ranks," Renee suggested. "A soldier he trusted with the information, unknowing that the man had Gevari connections." Onedu pounced on that possibility, though Zia looked dubious. Renee went on. "At any rate, we agree: The matter should be thoroughly examined."

"As it will."

"Most High," Martil said, his patience wearing thin. "What of the conference of Niandian leaders? Has it assembled yet?"

Zia, her tone chilly, answered him. "When we thought Chayo was dead, and that you Arbiters were, plans for the conference were temporarily suspended. Then, the search to root out the Gevari faction triggered a near–civil war on some of our colony planets. We have had much to do, putting down those uprisings."

"And the conference?" Martil persisted, a terrier with his teeth in the princess's leg.

"Thirteen of our colonial premiers are at present here on the mother world, ready to begin discussion of a truce. Wisi of Corlane, a powerful leader of our largest colonial branch, is due to arrive on Niand today," Zia said, glowering at the dark-haired Arbiter.

The matriarch took up the explanation. "Seven premiers who were en route to Niand were forced to turn back to put down Gevari insurrections on their planets. Four of them have since informed me that they are now, once more, free to attend the peace negotiations. I will contact the remaining leaders immediately and command them to begin their journey. However, if they are not able . . ."

"Proxies?" Martil asked hopefully. He waited until Onedu and her daughter had mentally converted that into something understood in Niandian culture, then said, "We appreciate the problems caused by Niand's far-flung interests. But is not further insurrection better dealt with after your Federation is finally at peace with the Green Union? Then your enemies can no longer strike at you simultaneously from without and within."

Renee recalled Martil's previous sour put-downs of Niand's "far-flung" interests, and his scorn of such a comparatively primitive culture. Diplomacy spoke with forked tongue!

And his mention of the war dredged up other memories, less amusing ones. Watching the Arbiters' gruesome holograms, the ones with an extra whammy. Her Ka-Een pendant throbbed gently, and Renee sensed that sooner or later, she'd have to participate with Martil and Tae in repeating that same gut-wrenching show for the Niandian peace conference delegates. As the other Arbiter team, the one assigned to the Haukiet empire, had been forced to use that tool to convince shape-shifter warmongers to close up shop, so this team had to convince Chayo's people.

It wasn't a demonstration Renee looked forward to. To participate, she'd have to push her newfound apprentice-Arbiter skills and knowledge hard. And it was going to

be damned unpleasant, seeing those awful scenes of carnage—and feeling them so intensely—again.

Could she help the men use that particular tool? Did
she have the necessary training? Had all that forced education during her sleep done the trick? Was that possible, even for the Arbiters' futuristic technology?

As if in answer, those scenes of carnage blurred in her
mind's eye, replaced by other images. Three Ka-Eens,
and herself, Martil, and Tae possessed by those Ka-Een
entities—a team. A team with six members. Apprentice
or not, she was in this, up to her neck and higher, if
need be. She trusted the little gray-green-gold critters to
give her a boost, if called for.

"There is much wisdom in what you suggest, Martil of
the Bright Suns," the matriarch was saying. "This conflict, it costs my children, my people, too much. The
treasure required to maintain the forces is almost incalculable. But the cost in blood and suffering has become
past bearing. We have our pride, territorial claims we
cannot—we *must* not!—relinquish easily. But . . . if there
is the slightest chance of compromise, of peace . . ."

"Summon your absent premiers home to the mother
world, Onedu," Renee said gently. "Gather your leaders. Let them hear us, and let them decide with you
whether it shall be peace or further bloodshed. Do this
for your children's sake, for your citizens are your children, Most High."

Niandians. Ordinary beings simply trying to get by.
They always took the brunt of these collisions, whether
those were between two of Earth's nations or two vast
stellar empires. The little people. For several years, in
the life she had known before, Renee's heart and soul
had been devoted to helping those little people. Dammit,
someone had to take their part! Otherwise, they continued to get stepped on, ground into the mud. It wasn't
fair! On Earth, or here on Niand. Or even on a Haukiet
world, where the green-furred shape-shifters undoubtedly had their own versions of the little people. If for no
other reason than to give all of them a break, this conference simply had to come together.

"Yes. Yes. I will," Onedu vowed. "You are right. I
must. This killing must stop." The matriarch bent over

the arm of her chair, speaking into a mini-communicator that suddenly appeared there, popping into existence. The Niandian monarch's voice was heavy with sorrow for past agonies as she relayed the orders.

Renee felt a tug on her emotional strings. She hadn't felt such caring rapport with an older woman since her own mother had died. This was no place for succumbing to sloppy sentimentality, though. The Arbiters had too much to do. There was no time to waste in getting all gooey affectionate over a woman not even related to her, and an alien woman, at that.

Sighing, Renee shifted her gaze, and caught Zia staring worriedly at the matriarch. Concerned for her mother's distress? Or was something else eating at the princess? Zia became aware that she was under the Arbiter's scrutiny and hastily changed gears, trying to plaster a polite smile on her perfect features. It didn't work. That was no poker face. Zia didn't dissemble at all well. She'd never had to learn how. No need for her to adopt a noncommittal, uninformative expression. She wasn't a member of a sexual or racial minority, playing humble games for the bosses. Zia didn't even have to bat her eyelashes and pretend fascination with economically powerful but utterly fatuous men. Not on this world, and not with this species. Women here ran the entire show, from bestowing their smiles on a would-be suitor to deciding if a prospective father was worth their cooperation to put something in the uterine oven. Plus Princess Zia was the second-highest-ranking female of her race, a race ruled by a biologically dominant woman.

"It is done," the matriarch said, and shut off the chair-arm communicator. "And I have additional news. Wisi of Corlane will be arriving within the hour. She wants to make your acquaintance, Arbiters, if you would be so kind. Would you meet her?"

Zia perked up, delighted. "Excellent! A deft political move. Wisi of Corlane, Renamos, wields enormous power in our Federation. Her vote at the peace conference will be crucial. If she is favorably impressed with you . . ."

Renee darted an inquiring glance at her Arbiter partners. Tae was nodding his approval of the suggestion.

Martil was shrugging, not wanting to concede whole-hearted agreement on such short notice. "Thank you, Zia. We shall be happy to meet the Esteemed Lady."

"And perhaps I can show you a few of Niand's architectural and cultural achievements, along the way," the princess went on with growing enthusiasm. "You had no opportunity to view these things on your earlier visit, to our shame."

"To the Gevari rebels' shame," Renee corrected, smiling. "Chayo, are you coming with us?" Zia bristled at that, as if annoyed. Did she object to her brother butting into an excursion she was hostessing? Sibling rivalry, on a social level?

The matriarch pressed her son's hand. "No, Chayo must contact his loyal subjects and give them the gladsome news of his survival. We will arrange a Federation-wide broadcast while you meet Wisi. Do go on. And please enjoy yourselves, Arbiters."

Chayo made a fuss over Renee's hand, kissing it, an act that made Zia raise her delicate eyebrows. "My Lady Renamos, my apologies for not joining the party," the prince said. "But as my mother has said, I have duties to perform."

"Most commendable."

Onedu regarded him dotingly. "Chayo has ever been an obedient son. Was he not willing to make the first approach to the Arbiters for my sake? Knowing the dangers, he still took the risks."

"Yes, ever the brave gallant," Zia said brusquely, then gestured to Renee and the men. "If you please, Renamos, will you and your . . . companions follow me?"

They did so, leaving Chayo in a whispered conversation with the matriarch. Renee did her own share of whispering, telling Martil, "Fulfilling his end of the bargain, huh?"

They and Tae were trailing Princess Zia along a palace corridor. Servants scuttled out of their way and armed guards snapped to stiff attention, saluting.

"Chayo is a useful ally, no argument," Martil muttered.

So he backed up Renee's speculations—that Chayo intended to get in a bit of propaganda during his broadcast to the Niandians. And it was likely he'd throw in some private stuff to impress upon the matriarch just how powerful the Arbiters were. He'd been convinced, thanks to all those tours of the Arbiter worlds Martil and Tae had dragged him to. Now it was Chayo's job to pass on his discoveries to his people's absolute ruler.

Corridor after corridor. Hundreds of wide-eyed, busy servants. Ranks of uniformed soldiers, eager to serve. Finally, Zia led the Arbiters out into a colosseum-size room. The place was jammed with Niandians. All shapes and sizes and a variety of colors. Some had the ivory, butterscotch-colored, or burnt-caramel skin tones Renee had already encountered. Others, though, came in hues she had to hope were natural, and not the product of a hideous disease.

Petitioners pushed forward as soon as Zia entered. One especially aggressive fat man with a startling mauve complexion fought his way to within touching distance of the princess. "Your Eminence! If you would just look at this trade agreement I'm proposing to the Sush Cluster worlds . . ."

"Not now, Deputy Premier," Zia said, sniffing.

Other petitioners and favor seekers crowded in. Renee, Martil, and Tae were hemmed in tightly by a cordon of soldiers; the men and the princess did okay, but Renee, much shorter than those three, was beginning to get an attack of claustrophobia. She couldn't see anything but shoulders and waving hands and Zia's back, and the air was getting stuffy, here in the middle of the melee.

"Eminence! The delegation from Taja wishes . . ."

"Eminence! The launching of the . . ."

"Daughter of Onedu! Her Excellency the submatriarch of Esher requests . . ." That was the fat man, again, screaming to make himself heard over the crowd.

Zia glanced around nervously. The crush was getting out of hand. There was a noise behind the princess, someone bulling her way through the mass of court favorites. More soldiers appeared, thrusting aside the pushiest of the pleaders, and the matriarch's ugly servant, Beyeth, edged past the Arbiters, tugging at Zia's arm. As the guards emphasized the order, Beyeth roared, "Her Eminence will hear your petitions later, at the

proper time, during the regular procedural audience."
Her voice was strident, slicing past the babble quite effectively.

As the hangers-on fell back, Zia started forward again, saying, "I beg your indulgences, my loyal subjects. Duty demands my attention elsewhere at this moment."

Renee thought of the "bad cop, good cop" shtick; Beyeth and the princess played that expertly. The servant growled and chased people off while Zia blew verbal kisses, keeping taut the bonds of affection between herself and the Niandians.

Efficiently, and with minimal violence, the soldiers cleared a path clear across the room. Renee was awed. Mob scenes on TV usually showed a platoon of troops doing that. Here, all that was necessary was a royal command, a bit of yelling by ugly-faced Beyeth, and a bit of firm line-holding by the guards.

Even so, it took Zia's group quite a while to reach the far end of the huge chamber. She led them through another door, into another gigantic room, and a meeting with yet another batch of favor seekers. These plaintiffs, at least, were quieter, politer, and fewer in number than the pushy bunch right outside the royal suite's halls. Renee noticed that these particular petitioners weren't so richly dressed as the first gaggle, either. Presumably, they were of lower rank. They backed up meekly when Beyeth put her leather lungs to work. Bowing, the hopeful citizens stood on the sidelines as Zia paraded past. The bolder onlookers shouted compliments, and many cried, "Remember me at the audience later, Eminence!"

Beyeth sized up the courteous crowd, softening. "Child, maybe we could stop here and you could speak with them a moment."

"We are in a hurry. There is no time," Zia said. "Besides, would you inflict their whining and wheedling on our guests?"

"Your mother would."

"Far too often," the princess retorted. "That is why she is so weary so often. They demand too much of her." Making a sudden decision, the young woman said, "Beyeth, inform security that I want no further such outrageous scenes as that one leading to the presence corridors. Disgraceful! Those people presume on their ranks. And I especially do not want my mother disturbed by them. Not now, while so many of Niand's premiers are visiting us.''

''Yes, Eminence,'' the servant murmured, her face stonily disapproving as well as ugly at that moment.

Beyond the second big room there was a third, and then a fourth, and a fifth. Chinese boxes; each one was a bit smaller. And in each there were fewer applicants for Zia's attention. Eventually, the rooms ended in another corridor, this one a ramp, sloping down. The princess, heading up the pack, led the Arbiters and soldiers and Beyeth to the bottom and executed a sharp right turn, halting facing a wall decorated with sparkling tiles. The others stopped—with varying degrees of neatness—all around her, bumping into one another. The troops took positions in a box formation, bracketing Zia and the other civilians. The princess prodded at one of the tiles. Nothing happened. Renee wondered if the door was stuck, or if Zia had forgotten its combination.

Then, abruptly, all of them were somewhere else.

chapter 8

Renee's stomach did a lurching flip-flop. She groaned, clutching her midriff, and gawked. The soldiers were fanning out, forming a protective cordon along a balcony railing in front of Princess Zia.

The group now stood on a mezzanine level in the midst of a giant's barn of a concourse. The ceiling arched cloud-high above their heads. Immense transparent walls bracketed both ends of the structure. Zia stepped out of a kind of three-sided box lined in tiles—very similar to the alcove they'd entered wherever they had been.

Correction: wherever they had come from. Obviously, they were no longer in Niand's palace. No subterranean passageways in this place. No sign of baby-blue egg vehicles. Or corridors. The ambience was that of an above-ground artificial cave, and sunlight shone through those glass walls. A ramp escalator angled down from the mezzanine. Below, on the main floor, literally thousands of Niandians were hurrying about on their business. It was Union Station cubed. Commuter central for an alien world, complete with vendor's booths, what seemed to be ticket sellers, and an ongoing blare of a PA. Was that last announcing train or flight departures and arrivals?

She muffled a hiccup, rubbing her stomach some more. "Damn. I wasn't prepared for that," Martil was saying through gritted teeth. Renee quit studying the indoor scenery and looked at him. He was red as a beet. Blushing up a storm! "Stupid of me, and after Chayo's constant warnings, too." Tae patted the smaller man's shoulder consolingly.

"Oh. That was one of their matter-relay units?" she guessed. "Well, it worked out okay. The Gevari didn't evaporate us. They couldn't: Zia's with us."

Martil sighed. "Still, it was stupid of me."

"Cheer up." Renee grinned, giving back one of dozens of sly leers he'd handed her ever since she'd met him. "You can't be brilliant all the time, even if that is what you get paid for." He rolled his eyes, his expression very sour, and she had to turn away to keep from bursting into rude laughter.

"Honored Arbiters," Zia was saying, "this is Niand's Federation hub spaceport. Premier Wisi of Corlane will arrive here soon. In the meantime, I would like to show you the numerous sections of this complex—our multi-world trade agency and some of our latest model space-craft."

More soldiers were galloping to stand attendance on the princess. They lined up smartly along the sides of the escalator, along the balcony as far as the eye could see, around the matter-relay box Zia and her party had just stepped out of. One young officer saluted her Eminence so smartly Renee was half-afraid he'd fall over backward. Spiffy uniforms. Boots polished to a mirror sheen. And weapons. Each carried an object that looked a bit like the cattle prods Renee had seen in some of Evy's films of early-day civil rights demonstrations. These prods, however, were fancy. Solid white, and accented with a tracery of fine gold wires twining about the barrels' lengths. At the tip of each weapon was what appeared to be a stinger.

Zia was still pointing out objects of interest on the floor below. Proud of her species' achievements and this evidence of a thriving interstellar travel-and-trade net-work. "Very impressive," Renee said, not having to stretch the truth to be polite. "Are we still in the capital city?"

"Not at all. We are seven sun-markings distant," Zia replied.

"Not line-of-sight, then," Martil muttered. Very softly, he added, "They *are* quite advanced."

Something was shimmering to Princess Zia's left. General Vunj took shape there. No, not Vunj in the flesh, Renee decided, after a close look; this was a three-dimensional image of the general. A hologram, and less convincing than the Arbiters' version of that science. That fact should help reassure Martil that the outsiders were still ahead of the Niandians in one field, at least.

"Eminence, Zia," the general's image said, "my intelligence and special defense forces strongly advise you to leave Traffic Central. At once!" His blustery tone hadn't changed a bit during Renee's absence from this world.

"We thank you for your concern," Zia said, feigning a bored yawn. "But it is unnecessary. As you can see, the royal bodyguards are here to protect me and our guests."

"It is not safe! You have not heard. Premier Wisi's shuttle will be delayed. An errand of mercy takes precedence," General Vunj went on, trying to emphasize his words with arm waving as well as volume. "The medical ship is even now making an emergency landing. There may be diseased or contaminated war victims aboard. You must evacuate that area, Eminence!"

He paused, and the image's head turned, its lips moving, but the sounds it made inaudible. Apparently Vunj was talking to someone off camera. Meanwhile, a persistent ache was building in Renee's ears. She became conscious of a distant, high-pitched mechanical yowl.

Vunj's image faced Princess Zia again. He quit trying to bully her and resorted to a coaxing manner. "I beg of you, please do not remain in such a dangerous area. It will be not only dangerous but most unpleasant for you . . . and for those Arbiters . . ."

The mechanical yowl had developed undertones. It was becoming a crescendoing hum, drowning out the rest of the general's appeal. Renee glanced around and saw that the enormous glass walls were transforming themselves into doors, folding back. The transparencies were polarized, making seeing through them a dark-glass challenge. Now, as they moved aside, miles of tarmac came in sharp view. They reached to the horizon. A runway for space-ships? It seemed to go on forever.

She could make out, with difficulty, a row of towers on the distant skyline. And coming from those towers— an optical illusion, no doubt—was a frighteningly large vehicle. It resembled a dirigible designed by titans. A yowling, thundering juggernaut. Renee hoped the pilots had good brakes, because whoever was driving was aiming straight for the concourse's doors, which suddenly didn't seem nearly big enough.

"Please leave the area!" General Vunj screamed, barely audible.

Zia ignored the image. She took Renee's hand and led the way to the ramp-escalator. The Earthwoman glanced over her shoulder nervously. Martil, Tae, and Beyeth were following her and the princess. So it must be all right. The five of them rode down to the main floor. Zia didn't appear apprehensive at all about the approaching space-ship.

She knew what she was doing, Renee saw with relief. The vehicle had finally decelerated noticeably. Now it was moving at a crawl, slowly nudging its huge nose in those large doors. A sea of waiting Niandians moved out of its way, eddying on either side as the craft whined to a complete halt.

"We had not intended that you should observe such terrible things, Arbiter Renamos," Zia said. "But per-haps it is best that you do, before the conference of our leaders assembles. I am afraid this is going to be one more awful example of an all too common occurrence in our Federation. The passengers are victims of the Green Union's attacks. For most, adequate care is not available on the frontier, and if we are to save these poor wounded people of ours, we must bring them here, to the mother world. Here they will have the best we can provide."

Curved door-ramps were being lowered on both sides of the spaceship. Crew members ran down, shouting or-ders at the waiting crowd of medical personnel. Soldiers were herding the concourse's regular commuters and off-world travelers back to the opposite side of the great building. Schedules were plainly being shuffled to ac-commodate the unexpected emergency. The immense new arrival was a spacegoing ambulance of gargantuan proportions.

Zia led Renee to where one of the ramps was now anchored to the concourse's floor. Guards swarmed around the two women, creating a living fence. Renee peered up the ship's ramp and saw that there were a number of bays with many different tiers inside. All of them bustled with activity. Niandians in gray-and-white striped uniforms were working feverishly in there. Renee knew without having to ask that the personnel were medical staffers. Their outfits contrasted strikingly with the soldiers' severe brown uniforms.

A steady stream of shiny cocoons were floating down the ramps, guided by the gray-and-white stripers. Renee craned her neck as the first cocoon went past her. A Niandian man lay inside. A wounded soldier? Perhaps a wounded civilian? Impossible to tell. He was nearly naked, and a shimmering transparent bandage covered his gaping wounds. The futuristic gauze kept out dirt and germ-laden air, but it couldn't hide the gore. Renee reflected that it didn't actually matter if the man had been a combatant or merely a hapless civilian caught in the interspecies crossfire; right now he desperately needed help.

So did the other passengers. Gray-and-white stripers were steering the cocoons into a nearby concourse area. That section had been roped off hastily to serve as a Niandian version of a M.A.S.H. unit. Local medical personnel were arriving by the dozens, moving in alongside the staffers from the ship, laboring to save lives.

More cocoons. More and more and more. Renee supposed the odd containers were sort of enclosed stretchers. She hoped they included life-sustaining medications to tide the victims over until the doctors and nurses could apply more thoroughgoing repairs. It was obvious the rescuers were confronting a major crisis here.

The setting—and the people—were alien. The huge ship and this spaceport an impossible fiction by all the standards Renee had once known, on Earth. And yet, there was a poignant universality to what she was seeing. A traveling hospital, transporting the injured to a central, expertly staffed home location. And as they would have on Earth, the healers were responding to the call, working frantically.

The situation reached out and grabbed Renee by the heartstrings. These victims weren't Afghanis, or African victims of brushfire war and starvation. In fact, they weren't human at all. Not Asians, Africans, or whites, but Niandians. Their skins were butterscotch or ivory-colored, a burnt-caramel hue or mauve, their hands missing one finger, naturally, by genetic design. Not Renee's race. But they were hurting. Hurting terribly.

There were some walking wounded, helped down the ramps by willing med staffers. A few victims didn't look cut up, but they had obviously suffered unimaginable emotional injuries. Psychic traumas, driving them to the brink of madness and possibly death. Renee had never seen such haunted eyes.

Zia waded slowly into the mess. Beyeth dogged her mistress's footsteps, Renee close behind, moving in a kind of appalled trance. Many of the victims in the cocoons recognized the princess and called out to her. Without hesitation, Zia took their hands, stroked fevered foreheads, got her delicate hands bloody comforting them.

"Mother-Sister . . . Eminence . . . oh, help us, help us . . . !"

"We will," Zia assured them, her voice tender. "You are safe now, my people, my children. You are on Niand, the mother world, and we will make you whole again." Beyeth beamed at the younger woman, nodding her approval. And then she, too, was doing what she could to solace the war refugees.

Hordes of whimpering wounded surrounded Renee. Now and then, she spotted Martil and Tae, yards away, on the other side of the line of royal bodyguards—who were still trying to maintain their protective cordon around Princess Zia. Neither Martil nor Tae seemed particularly agitated; they weren't struggling to break through the soldiers' ranks to get close to Renee. Apparently they didn't feel there was any risk involved here to the Arbiters.

But plenty of risk to the wounded being borne down out of the hospital ship. They had to be kept alive until the doctors could save them. It would be unbearable for these poor people to have been transported so far, to be brought into the bosom of their mother world, only to die.

Renee quit trying to keep track of where Martil and Tae were and pitched in to do what she could. She had no illusions that her CPR training and a basic Red Cross emergency first-aid course would perform miracles here. For one thing, she didn't dare attempt too much; what might help a member of *Homo sapiens* wouldn't necessarily be a good idea for a Niandian. There were enough options, though, that she was sure she could at least do a small amount of good.

Nearby, Zia was ordering some spaceport official, "The pilot will not be reprimanded for her precipitous actions. What was she supposed to do? Leave my people on some ill-equipped colony world to die? No!" The princess jabbed a blood-smeared hand at the captain of her bodyguards. "Make note. Prepare a commendation for the ship's pilot and crew. I do not wish them chided for excessive fuel consumption or other such nonsense."

"Right on," Renee said, wanting to applaud. But she was too busy at that moment, helping a gray-and-white striper steer one of the cocoons into the staging area. When they had it settled into an empty spot, the striper hurried back to the ship to fetch another patient. Renee knelt beside the cocoon-stretcher. A Niandian woman lay inside, a toddler and an infant nestled against her. All of them had been horribly burned. The woman blinked up at Renee. "Lady? You—you have come to help us?"

"If I can," Renee promised. Another gray-and-white striper bent over the mother and her babies, offering the mother a cup. "Here, I can do that," Renee said. "Go help someone else." The striper muttered his thanks and rushed off. Renee raised the woman's head and helped her drink, and together they persuaded the toddler to take a sip. When she touched the baby, though, Renee was distressed that there was no movement at all in response. A brief examination confirmed her fears. Fighting anguish, she told the woman, "I—I'm sorry. I think the baby's . . . dead."

The Niandian mother fussed over the infant for a bit,

sobbing, then cuddled her toddler closer. Renee tried to express her sympathy and insisted that the woman drink some more water.

"M-my gratitude, Esteemed Lady," the victim whispered. "It is . . . I loved him so . . . even though he was but a boy." Ignoring her painful, bandaged burns, the mother hugged the child still remaining to her and added, "But I have her yet, my precious darling."

Renee's emotions were torn. Empathy for the woman's tragedy, and a jarring sensation. Of course. Among Niandians, it was girl children who were valued. Did their ancient history include barbaric incidents of exposing or drowning or otherwise dispensing with comparatively "insignificant" male babies? In times of famine or war, had the little boys been the first to go? What a startling reversal from the patterns on Earth! And how very understandable, given the Niandians' biology.

Then she smothered her amazement. What was she thinking of? This was no time or place for analyzing the details of Niandian culture. People needed her help.

The liquid in the cup had obviously contained a pain-killer or tranquilizer. Soon, both the mother and her daughter were drifting off to sleep, and Renee moved to an adjacent cocoon to see what she could do to aid the victim in that one.

She lost track of the minutes. In this situation, those who were healthy became parts of a gigantic whole, all of them working together selflessly. She took orders from the gray-and-white stripers and pitched in cautiously. Always, in the back of Renee's mind, was the reality that she was dealing with alien physiologies and had to be sure she did nothing that would make their conditions worse.

Burn victims. Niandians suffering with awful wounds produced by shrapnel or bombs. People mangled in collapsing buildings. Some had breathed deadly gases. Others had witnessed things that had pushed them close to insanity. Occasionally, one of those last would suddenly go berserk. Renee helped the stripers restrain them until an aerosol shot of sorts could be administered to calm the trauma case down.

And all of them, whether physically or mentally

wounded, were in a form of horror-shock. Sinking in remembered misery, their own and that of those left behind on their colony worlds—dead.

Renee tried simultaneously to aid the stripers and stay out of the professionals' way. She steadied cocoons while the doctors worked. Comforted a victim here. Handed called-for gadgets to a med staffer there. Once, she got a bit too near the action; a striper was spraying one of the aerosol shots at a patient and the stuff saturated the air inside the partially opened cocoon. Renee was forced to turn aside and cough for several minutes. Whew! That medicine was foul! But if it helped the wounded, what did it matter?

She moved on, helping. It was her sometime job at SOS's clinic intensified, on a planetary scale. So much to be done so quickly . . .

"Renamos?"

Renee was tending to a tearful Niandian child. She finished giving the baby a drink before she turned around and saw Martil standing beside her. Tae hulked a few steps back. Like Princess Zia and Beyeth and everyone else who was assisting the injured, the men had gotten blood and bits of shimmering plastic bandages on their clothes and hands. Renee wondered why they weren't helping people out now, at this moment? What was so important that they had broken off their humanitarian tasks and bothered her? "What do you want?" she snapped.

"We appreciate your concern. We share it," Martil said. "But you must remember why we are here."

"I know why I'm here—to help these people." Renee glared at the pair. "Doesn't it mean anything to you, that they're hurting?"

Martil blinked, visibly aggrieved. "Of course it does. And we have helped. But what we are doing is superficial. Zia is being permitted to dabble at assisting the medical personnel, as are we. None of our aid is truly necessary, though. This is a form of show, to impress upon us the horrors of the Niand-Haukiet war, from a safe and sanitary distance."

"It does impress the horrors of war on me," Renee said with heat. "And it's affecting Princess Zia, too.

Haven't you watched her? She's bawling half the time. She really cares, cares so much it's tearing her up. Use some of that cold-blooded practicality you're so fond of, why don't you? Zia's more likely to persuade that assembly of Federation premiers to vote for peace—because of what she's seeing here. Now go away and let me work."

"Renamos . . ."

"Go away!" Renee deliberately turned her back on Martil, very annoyed with him.

As she did, a number of Niandian soldiers trotted by, on their way to relieve the princess's bodyguard. The troops didn't get in the doctors' path, but for a brief time they made the area extremely crowded. When they had cleared out, Martil and Tae were gone, too. Renee rather regretted that. She'd been having additional sour impulses, and had wanted to chew Martil out further. Couldn't he see what this shipful of injured Niandians meant? The Green Union was breaking the truce! So much for their promises to the Arbiter team. And these victims were paying the price.

A tiny stab of doubt prodded at her. Renee knew that Martil wasn't callous. And Tae definitely wasn't. Why had she been so quick to assume that they weren't emotionally involved in all of this suffering, as she had been?

"Esteemed Lady?" One of the stripers, looking anxious. "Could you . . . could you help me, please?"

"Sure." Renee got to her feet. Her back was beginning to ache from all this squatting and bending necessary to tend to people in the cocoons. She brushed hair out of her eyes and tried to hide her weariness. Odd. This moderate amount of exercise shouldn't have tired her. Especially not after the thorough conditioning she'd been through, sleeping and waking, on the Arbiter worlds.

The gray-and-white striper held out a hand. As Renee touched the woman's fingers, there was a sharp, biting sensation, and she recoiled.

"Oh! Esteemed Lady! My apologies . . ."

"Forget it. It's static electricity," Renee said with a lame smile. "I've been coping with that all my life. I'm a walking Leyden jar." The striper looked utterly blank, and Renee shrugged off any further attempt at explanations. "Just babbling. Lead on."

Where the striper led her to was a concourse anteroom crammed with children. For some reason, the kids had been segregated here. Renee suspected that was because these were orphans. Most of the kids were injured and all of them were terrified, badly needing soft voices and reassurances. Renee didn't ask questions. She got busy.

The striper hovered as the human took a sobbing toddler onto her lap. "It's okay," Renee said. "I'm pretty good with kids." Smiling, the medical staffer went to take care of other children, and Renee concentrated on cheering the frightened baby she held. Gradually, its tears abated. A chubby little hand groped at Renee's Ka-Een pendant, toying with it in infantile curiosity.

When that happened, Renee received an impression of something poking through a fog. Troubling questions twinged at her brain, and her mind began to race.

What had Martil said? That she should remember why she was there. That the things the Arbiters were doing were actually rather superficial, could be performed by any untrained Niandian.

A show. The hospital ship's arrival couldn't have been a surprise. General Vunj had known it was coming, and had tried to shoo Princess Zia and her guests off to an area where they wouldn't be dragged into the relief efforts. He'd said Premier Wisi's spacegoing flagship or whatever had been delayed, to make room for the emergency vehicle.

But . . . that situation must have been planned hours in advance. Had to be. Even as advanced a species as the Niandians' doesn't have instantaneous travel via Ka-Eens. Even when the matriarch was sending us here, didn't she know we wouldn't meet Premier Wisi? Was she setting up us and the princess? Trying to drag our emotions into the upcoming peace negotiations? So we'd be swayed over to the Niandian point of view and maybe tilt the truce to favor the matriarch's species . . . ?

"Kindly one . . . ?" A medical staffer had tapped Renee's shoulder and was offering the Arbiter a steaming cupful of what looked deliciously like coffee. Renee's questions fizzled out, swallowed up back into that veil of fog at the edge of her mind.

"Oh, thanks!" Renee took the coffee with care, not

moving her head too sharply, lest she jerk the Ka-Een pendant out of the baby's hands. But the kid had lost interest in the jewelry by now. Its eyelids drooped. The rosebud mouth made reflexive sucking motions. Smiling, the gray-and-white striper gently took the baby from Renee and carried it to a down-lined crib, settling it in for a nap.

Renee sipped at the coffee, or Niandian version thereof. It tasted halfway between tea and cola. But it was just right, not too hot, not too tepid, and it lifted her energy considerably.

When the striper asked her to assist other children, Renee was ready to go. She helped soothe a toddler while a plastic bandage was changed. Then there were other kids to calm down. Others to help out of their cocoons. Cribs to be prepared. Funny, elongated nursing bottles to coax the infants to take.

"We need more hands," the striper grumbled.

"You sure do," Renee agreed.

"Would you bring me a fresh supply of soothant, my Lady?" The woman pointed to a medical supply room at the far end of the makeshift hospital nursery.

Renee hurried to fetch the requested drug. It seemed like a very long way to the supply alcove. The enclosed area was as far as it could be from the door connecting the nursery with the concourse. A petite Niandian med staffer was working in the room, unpacking boxes. Her gray-and-white uniform made her look like a volunteer nurse's aide, an effect enhanced by her hair, which was gathered on either side of her head into two long, silky ponytails. But Renee reminded herself that she shouldn't jump to conclusions; for all she knew, this woman might be a famous surgeon among her people. "The soothant?" Renee inquired. "It's needed."

"Ah! This way, Esteemed Lady Renamos." The striper led her still further into the isolated room.

Again, something nagged deep within Renee's brain, trying to get to the surface:

Where were Martil and Tae and Princess Zia? How had she become separated from them? Maybe she should head back into the main part of the spaceport.

The striper opened a cabinet and took out some boxes

with squiggly Niandian writing on them. Renee started to thank her, but the woman's eyes widened in alarm. She was gazing past Renee in obvious dismay and anger. Intrigued, Renee turned to see what had drawn the med staffer's attention.

A couple of soldiers were out in the nursery. They were determinedly threading their way through the forest of cribs and cocoons.

"Dirga, they are coming." The striper was speaking urgently into a flattened pen-style radio, one much like the gadget Chayo had used in vain at Hell-All when he and the Arbiters were being bombed. Why was the striper carrying one of those? And who was she warning? Who were "they"? The soldiers? Those must be some of Princess Zia's bodyguards, come to check up on the errant Arbiter and make sure the royal guest was okay.

"Stand aside, Esteemed Lady."

The little gray-and-white striper was holding one of those billy clubs with the gold-wire tracery. She pointed it, and a red streak shot from its tip, lancing across the supply room. It caught one of the soldiers just as he stepped through the door. He clutched at his head and fell, flopping grotesquely, like a dying fish. In the nursery beyond, injured kids watched the scene with the intent, silent stare of the very young. Blood spread out under the fallen soldier's body, running over the doorsill.

The second bodyguard crouched behind his buddy and aimed a billy club weapon at the striper. Another fiery lance zapped across the room, in Renee's general direction this time. The bolt chewed pieces out of the supply cabinet.

"Here, Lady." The little woman yanked at Renee's arm, dragging her into a cramped cubicle standing next to the cabinet.

"What the hell . . . ?" Renee protested. None of this was making any sense. Particularly not a shoot-out in the middle of a hospital emergency room!

"They are assassins, Lady. Do not be fooled by their uniforms." The Niandian was muttering into her flattened pen-style radio again. "Do not fear, we will—"

The second soldier charged, firing his billy-club gun. Either he was in too big a hurry to take aim, or he was afraid of accidentally hitting an Arbiter. Every red bolt went wild. The gray-and-white striper, on the other hand, was an excellent shot, a dead-eye. The finger of red fire caught the man high in the chest. He staggered back, dropping his weapon, his eyes glazing. A hideous, gaping hole was where his heart and lungs should have been.

"Oh, my god!" Renee gasped, sickened and appalled.

Her stomach lurched, and she and the striper were somewhere else.

chapter 9

THEY were standing under the open sky with yellowish grass underfoot and funny-looking, droopy trees dotting the prairie landscape. A couple of gleaming towers were directly in front of . . . in front of where Renee was.

Where was *that*?

Dazedly, she glanced to one side, and regretted the action. Her guts and middle ears were in a turmoil. Gulping down a wave of nausea, she saw that she and the woman with the billy-club gun were standing in a tile-walled three-sided closet. One just like Princess Zia had led the Arbiters into earlier. Then, they'd moved in a second from the palace to the spaceport, maybe half a globe away. This time, Renee seemed to have stepped— without knowing it—into a matter-relay terminal at the concourse and come out here.

Farm country. Cultivated fields surrounding her. Maybe those towers were grain elevators.

The gray-and-white striper still held her oddly shaped gun ready. And with her free hand she gripped Renee's upper arm. Firmly. A steely touch. Renee wanted to tell the woman that she could let go. I'm not planning on running, at least not until my stomach quiets down, she thought.

She didn't get the chance. Her stomach flip-flopped

137

once more, and once more they were somewhere else. Renee was rapidly developing a bad case of heartburn.

This time, they had landed in a big room aglow with blue lights. A bunch of Niandians waited apprehensively in front of the cubicle. As the gray-and-white striper shoved Renee ahead of her, out of the tile-lined box, the welcoming committee relaxed, smiles blossoming. Immediately, the striper released Renee, and she smiled, too, a bit apologetically.

She *ought* to! There'd been no need for the rough stuff! Had there?

"Oh, Esteemed Lady Renamos, you have escaped them!" A skinny man clutched her hand, kissing it. Then he dropped to his knees, doing the same to the hem of her dashiki. A plump woman beamed at Renee fondly. Her mood was infectious, warm, maternal. How relieved she was! Her baby, home safe from the wars!

What wars? What the hell was going on?

All of these people had the same rich ivory complexion as did Matriarch Onedu. The blue lights didn't help their looks at all. In fact, the effect added painfully to the queasiness assaulting Renee's innards. That light on that tint of skin made the entire group look like beached fish. Her stomach flopped anew, and Renee said shakily, "I— I'd like to sit down, please."

"Of course, of course!"

They led her to a divinely soft sofa, plumped pillows for her, fussed, and offered her a drink. She shuddered, her nausea flaring. "It's only cold water," the skinny man said.

"Well, that might taste good, about now." Renee took a long pull, hoping the liquid would wash the acid out of her mouth and quiet her guts. It did, some. Feeling somewhat better, she asked, "Would someone mind telling me what this is all about?"

"Those men who attacked you at the concourse were assassins, Esteemed Lady. It was most fortunate that Pasyi was assigned there today to help the innocent victims of the Green Union's aggression. If she had not seen the danger to you . . ."

Renee peered owlishly at the gray-and-white striper. Pasyi was grinning, as if to say, "That's all right; you

don't need to thank me. Just doing my job, Ma'am.''
The woman was as petite as the Arbiter-trainer Soh, and
even more deadly. Especially while she was wielding that
billy-club gun. The thing was a hell of a lot more lethal
than the harmless stinger Soh had used to teach Renee to
defend herself.

Pasyi had either ditched the alien gun or holstered it.
It wasn't in sight. Renee tried, not too successfully, to
forget the weapon, and what it had done to the two soldiers.

"Why? Why would they want to kill me? I'm not any
Niandian's enemy.''

The plump, matronly woman sat beside her, patting
Renee's hand affectionately. "We know you are not, my
dear, but others are so witless, so fanatically prejudiced
that they cannot accept that. Permit me to make myself
known to you. I am Esher, and your family is mine. No
matter that those murderers struck at you. You are safe
now.''

"Why did they want to kill me?'' Renee repeated
plaintively. Wasn't anyone listening to her? It was nice
to be coddled and pampered like this; but confusion had
made her head ache, and her guts were still boiling. Om-
inous churnings going on down there.

"They tried to kill you because you will see the truth,
and judge fairly,'' the motherly woman explained. "We
respect your judgment, Esteemed Arbiter. Unhappily,
those Disloyalists do not.''

Renee wanted to tell them that she wasn't really an
Arbiter, just an apprentice, a tagalong. If they had a
warning for the Arbiters, they should be delivering it to
Martil and Tae.

That thought jolted her. "My companions! Are they . . .''

"Oh, quite safe, my dear. The Disloyalists had no need
to move against them, of course. They are mere men.''

Of course. This was Niand. And Esteemed Lady Renamos, mere apprentice in the true order of things,
ranked head and shoulders above Martil and Tae. In
Niandian eyes, she must be calling the shots. After all,
she was female.

Their tacit assumptions and attitudes were overwhelming. It was light-years past any reversal of cultural power

roles Renee had fantasized. And right now, it wasn't welcome. She'd have been glad to hand over all vestiges of her alleged authority. Let capable male hands take the reins and make the decisions. Martil and Tae had the experience to deal with this situation. Renamos of the Sisterhood of the Nine Worlds sure didn't. Not while her stomach was declaring World War III and her head was spinning like this.

She took another long drink of water. "I—I'm sorry. I don't feel well."

"Oh, my dear. My poor dear." The Lady Esher looked around, saying angrily, "Those vicious hooligans! How they have distressed her. Quickly. Bring us a covering. This child must rest." She soothed Renee, encouraging her to stretch out on the comfy sofa, shushed the rest of the Niandians looking on, and lulled the Arbiter to sleep.

Or was it sleep? Sleep mingled with voices that appeared to come from the waking world all around. Dreams that were not quite dreams.

We will have it at last. Hard pressed. But they have not defeated us. They never shall.

She will be a marvelous living weapon for us.

Do you not think it is too much, too fast?

No, she is strong, this alien. You will see. She will help us succeed.

Succeed at what? But Renee couldn't hang on to the question, and for a long time she floated in nothingness.

Coming back to herself was a struggle, worse than any waking-up session she'd ever gone through. Swimming through tons of maple syrup and sticky tape. She pushed tiredly at the fluffy blanket the Lady Esher had placed over her. Renee's yawn became a soft groan. Her head hurt far worse than it had before she'd gone to sleep.

And the voices were still there. Not dreams. In the room with her.

Moving unsteadily, she forced herself into an upright position and squinted at her surroundings. Nothing had changed. The same ugly blue lights. The same bunch of ivory-skinned Niandians.

"Are they ready?" The skinny man waggled his chin and gazed worriedly at the gray-and-white striper, Pasyi.

"Very nearly, yes."

"Ah, my dear! You are awake!" Lady Esher pounced, taking Renee's limp hand. She exuded motherly concern, something Renee hadn't enjoyed since she was a teenager. That touch and gentle voice were very lulling. They almost, but not quite, banished the Arbiter's nausea and headache. She was grateful for the kind attention.

Somehow, she was on her feet. More or less. As wobbly as a newborn kitten. Lady Esher tucked a plump arm through Renee's and led her into another room. To Renee's relief, the lighting in here was normal. The place was crowded with Niandians, all of them eager to greet the Esteemed Arbiter. Men knelt and kissed her hem. Women embraced her, gushing.

"We were so afraid . . ."

"There were rumors that the Arbiters would be alien males, and be cold, unfeeling brutes, ignoring our suffering and our rights. But you, Esteemed Lady, you will have the beloved gentleness common to all your sex. You will not be cruel. We can trust you."

"So kind, as you were kind to the wounded children . . ."

"Yes, of one heart with her Eminence. It was shown on the newscasts. Both of them, ministering to the injured, not afraid to dirty their lovely hands . . ."

"Sisters of one soul . . ."

"Tender . . ."

"Nurturing . . ."

"She will know the right thing to do, yes, yes . . . !"

Renee was having trouble focusing and remaining on her feet. A sea of faces circled her. Not only ivory-skinned Niandians, now. This was a cosmopolitan gathering. Butterscotch-colored people, those with burnt-caramel complexions, and some of the mauve-hued sub-race. All of them fawning on her, complimenting her endlessly. Lady Esher was leading the chorus, as doting as if Renee were her protegee.

"I—I don't understand what it is you expect of me . . ." Renee said, her words a feeble croak.

Lady Esher hugged her. "Only your womanly duty, my dear. We know you will be fair. When you speak to our premiers in assembly, you will tell them the truth, won't you?"

"Truth . . . sure . . . nothing but the truth . . ."

A Niandian punched a control panel nearby, and holograms took shape. The herd of well-wishers edged back so that Renee could have a clear view. She blinked and leaned unashamedly on Lady Esher, trying to pay attention to the sharpening three-dimensional figures.

She'd seen better holograms somewhere else recently. But she couldn't pinpoint the occasion and place.

These weren't bad, though. Close-ups of refugees. Niandians. Being ordered about. Forbidden to get on board a spaceship. They weren't being permitted to escape from disaster.

"But . . . but those are Niandian soldiers, preventing Niandian citizens from getting to safety, leaving the war zone," Renee said thickly.

"Those are traitors, an appeasement faction within our own military forces," Lady Esher explained. "Look at them! They told those colonists that they had no need to fear the Green Union!"

"Motherless collaborators," an onlooker growled.

"May they rot in whatever hell the Great Nurturer consigns them to for all eternity!"

New holograms formed, and the Green Union was now on the scene. Tall, green-furred, shape-shifting creatures. Another close-up, as something was exchanged between the invading Green Union forces and the traitorous Niandian troops. Not money. The exchange medium gleamed, like precious gems.

And then the refugees were shown again as the Niandian soldiers and the Green Union ones forced the hapless civilians into a dark cavity. A spacecraft's maw. An alien equivalent of those terrible World War II newsreels—captive peoples, thrust into cattle cars, to be carried away to concentration camps, and worse. The dark cavity sealed itself, and the hologram shrank so that Renee could see the entire picture. The ship was launching, leaping up into space, nearing hyperdrive status. Then it winked, entering light-year–spanning speed ranges, stars blurring as the interstellar ship rushed toward its destination.

Renee put a hand to her throbbing temples. Why didn't someone at least offer her some aspirin? If Tae were here, he'd know that . . .

Tae?

But he was a Haukiet, a Green Union species type. Once he had been one of those green furred shapeshifting monsters. The beings who herded helpless Niandians into a slave spaceship—after buying them from Niandian traitors.

Voices, underlining her sudden wariness of what Tae represented. "Those slimy abominations! Our prisoners of war will never escape from them."

"Inhuman! To them, we are no more than animals, mere living tools to labor for them . . ."

"I have heard it whispered that they *eat* us, too . . . !"

"And the Niandian appeasers are no better . . ."

"Sellers of their own kind! They want the war to end . . ."

"Yes! Want it to end now, before we are able to press home our recent victories and perhaps reach some of those prison camps before it is too late . . ."

"Why should the appeasers, the traitors fear a peace that favors the Green Union? They will have everything to gain . . ."

"The invader has already dealt with them . . ."

"Perhaps they even plan in secret to continue their loathsome slave trade . . ."

"And the appeasers have guarded their tracks well. They hope to strengthen trade bonds with those alien monsters . . ."

"Oh, yes, *their* future will be rich, while Niand as a whole suffers, groaning under crippling reparations the traitors and the Green Union will exact upon us . . ."

"Our only prayer is the Arbiter Renamos. If she is fair . . ."

More holograms. Green Union forces moving through masses of kneeling Niandians, picking and choosing. Separating the sheep from the goats, the healthy from the sick or injured. Every so often, a weapon was pointed at a captive, and that Niandian became a pitiful heap of ashes.

Renee clenched her fists, swept with hate. No wonder Lady Esher and the rest were so angry. They had a right to be! Look what their people had been through at the ruthless hands—shape-shifting limbs, rather—of the Green Union.

"And those who are spared . . . oh, it is worse," Lady Esher said, her eyes brimming. She and Renee cried on each other's shoulders for a moment. The Niandian went on, "Our poor females, in particular. Those—those terrible creatures, our enemy, can assume an almost human form, you know. And they . . . they . . . they have a sexual strength far beyond our species' males. They can— oh! I cannot utter such filth!"

No need for her to do so. Renee got the idea, all too clearly, and shuddered.

"Disgusting! Awful!" Renee murmured, swallowing a hiccup. She felt like a wreck, and not just a physical one. She agonized for the Niandians, empathizing deeply.

An unseen finger poked through the cotton candy clogging her thoughts. A memory. Difficult to get ahold of.

Someone else has suffered, too. Suffered just as badly as the Niandians have. I've seen it, in other holograms. Somewhere . . .

"We know how this upsets you, my dear, but we had to make the situation plain. The Arbiters' fairness is famous. We know we can trust you. You will not betray us as the others have."

The nagging memory wouldn't leave Renee alone, but couldn't quite be brought into focus. It lingered, prodding her subliminally, stirring suspicions.

And then her attempt to recall was swept away.

A figure was plowing through the mass of Niandians. Not a hologram, this. Solid. Real. Huge and hulking. An amorphous upright shape with shimmering green fur and enormous blue eyes.

Niandians screaming, running in panic . . .

The Haukiet approached Renee and produced appendages—fingers, of a sort. Those closed about her throat, bearing down. Those blue alien eyes peered directly into hers and a gash of a mouth opened, displaying oddly beautiful pink fangs.

She beat frantically at the hands encircling her throat. The room was spinning, her vision darkening as air got scarce.

Someone had to help her! And fast!

Suddenly, those huge hands fell away. Renee squirmed back a pace and fought to clear the dancing colored lights from her sight.

The Haukiet was still standing almost on top of her, his pink mouth agape. The skinny Niandian man was next to the alien, pressing one of those billy-club guns against the Haukiet's side. After an interminable moment, the Haukiet started to crumple. Pink liquid spumed down his side and onto the floor. Blood. Haukiet blood.

The alien toppled forward onto Renee, and as she wriggled out from under his collapsing weight, the sensations were shockingly familiar. Another, similar collision. A Haukiet—though not looking at all like a Haukiet—falling on her. But that member of the Green Union species had been protecting her, shielding her with his own big body. And he had ended up with a back full of shrapnel gouges, as a result. His blood, too, was pink and foamy.

A great tree of green-furred flesh, the Haukiet's form crashed to the floor.

Renee massaged her aching throat while the Lady Esher petted and caressed her, sobbing. "Oh, my poor, poor dear! Here!" and she handed Renee another glass of something. The liquid felt wonderful going down—icy and soothing. "He might have *killed* you!"

"Tampering!" someone shouted. "That is how he got in here . . . !"

"An agent! A spy within our ranks . . . !"

"We must guard the Esteemed Arbiter from . . ."

"She was his target. He wanted to slay her . . ."

"He certainly tried hard enough," Renee whispered huskily. "In another second he . . . he would have mashed my windpipe. But why? And where did he come from?" Pasyi, the gray-and-white striper, pointed to a tile-walled cubicle, one of the stomach-looping Niandian matter-relay units. "I—I don't understand. How . . ."

"An assassin," the skinny man said quickly. "A suicide mission. It has happened previously. I cannot tell you of the critical losses we have suffered, and in very high echelons of our military and our matriarch's trusted advisors. The traitors and the Green Union manage to penetrate, every so often."

"They will risk all, even their lives, to cripple us," Esher told Renee. "They strike at our leaders, our heart, to leave us helpless. They want to slant any truce negotiations before they begin. And you, my dear, are such an influential person, they *had* to attack . . ."

"Me?" Renee said, incredulous. Her head hurt all the way down to her neck and shoulders now.

"Again and again! They fear you will influence the assembly of premiers in Niand's favor."

"That's—that's not how the Arbiters work!"

Esher hadn't heard Renee's weak protest. "That is why they tried to kill you at the spaceport, why they still try to kill you, using this suicide agent. Oh, we must save you!"

"I hope somebody does." Renee's knees sagged, and suddenly people were supporting her, helping her over to a sofa, urging her to lie down, to sleep.

But this is ridiculous, her mind seemed to say to her. I just woke up. Just in time to be nearly strangled by a Haukiet. Everything is so damned mixed up!

Voices. Soft. Insistent. Worming their ways into her brain.

The Green Union, butchers, killers of children, despoilers of women not of their race, slavers! They must be destroyed. You are the only one who can do it. Tip the balance of the assembly, rid the universe of this inhuman menace . . .

Other voices, not so soft, but equally insistent.

"Do you think it's been enough?"

"That's four now, plus the radiation. That will heighten the effect of the ingested distortants. It is working."

"But she is ill."

"That will pass soon. It is mere alien weakness."

The voices died away to an incoherent muttering. *Real* muttering, not like the dreamy sounds Renee had been hearing earlier.

Or *had* she heard them?

She couldn't be sure. Not of anything. Sick and exhausted, she let herself sink into nothing.

And eventually had to swim back to the surface once more, up through the maple syrup and sticky tape. She rolled onto her side and peered at the world through bleary eyes. A knot of Niandians was in the corner of the room. They were bent over a machine with lots of twinkling lights. A Niandian supercomputer? Whatever it was, they were unhappy about the readings they were getting. One of them spat a graphic obscenity.

Lady Esher was helping Renee to sit up, against Renee's mumbling objections. "My dear, for your safety's sake, we must leave."

The Niandians towed an unwilling Arbiter toward a matter-relay cubicle. Pasyi and the skinny man crowded close, pushing Renee along. She wanted to put her foot down and shout, "No!" Those tile-walled things were bad news. They shouldn't use them. Among their other drawbacks, they tended to make one as sick as a dog.

"Wait a minute!" she finally got out. The Niandians did, though they fidgeted with impatience. Renee struggled to compose her thoughts, grabbing at them as they floated by, like brass rings on a carousel. "The—the Gevari have sabotaged these matter-relay systems. Monkeyed with them. Dangerous. Shouldn't travel that route . . ."

Lady Esher laughed, a jolly, breast-jiggling chortle. She took Renee's face between her plump hands and patted the younger woman's cheeks gently. Very much like a Jewish mother. "Oh, my dear. My dear! Don't you see? We *are* the Gevari. You have been so misguided by our enemies' accusations. They lied to you, about that, about everything. Come now, and you will understand."

Reluctantly, Renee got into the cubicle with the others. Her stomach lurched again, and again they were somewhere else.

"You see?" Esher crowed. "Nothing happened." She led Renee out into that particular terminal's adjacent room.

"Aah, they have . . ." The skinny man was flinging up his hands in alarm, squeaking.

"You are not the only ones who can interrupt the matter-relay procedures."

General Vunj awaited the new arrivals. Vunj and five soldiers. All of them had billy-club guns and were pointing those straight at Lady Esher's group.

Fear was a net, wrapping itself around Renee. They had been caught. Someone had made a mistake, and they had been caught.

Had she suspected General Vunj of being a secret Gevari? Nothing so helpful. Actually, he was the enemy.

"What a pleasure to behold your treasonous face in these circumstances, Hij," the general said. He moved toward the group and seized the skinny man's jumpsuit, shaking Hij like a rat. "You have tricked yourselves, finally."

"Don't hit him," Renee pleaded.

"You ask for their lives, Esteemed Arbiter, after what they have done to you?"

"They haven't done anything to me except show me the truth. You're the one that's the traitor," Renee said, outraged. "You and all those who wanted to tilt the peace process toward the Green Union."

General Vunj gawked, momentarily speechless. Then he studied her escorts with narrowed eyes. "So that is what they told you? It is as the matriarch feared. You fools!" he yelled, venting his wrath on Lady Esher and the others. "You dare do this to an Arbiter? To a guest of Niand? A guest who put her life in our hands? Fanatics! Idiots! Don't you realize that the Arbiters can destroy us all if any harm comes to one of their representatives?"

Nagging reminders were poking their way through Renee's headache. Scratching fingernails along her gray matter. That increased the pounding in her temples and hurt her raw throat. Nor was her stomach behaving at all well.

"I guessed what they were up to when my operatives informed me of your abduction, Esteemed Lady Renamos," the general said. "But I thought even the Gevari would have the sense to avoid such an intolerable act." Vunj's fist was still locked in the skinny man's jumpsuit lapels, and the general shoved Hij this way and that as he spoke, like a living swagger stick. "Things had gotten so confused that the matriarch was wary of me. Of *me*! Well, this will set her mind to rest on that score. You are all under arrest."

There were more people in the room, loping past Renee. Vunj's soldiers fired their weapons, and the newcomers fired back. Men shrieked and fell, writhing. Renee stared in dismayed astonishment. She recognized some of the newcomers. They included the Gevari who had been bent over the computer machine back in—the other place she'd recently come from.

A Gevari shoved a white billy-club gun tight against General Vunj's neck, preparing to fire. Lady Esher threw up a hand. "No. We need him alive. He will be very useful." Vunj rolled his eyes at her, furious, struggling futilely. Esher said, "You know a great deal that can hurt us, but far more that will help us. Yes, I think you will make a most valuable tool."

Lady Esher didn't sound a bit motherly now. Appearances had been deceiving. Renee began to have reservations about her. Esher. Wasn't that name familiar, somehow?

So damned many things were. And all of them kept whirling around dizzyingly, not quite within reach.

She was being hustled into the matter-relay unit once more. Everyone crowding in. General Vunj, too. Where were his soldiers? Renee had a shivery feeling that they were dead.

Lurch!

They were somewhere *else*.

Renee moaned. The lighting here was red. Lady Esher and the other Niandians looked magenta-skinned, and their clothes were garish hues of burgundy and scarlet. Just like the inside of Renee's gut.

"You will never succeed!" Vunj blustered as they forced him across the room. "My people are efficient, and I am not a willing subject for your devious tactics."

"Ah! But we can be very thorough," Esher retorted. She smiled at Renee. "Are we not, my dear?"

"Excuse me. I'm going to be sick."

She was. Very. Something resembling a super-ashtray sat on a nearby table. Renee lunged for it, retching, feeling worse than she could ever remember. Friendly hands patted her on the back, fetched a tissue to wipe her mouth, soothed her. It didn't help much. Her stomach was a tortured lump, and everything got very, very dim.

Darkness. Nightmares. And then . . .

Waking up. Not by choice. She was half sitting, half

lying in a hammocky chair. The headache still pounded at her. Renee longed for something sharp; with that, she could poke a hole in her forehead and maybe let some of the pain out.

Had she fainted? She must have. It felt like it was hours later. It felt miserable—wish-I-could-die miserable. Renee tried to sit up straighter and held her throbbing head, wondering how soon she'd have to throw up again. That diaphragm-knotting pain was still down there, still active. Either she had the worse case of flu on record or somebody had slipped her a Mickey Finn.

"You do understand now?" Soft voices, nearby. General Vunj was being held by the Gevari. No, he was being propped up. He was also being caressed and made over by Lady Esher and Pasyi. Vunj was glassy-eyed, but his jaw was stubbornly set. Continuing to resist to the last breath.

Why didn't he just give in? she thought. It was easier.

And yet, why should he cooperate? That didn't make any sense. None of this did.

Cobwebs, melting within Renee's thoughts.

They've got to be kidding. This one-sided propaganda—All this hate for the Green Union. I know a Green Union type pretty well, and he's a sweet guy. Haukiets. Niandians. They're both civilized, highly intelligent species. So what's all this nitpicking over names and alienness? The universe is big enough for them to live in peace for thousands of generations to come . . .

That was the important thing. Stopping the killing.

The propaganda had been solely for her benefit. And now it was being twisted sideways and applied to General Vunj. The Gevari kept harping on the Green Union's having committed atrocities. Well, what about the atrocities the Niandians had committed? Those *had* taken place. She'd seen them in the Arbiters' holograms, and Renee tended to believe their accounts of events a lot more than she did those claimed by Lady Esher and her fanatics.

Tilt the peace negotiations in Niand's direction. Better yet, from the Gevari's point of view, forget peace negotiations entirely; they wanted to persuade the Arbiters to use their superweapon to wipe the Green Union out of the cosmos.

Let us do their dirty work for them, she thought.

Use our weapon, the scalpel, and forget about the other weapon, the ones the Gevari and top-dog Niandian leaders were holding in reserve. A weapon that could destroy not only the Green Union but all other life in its path.

Including Evy, Susan, Tran Cai, and billions of others back on Earth.

Brainwashing! That was what the Gevari had been doing to her! Sheep-dipping her mind. The previous time she'd been on Niand, the Gevari had tried to kill her, Martil, and Tae. This time they were concentrating on messing up her thoughts so completely she wouldn't be able to think straight at the peace negotiations.

A few implanted prejudices fought the broom sweeping away the cobwebs. The Gevari. Weren't they the good guys? They'd saved her from that Haukiet assassin. Or had they? Was the Haukiet a drugged dupe, programmed to do what his captors commanded, and then killed so that they could convince Renee of their good intentions?

But, remember all the Niandian babies, wounded . . .

The Haukiets' babies had suffered, too. They had been wounded, had died.

No, it was all some sort of plot by the Gevari. She had to get away from them. Now, while her mind was fairly clear.

How? There were so many of them, and she was alone. The matter-relay unit? Renee peered around and spied the cubicle. Her stomach heaved at the sight of the thing. Even if she managed to make it that far before the Gevari got to her, how did she operate the unit? Chayo had said, too, that the Gevari could interfere with matter-relay systems. Escaping in that direction might simply mean she'd be evaporated.

Nevertheless, she knew she had to try. Slowly, Renee got to her feet. Her legs trembled, threatening to fold under her. At least no one was watching her; the Gevari were concentrating on General Vunj. Poor Vunj! If she got away, maybe she could send a rescue squad back, before his brain was totally rotted. With infinite care, Renee edged toward the matter-relay cubicle.

Something stopped her. None of the Gevari had looked around or spoken to her. But she had to stay put. Why?

Wait. A subtle but clear plea. And in a strangely familiar tone. *Wait. Don't attempt it. Too dangerous. We will be there soon.*

Who would?

Abruptly, a wall disappeared, and people were charging into the room, aiming billy-club guns.

"Oh, lord," Renee gasped, "not another shoot-out."

A wild scramble. Gevari diving past Renee, heading for the matter-relay unit. And there was shooting, as she'd feared, and people screaming, falling, bleeding. One of the Gevaris grabbed her arm and started dragging her toward the cubicle. She twisted free and kicked him in the shins, hard. "Let go! I can't take any more of that stomach pump!"

A hand seemed to reach out of nowhere. It seized the Gevari's hair. The rebel fought to get loose. Renee hastily retreated and looked up.

A long way up. Tae was at the end of the hand trying to detach the Gevari's hair from his head. The big Arbiter wasn't smiling, for once. He looked positively nasty.

Renee ducked behind an overturned table. She suspected she was in no condition to participate in what was about to happen. Wary, she peered over the table's edge. The Gevari who'd been shoving her toward the matter-relay unit was fumbling at his belt, for a billy-club gun. Renee yelled a warning to Tae.

She needn't have bothered. Tae drove his free hand into the Gevari's belly, folding the man in the middle like a jackknife. Renee felt a trifle sorry for the rebel, and awed by Tae's strength. She had never imagined the big blond Arbiter striking anyone in anger and was glad he wasn't forced to do so often; that was one Gevari who wouldn't be abducting anyone else in the foreseeable future.

A couple of other familiar figures were very much in evidence in the chaos-ruled Gevari hideaway. Renee's stomach settled down a lot when she saw Martil and Chayo. They were flexing their muscles, enjoying all this masculine heavy action. She didn't mind playing spectator. Not at all!

A Gevari rushed at Martil, billy-club gun at the ready. Martil made no attempt to dodge, and for a heart-stopping

split second Renee was afraid that he'd lost all of his
common sense. He hadn't. The Arbiter deftly avoided the
stinger—just as a red bolt from its tip went zapping harmlessly past him. He grasped the weapon halfway down
its length and heaved it toward him in a startling display
of strength for such a thin being. The Gevari attacker
couldn't control his accumulated momentum. He kept
right on running, under Martil's arm and into a wall. The
deadly dance was almost comical. Martil had simply
helped his assailant along, to the point that the Gevari
knocked himself out cold.

More red streaks from the billy-club weapons were
shooting all over the room. Renee cringed down out of
the target zone again as one bolt ate a piece out of her
table barricade.

When she finally dared peer out from cover again, the
excitement seemed to be over.

Except that Chayo was aiming a Niandian gun point-
blank at General Vunj.

"Chayo, no!" Renee hurried around the table, leaning
on it and other furniture as she staggered across the room.
Tae moved in close beside her, one big hand under her
armpit, steadying her. "Don't, please don't!" she begged
the prince.

Chayo held his fire, but maintained his murderous, un-
blinking focus on the general. Vunj was a man in a
trance, unaware of his surroundings or his danger. The
prince's handsome features contorted with rage. "Let me
kill him, my Lady Renamos. If we had arrived but moments later, these motherless traitors would have had you
utterly within their power."

Renee plucked at his sleeve, trying to make him lower
the gun, which was pointed at the spot between the general's glassy eyes. "I know what they were up to. But
Vunj isn't one of them. He's not a Gevari. He waylaid
them at an earlier station on this matter-relay network,
was going to round them up, put them in custody. They've
been trying to frame him, all along, planting clues to
throw suspicion in his direction. Tell your mother that it
really wasn't him involved in the attacks on us."

"Are you sure?" Martil asked. He was stuffing his
shirt back into his pants. It had pulled out during his

rough-and-tumble exhibition with the Gevari. Renee had trouble meeting his gaze. She was remembering the last time she'd seen him and Tae, there in the spaceport concourse, and the shameful way she'd behaved.

"I'm sure," she said. "They drugged him, brainwashed him, like they did me. I don't know how long it went on. I've been out of things for a while."

"Four Niandian days," Martil said. Her jaw dropped and he nodded, confirming the shocking statement. "We had begun to despair of ever tracking you down. We feared the worst, and we suspected General Vunj knew something of your whereabouts. So we kept close watch on him, were following him. And then he vanished."

"They kidnapped him. He'd laid a trap for them, but it backfired." Renee gulped, mulling over what Martil had said. "I—I couldn't have been jerked around by these Gevari for a whole four days!"

"Do you remember everything that happened to you, my Lady?" Chayo asked. He continued to hold the gun on Vunj, but now his attention was primarily on her. "The Gevari have some very sophisticated drugs and mind-bending techniques at their disposal."

"Did they give you anything to eat or drink? Inject anything?" Martil wondered anxiously. "Something that might have been hidden by the flavor of ordinary tastes or smells?" His concern embarrassed her. She'd been a total bitch, accusing him of heartlessness. And all this time he'd been worried frantic about her. "When the guards separated you from us at the spaceport, where did you go?"

"Oh, lots of places. They lured me on beautifully. Let's see. Before the time when I—when I yelled at you, I think I inhaled something I shouldn't have. I thought I was helping out one of the doctors, but maybe I was being doped up, even then. And then I touched hands with a med staffer and got stung or bitten. I guess that wasn't static electricity after all. A Niandian hypo? Plus I don't know how much coffee and other stuff they gave me . . ."

Martil was aghast. Renee felt her ears getting hot from a chagrined blush. She had been a real ass, hadn't she? The Arbiter hugged her, his relief obvious. Martil's face

was much bonier and foxier-looking than usual, and there
were heavy circles under his eyes. "That was criminally
stupid of them! Didn't they realize that your body chem-
istry is different from a Niandian's?" He turned to Chayo
and exclaimed, "They could have killed her."

"Yes, but not deliberately. My Lady was far more useful to them alive."

"To shill for them at the assembly of Federation premiers. I know that—now," Renee said. "And I just
swallowed their scheme whole, thanks to whatever they
were feeding me. I guess it's a good thing I finally threw
up."

"Was that voluntary?" Martil asked.

Renee glanced up at Tae for a moment, then felt a
pulsing "remember me?" sensation at her breast. She
tried to alter the direction of her stare, to look down at
her Ka-Een—and almost fell over. Tae's hand tightened
under her arm. If he removed his support, she'd collapse.
Slowly, Renee said, "I think you ought to chalk one up
for my Ka-Een. It couldn't get through to me any other
way. So it made me get rid of all that drugged junk. Kill
or cure." She paused, studying the faces around her.
"You told me to wait, didn't you, Tae? You and my Ka-
Een. That's how you and Martil found me, too. Tracked
me down through my Ka-Een, working with yours."

The male Arbiters grinned, two not-very-small boys
sharing a not-very-well-kept secret.

"My prince," one of the Niandian soldiers interrupted, "I regret to report that two of the Gevari escaped: the small woman and the agent known as Hij.
And there is another matter I believe you must attend
immediately, Son of the Matriarch."

Chayo followed the man a few steps to one side. Renee, with Tae's assistance, swiveled to see what the problem was. It was Esher. The plump matron lay on the floor
near the matter-relay unit. There was no visible injury
on her.

"She stumbled, my prince," the guard explained.
"She could not reach the cubicle before we overtook
her."

Chayo knelt, taking Esher's hand and kissing it reverently. "Beloved of my mother, Noble Lady, how can this be? There is some mistake!"

"It's no mistake," Renee said weakly. "She's a Gevari big wheel. *The* Gevari, I suspect. Chief brainwasher. She handed out the orders."

The young prince gaped at Lady Esher in astonishment, shaking his head. "You are a fool," Esher whispered. "A fool, like your spineless weakling of a mother. The Gevari know how to die, and dead I am useless to you."

"My Lady! Don't!" Chayo cried, chafing her hand. She sneered at him, contemptuous of his pity.

"Fools—all of you." Those words were very faint, and then Esher's voice dribbled away into nothing; she stared unseeingly at the ceiling.

"Poison?" Renee said, deeply distressed.

Martil sighed heavily. "No doubt. She wanted to conceal information. Most likely the others we captured here don't know anything much. Lady Esher did. Probably the two who escaped were the sole other key operators in this plot."

"Hij and Pasyi," Renee said. "Pasyi was the first Gevari I met, there at the spaceport. She was in the room with the orphans, and she shot a couple of soldiers . . ."

"Agents," General Vunj said suddenly. He was drooling as he spoke. "Good agents! Tried to . . . dangerous! Dangerous!"

Martil leaned over the general. "Vunj! Chief of Niand's defenses! Do you know the hiding places of the remaining Gevari rebels? Tell us!"

Vunj was sweating badly, his bug-eyed gaze unfocused. Chayo left Lady Esher's body and hurried over to the officer. The prince shook Vunj demandingly. "Remember! You must remember! Why do you always keep these top-level intelligence strikes of yours to yourself? You are the only one privy to the information, aren't you, now that your people are dead? Tell us who besides Esher still leads these die-hard Gevaris. They will destroy us with their fanaticism!"

"Dangerous!" General Vunj repeated, a man trapped

in a waking nightmare, caged within his own mind, perhaps forever. "Destroy us! They will harm the Arbiters—and it is *death* to harm the Arbiters!"

chapter 10

Renee felt a little less blah than she had. A large amount of undrugged sleep, a leisurely "insta-bath," and a general absence of tension for the past Niandian day had done wonders. She didn't feel completely restored, by a long shot, but not too bad, all things considered. She leaned closer to the room's mirrored wall, squinting critically at her reflection. Passable, though hardly spectacular. It—she—would have to do.

A buffet of sorts was spread out on a nearby table. Renee eyed its contents warily and decided she'd already had a big enough snack, earlier that morning. Solid food had produced a definite improvement in her condition—solid, *untainted* food and drink. There had been a number of hours, after her return to the capital city and the palace, when the very thought of eating had nauseated her. Eventually, though, the queasiness had abated. And Martil had assured her that it was safe to indulge in the miniature banquet the matriarch's staff had prepared for the alien Arbiters. However, Renee hadn't felt like taking that chance until this morning.

She tapped a cup of Niandian cola-tea from an oddly shaped urn and sipped at the liquid, letting it clear some of the lingering cobwebs from her brain.

Four whole days—no, five—wasted! What an airhead she'd been! Drugs aside, she should have been suspicious. But, as Martil had noted, the Gevari were sharp; they'd played expertly on Renee's sensibilities and sympathies, there at the spaceport. Martil admitted the scenes of war victims had affected him and Tae, too. They had managed to pull themselves out of the trap, though, and had tried to warn Renee to do the same. Lacking their experience, she had let herself be suckered right in. In retrospect, she wasn't sure whether she was ashamed to be so gullible or proud that she wasn't so callous she could easily step back from suffering humanoids in need.

"Have you slept well, Renamos?" The matriarch and Zia swept into the Arbiters' suite, Onedu taking the lead with polite chitchat. While Zia inspected the buffet and the room's luxurious appointments, the matriarch quizzed their recently rescued guest. "I trust all is as you would have wished? If there is anything you desire, you have only to request it . . . ."

"Proper food and drink," Zia said, nodding her approval. "Not like that which those committers of outrage forced upon you."

"There doesn't seem to be any permanent damage caused by the Gevaris' drugs," Renee replied. She studied the royal pair thoughtfully, remembering some of the nagging doubts that had penetrated her befogged brain even while the Gevaris were pumping her full of alien chemicals.

"They were criminally stupid," Zia exclaimed. "Their zeal for the honor of Niand obviously overcame their wits. They should have realized one of the Arbiters might be killed by the application of those drugs." Her anger was sincere, and her contempt was withering.

"We must make amends to you," the matriarch said.

"You mean for sending me to the spaceport with Zia—when you knew that we wouldn't be meeting Wisi of Corlane but witnessing the tragedy of that hospital ship?" Onedu and her daughter exchanged startled glances as the Arbiter added, "That was a scheme that backfired on you, didn't it?"

"I—neither of us had seen that the situation would become so convoluted," the matriarch admitted. "We confess we had hoped to elicit your sympathies for our people, but—"

"And we are not ashamed of that," Zia cut in, her chin going up defiantly. "Niand has suffered so much. Her children, her helpless ones, those our family is sworn to protect." The princess's voice trembled. "Our concern always must be for them, for Niand. We do not know the Arbiters' viewpoint. We fear, justifiably, that you will not have our people's interests at heart so much as you have the enemy's. It is not wrong for us to wish to show you the pain our citizens have known. Is it?" Zia finished, challengingly.

Renee felt Tae's presence close by, in an adjacent room. He was feeding his support through his Ka-Een and hers. He and Martil, as Renee's "subordinates," had been housed in less elegant quarters. But their separation from her wasn't complete, as the Ka-Eens were at pains to remind her. Nudged by those incoming signals, she said, "No, it is not wrong to want to shield your people, your children. But you have to see that there comes a time when the best way to care for those entrusted to you is to give them peace. As you yourself note, Eminence, the Gevaris, too, were concerned for the honor of Niand. And their zeal has lead them to commit dangerous acts. Further acts, carried to extremes, could destroy the attempts at a truce, could plunge Niand into still more years of war."

Zia scowled. "Matriotism and love of our people is not to blame!"

Her mother laid a quieting hand on the princess's arm. "Be patient, my dear. Renamos, you must forgive her anger. The recent truce proposals received from the Green Union during your . . . your absence are difficult to accept. The enemy is asking us to withdraw from frontier colonies clearly established as ours."

"As they will be expected to withdraw from colonies they have placed within territories you claim," Renee retorted. "There will have to be compromise to attain peace. Compromise on both sides." Zia was gritting her teeth, resisting the concept. The young woman reminded Renee of a tigress defending her threatened cubs. Maybe they had misjudged Zia. She was no beautiful figurehead. She really cared about her people, every bit as much as the matriarch herself did. They were two tigresses, equally determined to get the best deal possible for their people. Renee gestured to a nearby screen, the Niandian version of a computer terminal. "While I was recuperating, I had an opportunity to study the Green Union's message. Are the counterproposals Niand will be putting forward any less chauvinistic? They want to protect their people, just as you do yours."

"Can the Arbiters promise that the Green Union will abide by any agreed-upon terms?" the matriarch demanded. Then she sighed and said, "I but express the fears many of my cabinet and premiers hold. This process will not be easy."

"It was not supposed to be," Renee said gently, commiserating. "It never is. But peace is worth it, Onedu, Zia. Truly."

A door leading to the suite's outer rooms stood ajar. A gaggle of palace servants was visible through the crack. Some of them, notably Beyeth, were peeking in. Eavesdropping. Their faces showed their loyalty, their desire to back up every word their leaders said with fervent cheers. Undoubtedly, most Niandian citizens felt the same. Whatever the matriarch decreed, they'd obey. Even if it meant rejecting peace and continuing this bloody interstellar war that was ravaging their Federation and the Green Union.

Martil had said it was tougher to stop a war than to start one. And how! But the matriarch would have to, despite the Gevaris, and despite stubborn holdouts among her political factions. If she didn't, if she and Zia couldn't call a halt, neither side in the conflict would win, and millions more would die.

"We need a bit more time," Onedu said, and her daughter nodded earnestly.

"Time?" Renee exclaimed. "To do what? To reconsider your people's weariness? To throw more obstacles into the negotiations? To allow the Gevaris time to try to wreck the entire process—again? Perhaps you would rather they had killed me? That would have given you all sorts of time—is that what you're thinking?"

Matriarch and princess recoiled, and Onedu cried, "No! I swear upon the spirit of the Great Nurturer, the Gevaris are finished. They will not strike at you or at anyone else ever again.'' Zia eyed her mother sidelong, frowning. Apparently, she wasn't quite so confident on that score as the older woman was. Onedu went on, ''We cannot tolerate the Gevaris. They are an internal threat to Niand that must be utterly abolished. When Hij and Pasyi are captured . . .''

''You haven't had much luck doing that, I gather,'' Renee said dryly.

''Please leave such matters to us, Arbiter. As soon as the healers have penetrated General Vunj's mental confusion—''

''That will take too long,'' a male voice interrupted. The Niandian females stiffened, annoyed by such rudeness. Martil, Tae, and Chayo stood in the archway linking their room with this one. Chayo glanced ruefully at Martil, plainly wishing the fox-faced man hadn't barged into the matriarch's statement. ''The assembly of premiers must be convened now,'' Martil insisted. ''As I understand it, all of them and your cabinet—a full quorum—are in the capital now, are they not?''

The royal women bristled and glared at Prince Chayo. ''You have told them this?''

Chayo put on a hangdog expression, shamming apology. Beneath that mask, though, Renee detected a grim satisfaction. He might put on a groveling pose, but his personal feelings had a touch of shin-kicking to them. ''Did you not wish peace? I was instructed to—''

''Oh, it is of no matter,'' the matriarch said curtly, waving a hand. ''It is done. Yes, Martil of the Bright Suns, a quorum is gathered, finally.''

''The meeting must take place at once.''

Renee sensed the monarch's hackles rising. Zia, too, was on the verge of erupting. Smoothly, the female member of the Arbiters stepped into the discussion, punching Onedu's and Zia's buttons. ''The people's suffering should end. As soon as possible. And this can only be accomplished if Niand's leaders accept a truce. Is not the reward worth the sacrifice?''

''No one can predict how long it will take for the healers to break down the damage the Gevaris did to General Vunj,'' Martil said. All three Niandians peered at him with dismay. They didn't argue the statement, however.

He'd spotted the stalling tactic and torn away the verbal curtain the matriarch and her children had thrown up. "Therefore, we will proceed without further delay. Time is precious. We will expect the Niandian premiers to be assembled *today*."

Onedu opened her mouth to protest, then thought better of it. Apprehensive, she surveyed the Arbiters. Renee could all but see the wheels turning in the matriarch's mind. Fear conquered her defensive urges. Fear that the Arbiters, now that they were committed to the peace negotiations, could cause more damage to Niand than even the Green Union had.

"I see that there is no choice in the matter," the matriarch said with audible resentment. "Very well. The assembly will be convened. My son will conduct you to the appropriate chamber, when all is ready."

"Thank you," Renee said, inclining her head courteously.

Zia and her mother mumbled the usual insincere parting phrases and headed for the door to the corridor. Beyeth fell into step behind them—after sparing one fierce glower back into the room, aiming her mother-tiger gaze directly at the Arbiters.

Chayo waited until the ruler and her entourage were out of earshot, then grunted unhappily. "They blame me. I shall hear more of this, no doubt."

Renee perched on the edge of the computer table. Tae decided to sprawl at her feet, typically, doing his imitation of a humanoid blond Great Dane. "Vacillation, thy name is woman." The men peered at her curiously and Renee shrugged. "The matriarch's entitled to have second thoughts, I suppose. She wants the peace, and she's afraid that it's going to cost her people too much. Wants to have it both ways, and so does Zia."

"And there is the matter of Vunj," Chayo said. Martil seemed ill at ease, scratching the mole on his chin. The prince went on glumly, "That situation has distressed my mother badly. The physicians can give her no assurances that the general's mind will ever be normal again. It is not merely the knowledge of Gevari plans he holds locked in his brain which makes this an agony. It is a . . . personal response."

Personal. As in family? Renee bit her lip, moved for Chayo's sake, and for his mother's and sister's. The matriarch's edgy attitude tended to confirm Chayo's speculation that his father was General Vunj. In that case, the matriarch had not only lost a valuable military leader, she might have lost the man who was the chosen father of her children. Little wonder her feelings were in a muddle!

"They still haven't been able to coax anything out of him?" Renee asked. "Didn't he put anything on paper? Er . . . on a computer?"

Chayo was sourly depressed. "He did not trust anyone. It is likely he intended to capture the Lady Esher and all her cohorts and present them to my mother as trophies. That is the sort of operation that appeals to Vunj. Unfortunately, he kept his counsel utterly private. And now . . ."

Martil waved a beringed hand, shooing invisible insects. "It is done. We must proceed as we planned. It's possible that once peace is in place, your mother's researchers may be able to come up with new techniques to cure the general. For the moment, the negotiations will take precedence even over the most painful personal tragedies." Tae stared solemnly at the smaller man. The blond's heavy jaw set with determination. Martil glanced wanly at him and at Renee. "Indeed. The mission takes precedence over everything. With each time measure, more beings die. We will not—must not—allow further repetitions of that appalling emergency at the spaceport. The only way to prevent more bloodshed is an immediate truce." He narrowed his eyes, regarding Renee intently. "It will not be easy. How do you feel?"

"I'm recuperated," she said. "I ought to be. I've been eating like a horse this morning. Doing my best to make up for those four missing days." Pausing, she added worriedly, "You did say this food was safe?"

"Quite safe."

Renee turned again to examine her image in the room's not-exactly-a-mirror. The palace's wardrobe women had cleaned up her clothes, removing the vomit and sweat and other evidences of her ordeal. They hadn't been happy, though, with her insistence that she wanted her own garments back, not fancy new Niandian ones. By now, Renee was aware that one never could be sure when a ride on the Ka-Eens' essence transfer would occur. And if that happened, she had better be wearing guaranteed organic materials. To placate the dressers, she had agreed to wear a lacy top-layer white dashiki over the orange one her motel room on the Arbiter world had provided. The effect was a nice touch.

Yes, she'd get by. Renamos of the Sisterhood of the Nine Worlds.

Sister pride? No, Renee pride, which was something better.

"I'm not sure you should let me attend the premiers' assembly with you," she said ruefully. "I'm a flop as an Arbiter."

Martil plucked a square-shaped, magenta-colored fruit from a bowl on a side table and bit into it with a loud crunch. Talking around the bite, he said, "Do not be ridiculous."

The prince had sidled around behind Renee, and now he began to massage her neck and shoulders with a strong but gentle touch. He was very good at that. She found the sensuous rubdown distracting. Nevertheless, she felt obligated to hammer home the obvious. "I'm not being ridiculous. I'm simply stating the facts."

"Are you making fun of Tae and me?" Martil asked. "Is that not your phrase? You are invaluable to the mission. These past days have proved that."

"How? By showing that I'll stupidly breathe and drink and eat things I shouldn't? By letting the Gevaris kidnap me? By making you guys and Chayo risk your necks to rescue me?"

Chayo's thumbs stroked the nape of her neck, and Renee made tiny, reflexive sounds of contentment. He leaned over her shoulder and said, "My mother and Zia guided the search. They were the first to understand that Vunj might provide the key to your whereabouts. They put the full might of Niand's intelligence-gathering divisions behind us."

"Thank them for me—again. Will you?"

"No thanks are necessary," Chayo insisted. "It was a matter of utmost urgency to all of us. Martil is correct.

Your presence is essential to the success of these negotiations. The attitude you have taken in speaking with my mother and sister, your gift for going to the heart of our hidden motivations—these are far more than any Niandian could have anticipated.'' The prince looked at Renee's fellow Arbiters and added, ''It is possible they might make some of the same points, but without your particular touch. It is . . . I do not know the term. A feeling exchanged between you and my mother and Zia. A thing common to your gender.''

''Female intuition?'' Renee muttered doubtfully. ''A magical bond among sisters? Hardly likely. Certainly not across species lines.''

''It exists, my Lady. I tell you only what is so,'' Chayo said, his tone adamant under the deferential words.

Martil flipped the core of the magenta-colored fruit away; the rug promptly swallowed it. ''There is a lot of truth in what he's saying,'' the Arbiter noted. ''It was you the Gevari tried to take control of and manipulate, Renamos, not us. Rightly so, from the Gevaris' point of view. Here, your sex is more than a mere status factor. Lady Esher and her fellow rebels seized upon that—and upon you. At least it was a saner choice than the one they used previously—trying to kill all of us. Saner, and more devious. Considering that, we must remain on our guard against any attempt at repetition. The closer we get to obtaining a truce, the more desperate the Gevari and their sympathizers will become.''

The massage had lulled Renee, but not so much so that she didn't feel alarm at hearing his final comments. ''Desperate enough to use their ultimate weapon?'' Chayo's hands stiffened. He, too, was apprehensive.

''Not if we perform our mission well,'' Martil reassured them. ''And now that you are free of the Gevaris' noxious potions, you will be able to think clearly at the assembly of premiers, Renamos. Most important. You will speak for the Arbiters—with our assistance, naturally. The Niandians will heed what you say, in all likelihood. They will ignore me. They'll regard Tae with deep-seated prejudice.''

Tae craned his neck, grinning up at her. How had she been deluded, even for an instant, into believing that all

Haukiets were murdering monsters? Drugs and brainwashing seemed pretty insufficient reasons for her gullibility, in retrospect.

"That assembly is going to be rife with male and female bias, as well as prejudice against the Green Union," she warned.

"Indeed!" Martil sighed. "Your earlier point was well taken: We should have sent a team of women Arbiters. If such a team had been available, which it wasn't and isn't. And if we'd been inclined to cater to the Niandians' biological and cultural hang-ups, which we aren't. But you were a bonus package, Renamos. It is almost as if the Ka-Eens sensed your essence, somewhere along their transference beam, and arbitrarily brought you into this situation in hopes of ending the war."

Smirking, Renee asked, "You mean I really was kidnapped? First by the Ka-Eens, then by the Gevaris . . ."

"The incidents are unrelated," Martil said, very huffy.

"Struck a nerve, did I? Interesting. The matriarch and Zia got testy when I suggested that their ideals weren't that much different from the Gevaris'. Now you're bristling at the suggestion that the Ka-Eens grabbed me for their own purposes." Martil scowled at her, and Tae's big shoulders heaved with silent laughter.

Prince Chayo cut in, on the defensive, "My mother and Zia may have been ill advised to send you to the spaceport to witness our war victims' pain. However, their motives were honorable."

"Zia's reactions certainly were," Renee said. "I saw how affected she was there, and that she wasn't afraid to get her hands dirty, helping the medics."

"She is the daughter-matriarch," Chayo explained, sounding surprised that the Arbiter was surprised. He quit massaging Renee's neck and moved around where she could see him. "Our people are her children, as they are my mother's. The rulers of Niand are the nurturers of our entire species. They care for us, at any cost, even that of their own lives."

"Okay. But I do wish they wouldn't let that caring and concern hamper peace negotiations. They want a truce, and they're afraid of it, afraid of letting the Haukiets get an advantage on Niand's defenses." Renee shook her head slowly. "No doubt the Haukiets feel the same way. Both sides are afraid to be the first to back off. If you only had fast interspecies communications, we wouldn't be teetering on this tightrope. I sure hope this doesn't end up with another Battle of New Orleans." The men looked bewildered, and she added, "It was a battle that happened on my home world. One that took place after the war was over. But the participants hadn't yet received word of the truce, and they kept on fighting, and people died as a result, people who might have lived, otherwise."

"A valid simile to this problem," Martil said. "The example is pertinent. Use that knowledge to guide you when we remind the assembly of premiers of the time differential involved in these peace negotiations. They must not seize upon the Green Union's inabilities to halt hostilities everywhere simultaneously throughout the sector as an excuse for continuing the conflict. Any more than the Arbiters will allow the Green Union to pounce should Niand agree to a truce and then have difficulties in contacting all of its various military units and ordering them to lay down their arms. Fortunately, as yet, the Niandians do not know that the Green Union has accepted the Arbiters' proposal for a cease-fire."

He, Tae, and Renee all glanced at Chayo. The prince was the picture of injured innocence. "You would not think that I would tell them?" he asked, offended.

"Haven't you?" Renee wondered. "Not even your mother and Zia?"

He shook his head vehemently. "I know that might interfere with your plans. What we observed on the Arbiter world—the success of the Arbiter team's work on the Haukiets' core planet—must be kept a secret, lest it tip the balance toward the Gevari sympathizers at the assembly."

"Indeed," Martil said tonelessly. "An excellent reason for keeping one's own counsel."

"But what if—?" Renee sucked in her breath, then plunged ahead, "What if some of the Gevaris who are still at large move without waiting to hear about the truce? What if they decide to push that doomsday switch while the negotiations are going on? How do we stop them?"

"You don't," Martil replied.

"Oh, I see. I'm merely the team's decorative female facade." Exasperated, she said, "Look, can't you and Tae imagine a situation where I may discover something you haven't? Something critical. I might have to make a decision fast, without consulting you. I'd have to know how to prevent the Gevaris from blowing up a big chunk of the cosmos."

In the most solemn tone she had ever heard, Martil told her, "You are not being excluded from our partnership, as you seem to fear. This has nothing to do with your femaleness. Do not be so oversensitive in that regard. If you are ready for the ultimate responsibility you have just described, it will be entrusted to you. If you are not, it will be withheld. And I am not the one who will give it or withhold it. Neither is Tae."

chapter 11

WAS that all he was going to reveal? Apparently. The man could be so damned infuriating! But he'd sounded deadly serious. No teasing note in the words at all. Well, if she waited, probably enlightenment would gradually filter up from the recesses of her mind into her consciousness, answering this riddle. A lot of that had been happening to her lately. She tried to conceal the fear his statement had caused by saying lightly, "So I just have to hope, huh? That I won't have to play hardball referee with Gevaris."

"There is no reason to worry, my Lady," Chayo said confidently. "My mother's security staff already has located the four relays for the forbidden devices. Crack troops have been posted to guard each one. Any Gevari who tries to breach those defenses will be cut down without mercy."

"Are you sure there isn't a fifth Bender Principle weapon hidden around here somewhere? In some palace hidey-hole or nook?" As Renee asked that, Martil's mouth quirked with sly, approving amusement. Obviously, the same possibility had occurred to him, too.

"No. There are but four," Chayo insisted. "Fully secured."

"Let's keep our fingers crossed that they stay that way."

"Rather more ammunition is available to us than primitive superstition," Martil cut in. "We are not alone on this mission. With certain problems, we must trust to our non-anthropomorphic companions to identify potential peril before that peril becomes acute—or insoluble."

Renee's hand stole to her Ka-Een pendant. The jewel nestled in her cleavage, exposed by the dashiki's provocatively low-cut neckline. "Our backup team, huh? Go get 'em! Find out where the Gevaris are hiding. Squash 'em if they stir a centimeter in the direction of that weapon." She paused, then murmured, "It always comes back around to the Ka-Eens, doesn't it? Is mine a male or a female?"

Tae chuckled and Martil exclaimed, "Ka-Eens do not . . ." His contemptuous smile slid off slowly, replaced by doubt. "That is, I don't think they are sexual entities. No, of course not! It's absurd!"

"Is it?" Renee caressed her inhuman little partner. "You admitted that you don't know everything there is to know about them."

"That's not required," he said, sniffing. "However, feel free to anthropomorphize your Ka-Een, if it makes you more comfortable. Many humanoid species, under stress, feel compelled to fantasize. You may even look upon your Ka-Een as a pet, if you choose." His hazel eyes twinkled mischievously. "Bear in mind, though, that it may regard you as its pet."

"I have no objections if it does," she said, annoyed.

There were several minutes of strained silence. Chayo finally broke it, clearing his throat noisily. "It will likely be some while yet before the premiers have gathered in the palace conference area. How may I amuse you until then? Perhaps a tour of the capital."

"No tours," Renee said hurriedly. "I've seen more than enough Niandian scenery to last me for months, even years."

"Then I could call for professional entertainers."

Martil waved a hand, dismissing the Prince's suggestion. "We stay here. We don't want to be at any distance from the conference when the hour arrives. Nor do we really need the distraction of local actors or comedians.

Let's watch updates on your newscasts as preparation for the meeting.''

Shrugging, Chayo cued one of the room's walls, and it converted itself into a giant-size TV. The screen was fragmented into a series of geometrically framed scenes. Squiggly Niandian printing and muted voice-overs accompanied the pictures. Renee sat back and tried to absorb the flow of information. Not easy. It was visual and audio hash, to a degree. The same technique some of Earth's film producers used when they wanted to create an impression of chaos.

Neither Martil nor Tae seemed overwhelmed by the dizzying flood of images and sounds. Nor was Chayo. Renee yielded to the humbling realization that such a high-speed broadcast was normal fare for audiences at the men's level of civilization. The best she could do was attempt to match their pace and hope that the subliminal conditioning the Arbiters had put her through would assist her.

Chayo sat beside her and occasionally pointed out certain pictures and commented on them. Now and then his arm brushed against hers or he touched her fingers briefly, withdrawing the instant he made contact. Staged, ''accidental'' grazes? There was a shy undercurrent in his actions. This was a Niandian version of a flirtation, made semiprivate by the room's dimmed lighting.

A hell of a long way from a gross grope in a darkened movie theater!

The situation wasn't surprising, given Niandian biology. Chayo wasn't precisely afraid of her, at least not physically. Niandian males were no more capable of being raped than human males were. But on the other hand, the females Chayo had known couldn't be raped, either. And they called all the shots during every phase of his species' initial flirtations, courtships, and intercourse, not to mention the essential process of actual reproduction. His culture had developed its own little rituals in this game of male and female, a game that had begun millions of years ago when the Niandians' hominid ancestress had evolved physical control of those processes.

The prince played the game very skillfully. No doubt he'd had plenty of practice. As cute as he was, and with his rank, there must have been a number of Niandian women who found him attractive.

Renee did, also, but wasn't sure how to respond. She was flattered and intrigued, yes. But her reactions couldn't be based on millions of years of absolute certainty in her control over *her* reproductive life—and on a male's abject passivity to her because of that control. Lifelong patterns, bred in her hormones and locked into habit by social custom, refused to disappear and left her feeling awkward and edgy.

Then, while she gazed at the TV images, she seemed to step outside her body, studying the situation from a distance. A woman from Earth. A Niandian male. And Martil of the Bright Suns, who had also, quite unexpectedly, acknowledged a sudden sexual tension between himself and the Ka-Eens' "hitchhiker," Renamos of the Nine Worlds. There was even Tae. He'd shown no such reaction to her presence, but he was an inescapable part of this crazy equation, a prominent factor, always there, always observing—and touching her mind.

The four of them came from such very different backgrounds. Light-years apart. Separated not only by their origins but by their individual experiences before they'd met here, on this world. It was truly astonishing that they'd found anything whatsoever in common—mind-boggling, when she stopped to think about it.

And yet they had. There were lumps in the mix, admittedly. Often they were on opposite wavelengths, in angry disagreement. Not even Martil's training in arbitrating interstellar wars could prepare him for every quirk other humanoid species could come up with to irritate him. Plus his personality and impatience tended to get in his way, at times. But somehow, they'd made it work. The four of them. The Arbiters and their Niandian ally.

That was the cosmic viewpoint Martil talked about, and Renee was using it, right now—stepping back, mentally. Grasping at the complexity of life in this universe. They were all trying to ensure that the Haukiets and the Niandians could function together, could share.

Could a Niandian man and an Earthwoman?

Renee didn't know. Nor was she sure how she felt, deep down, about this gentle flirtation. It was pleasurable, and damned unsettling. Every so often, her reflexes got a hard, painful jog, as if her instincts were reminding her pointedly that Chayo was an alien.

If she was having trouble accepting these friendly little attentions, how much tougher was it going to be for Chayo's race in general to accept the Haukiets? To abandon hatreds they'd nursed for decades? How could the Arbiters convince them to agree to make peace?

The cosmic picture.

The Arbiter team to the Green Union had used those eerie, lifelike holograms with the super-emotional whammy built in. In effect, they'd hit the Haukiets' high council with a tremendous psychological trauma. If the Niandians didn't move ahead with truce negotiations on their own, they'd be due for the same awesome treatment. One that they might resent fiercely, and with good reason. They could feel they were being coerced into a truce by Arbiter tricks. Solid, extremely persuasive trickery indeed. But an outsider's tactic, nevertheless.

The Arbiters' peacemaking mission no longer appeared quite as straightforward to Renee as it once had. Their work was complicated by all sorts of twists and turns. They'd have to figure it out and find ways to get around the obstacles, if they wanted to save innocent lives . . .

"My Lady?"

The wall screen had gone blank. How long had she been staring unseeingly at it? She hoped she hadn't hurt Chayo's ego; but how could she not have, ignoring him like that while she was mentally probing the riddles of the universe?

Well, sometimes plain old-fashioned sexuality simply had to take a backseat, so to speak, to more immediate, crucial matters.

"Wh-what is it?" she asked, aware she was reddening with embarrassment for her rudeness.

Matriarch Onedu's face winked into view on the formerly vacant screen. She announced, "The assembly has convened. We await you, Arbiters. Chayo, you will escort them. The guards are ready."

As the TV wall returned to a visual version of Muzak,

Renee said, "That was quick. I figured we'd be cooling our heels here for hours yet."

"Our matter-relay units, when properly protected, facilitate rapid gathering of a group from anywhere on our world," Chayo said with chauvinistic pride. He didn't seem hurt by Renee's earlier wool-gathering. His smile was sunshine as he bowed to her, offering his hand, and went on, "May I show you, Martil, and Tae the route to the conference area?"

They walked out into the corridor, which was lined on both sides with heavily armed soldiers. Renee fought an impulse to peer up at the ceiling and see if there were any more there. Royal bodyguards led the way, brought up the rear, and marched on either side of the foursome as they proceeded along the hall. At the end of the passageway, Chayo courteously handed Renee aboard one of the Niandians' ramp escalators. Martil and Tae stepped on behind them. Ahead, riding up the slope to the next level, soldiers stood at the alert, their weapons held at the ready.

"This is more like it," Renee told Chayo. He bent his head to hear her; there was a constant clatter of boots at the bottom of the escalator as more troops stomped onto the ramp to begin their ride. "I'm sorry," she said, raising her voice. "But I don't want to see your matter-relay units, ever again. They give me indigestion. Let's stick to this form of transportation from now on."

The prince grinned. "I had wanted to show you the beauties of my planet, via matter-relay units, when the war ends."

"We'll take an egg vehicle for that tour. It'll be slower, but then so am I."

The escalator seemed to go on and on, a very gentle grade, bearing them steadily upward. Additional royal guards stood at attention at the far end. Bodyguards everywhere! The matriarch was taking no chances on another kidnapping. The troops must be assigned on her personal order; the orders couldn't be coming from General Vunj. Poor Vunj! Too bad. And the old boy had been starting to show some promise, too.

Another corridor lay beyond the top of the escalator. Then there was a series of connected, traveling slide-walks. For quite a few minutes, the Arbiters followed their native guide through the maze of the palace. At last they entered a large room. The doors sighed shut, sealing them in.

Renee stared about curiously. A number of platforms hovered centimeters above the gleaming parquet floor. The strange daises floated about at a snail's pace, their seated riders striking up conversations with riders on neighboring platforms for a minute or two, then drifting on to another contact.

The room's walls swam with realistic holograms. Scenes of the Niandians' home world and her colony planets. Alien terrains and seascapes and skies. It was an impressive, ever-shifting illusion.

"My Lady, will you and your companions honor my mother and sister with your presence?" Chayo escorted his guests to the room's center and the largest of the floating platforms. The matriarch and Zia invited them aboard with gracious words and gestures. As Renee stepped up onto the thing, she prayed that her stomach would behave. It had been through a lot, recently. But the movement didn't disturb her innards in the slightest. Chayo guided her to a seat at the matriarch's left. Martil and Tae took chairs further to Renee's left, and Chayo sat at the end of the curving line. That was probably Niandian pecking order. Zia, in an obvious position of power, sat to the matriarch's right.

Scenes of distant seashores, strange yellow grasslands, and blue-black mountains light-years from Niand faded. The full circle of the surrounding wall now depicted the mother world—dark green foliage, a pale blue umbrella of sky, towering cities, and parklike regions where Niandian picnickers laughed and played and creatures resembling unicorns scampered beneath trees thick with wind-tossed fronds. Renee whispered to Martil, "Scenery to remind the premiers of their roots? So they'll be diligent in defending Niand?"

He pursed his lips, looking smug. "You adapt marvelously. Very astute. That is why you're an Arbiter."

The matriarch began speaking to the assembly. "Greetings. Welcome to our glorious conference. We appreciate the severe difficulties many of you have been forced to deal with in order to attend this gathering. It has been too many years since we have come together to express our mutual concern for the welfare of our people, our children.''

Politicalese. It went on at considerable length. Renee had a jabbing moment of déjà vu. Sitting in the audience at the Metro Council hearings with Evy at her side, both of them trying not to show their boredom—and their deeply felt anger.

Words. Political gobbledegook. Dragging out the hearings unnecessarily. Cluttering up the agenda with the council members' personal axes they wanted to grind. This one was running for reelection. That one was angling for a favor for some businessman crony. Another one was hoping his speechifying would get back to the mayor and earn him a promotion to a cushy job higher up in the city's echelons.

And meanwhile, the citizens—the children of these titled, axe-grinding fat cats—were waiting. The little people. The ones who'd been stepped on by society or the government. The needy. The people who just wanted an even break and a chance to work. The battered women. The homeless kids. The down-and-out men with that apprehensive, whipped-dog look in their eyes. The ones the politicians preached to—and far too often forgot when it came time to think about answers.

If only I had a magic wand, she thought.

She'd wished that, hadn't she? Thousands of light-years and not very long ago. She'd come so far, and things were remarkably the same. Maybe it didn't change. Not that part of humanoid society, anyway.

Renee adopted a polite expression, watching the matriarch and filtering the guff out of the speech. If Martil and Tac had to listen to this sort of thing on one mission after another, how did they do it without falling into a stupor?

Introductions. Those went on almost as long as the opening address. The matriarch's platform revolved slowly so that she was facing in turn each of the premier's daises. Every one of them had to return her remarks and introduce her staff.

Her. Most of the time it *was* a her. Their names

blurred, after a while. Galei of Xurn. Pia of Taja. Wisi of Corlane.

The ruler's platform shifted, lining up with that containing a group of three Niandians with mauve complexions. The woman leading them said, "Kilar, Matriarch of Rian. My deputy premier Fel. My statistician, Siu." Deputy Premier Fel looked familiar. Suddenly, Renee placed him: he was the fat man who had opportuned Zia in that big room outside the palace's private quarters, on the day Renee had been kidnapped. Kilar went on, "We must convey our sincere apologies to you, Most High. The behavior of her Excellency our sub-matriarch, the late Esher, has brought terrible shame and grief to our colony. She was the ultimate traitor, the defier of the Great Nurturer. We are appalled that she dared to act against you, Most High. We beg your forgiveness, and we pledge there will be no recurrence. The colony of Rian is utterly purged of all Gevari influence. They have been executed, to the last treasonous woman and her minions."

chapter 12

THE bloodthirsty satisfaction in Premier Kilar's announcement chilled Renee to the marrow. But something intruded, dissipating her revulsion and turning her attention elsewhere. The beginnings of a frown tightened her forehead. What was lurking down there in the shadows of her memory? She couldn't quite get hold of the thing. Martil noticed her distraction and peered at her sidelong, his expression very intent. He raised a questioning eyebrow.

Whatever the errant memory was, it skittered out of Renee's reach as the peaceful scenery decorating the walls was suddenly replaced by images of destruction and outrage. The war in progress. Niandians battling Green Union forces and, here and there, renegade Niandian bands. Like those collaborators and black-market Niandian traders in those holograms Lady Esher had shown Renee, days ago? Maybe not all of those images had been fiction. It seemed likely that in that respect Niand was no different from Earth. And throughout Earth's long, warlike history, there had always been humans who were only interested in looking out for themselves. Loyalty to their nations, leaders, or ideals never cluttered their agendas. They'd willingly betrayed their countrymen, sold their own people into slavery, or did whatever else would earn them a fast buck—and the hell with who got hurt. Logically, all Lady Esher had to do was dip into the news files and pull out some prime Niandian examples of the same sort of back-stabbing treachery among her species.

The images on the walls flowed rapidly. Scenes of Niandians fighting and dying amid the alien beauty or stark landscapes of a dozen colony planets. The holograms had their impact, yet carried with them a faintly artificial quality. The premiers and their aides made appropriate noises of wrath as they watched. Bubble-domed habitats on a planet rich with yellow soil—blown apart, the domes crushed, the occupants killed. Explosions, tearing at a city on a rocky plain beneath a fiery sky. The view from space, with mighty ships blasting away at the enemy, sending coruscating energies hurtling across the vacuum—energies that were still mere fiction back on Earth, or at least no more than speculation in scientific textbooks.

More conflict. Long views and close-ups. Civilians and soldiers being attacked or counterattacking. The "slimy abominations" from the Green Union either rushing to overwhelm a Niandian outpost or falling back as Niand's "brave troops" struck hard against the foe.

Something was missing: any tinge of a balanced presentation. This was blatant propaganda to point to the righteousness of the war. *This is what the Green Union and the treacherous collaborators have done to us! We must have revenge! Make them pay! This is a cause worth dying for!*

A cause the ordinary people could die for. There were no premiers or generals being mowed down in those scenes of carnage. Just thousands of everyday Niandian citizens.

The ones who did the paying, with their blood and tears. While the political top dogs stayed safe at home and made rabble-rousing speeches, propaganda holograms, and prated about the sacred honor of their race—which demanded yet more sacrifices from the little people.

"Where are the other worlds?" Renee whispered under the babble of the assembly, as the delegates reacted to the powerful scenes. Martil leaned toward her as she went on, "There ought to be twenty-five planets shown, if the mother world is included."

Chayo had overheard and supplied the answer. "The conflict does not strike at all our worlds equally. And some colonies are, quite understandably, weary of this senseless war. They declined to send holographic records for the committee which prepared this display. What you are seeing is the belligerent posturing of those premiers still willing to fight on. Victory or death, they proclaim. No matter what the price may be to Niand's people."

Renee nodded, agreeing with his bitter summation of this three-dimensional war poster. Her Ka-Een throbbed. She sensed its disgust, or a Ka-Een version of that emotion. Plainly, those nearly omnipotent little entities didn't think any more of this propaganda than their humanoid partners and Chayo did.

As the holograms faded, the matriarch resumed speaking. Though she couched things in political terms at first, as she continued there was a promising tilt in the direction of a truce. "We have seen the horrors wrought upon our colonies of Ther, Fiwa, and their sister worlds. And yet, we must confess that the desire of certain of our premiers puzzles us. Why do we go on? Why do we insist on further infliction of suffering? Can the cries of our people, our children, sound unheeded? Do we offer them only greater pain and greater slaughter? More privation? More criminal waste of their precious resources? Shall more thousands of our finest daughters and sons be thrown into this bottomless pit of death? Is it not time to consider . . ."

Renee almost expected to hear "de-escalation." Instead, the matriarch said, as translated by the Ka-Een, "abatement."

"The cost factor alone is increasing exponentially, Most High," volunteered a handsome, thirtyish woman. She reeled off a long string of statistics to prove her point. Even if it had been framed in dollars and cents, it definitely wasn't a low-side report. And the assemblywoman was no amateur. Far from it. The rest listened attentively, visibly awed by her expertise and reputation.

When the number cruncher concluded her argument, the others jumped in, carrying the ball forward loudly and with some heat. This time, there seemed to be plenty of solid, no-nonsense stuff mixed in with the propaganda.

The debate fascinated Renee, from an Earthwoman's, outsider's viewpoint. How Evy would have loved this! Women, wielding power freely. Not bound by any of those careful little rituals most upscale human women had to observe. No need for the Niandian females to worry about accusations that go-get-'em aggressiveness dented their femininity. No societal judgments of "Yes, she gets the job done, but she's abandoned her nurturing side and even her sexuality to reach the top of the ladder." Not here! Niandian women were totally confident, and firmly in control. They'd never had to resort to tricks or cater to male colleagues' egos. No eyelash batting or simpering in evidence at this assembly. The premiers used their brains and skills openly and didn't hesitate to stomp each other's toes if they had to. On Niand, there weren't likely to be complaints that they were "trashing" or "not sticking together for the sake of the movement." A women's movement wasn't necessary, thanks to Niandian evolution.

The male assembly delegates were another story, one that increasingly made Renee squirm inwardly as she observed the scene. The gathering was holding a warped mirror up to the human race. The men participating in the debate were definitely male; they raised their baritone and tenor voices and pounded fists on the chair arms and tables and generally carried on as Earthmen would have during such a discussion. But they behaved in that way only when dealing with other *men*. Their no-holds-barred, typically masculine aggressiveness took a sharp turn whenever the women entered the conversations— usually by cutting in without asking so much as a by your leave. And when that happened, Renee saw a painfully familiar, yet somehow skewed pattern emerge. The men clenched their fists subtly, stiffened, traded resentful, resigned glances with other men. A few of them resorted to the male equivalent of eyelash batting: flattering their women bosses shamelessly, becoming yes-men in a vividly demeaning way. They sidestepped the power-wielder's position, trying to outflank her with sweet talk and wheedling.

To Renee, the result was repellent. As repellent as what she, Evy, and millions of other Earthwomen had often endured while participating at conferences dominated by men.

Wasn't there any humanoid culture where people could just be people? Without all of these biologically ordered games. No devious tactics applied by either sex. No dominance or groveling subordination. Simply . . . balance.

A sad, knowing smile curved Martil's mouth. He was studying her, sharing her reaction. As she met his gaze, he nodded, empathizing. Tae glanced at the two of them and shook his head, in complete agreement with their dismay. Renee's Ka-Een throbbed, communicating the opinions of the entities. Unanimity. The six of them were outside. Not playing the game.

Umpiring.

That reminder made Renee push aside her musing on Niandian—and Earthly—cultural and sexual quirks. The Arbiters had a job to do here. These one-upmanship internal maneuverings by the premiers and their aides were mere window dressing. She couldn't allow them to throw her off course. It was crucial for her to keep her focus on the main problem: the War.

The arguments went on and on—point, counterpoint, statistics answered with refuting statistics, and appeals to matriotism and to the Great Nurturer's agony at her people's suffering.

And again and again, debates about the money it took to maintain an enormous, interstellar battle fleet and thousands and thousands of troops at top, fully-supplied fettle.

"When do they get around to reciting the latest figures on their gross Federation product?" Renee grumbled softly. Out of the corner of her eye she saw Martil grinning nastily, amused by her sarcasm. Then she reflected that money, after all, might be the key. Some premiers flinched when they heard the economic facts of life and death involved. The peace supporters seized on that, hammering the money element, underlining it constantly.

On and on and on. An hour slipped by, then two, perhaps three.

The "victory or death" adherents weren't the most numerous, but they were the loudest and the toughest to sell on compromise. Their arguments sometimes threatened to overwhelm the Niandian leaders sitting on the fence and pull them across to the war party's side. Now and then, Renee feared that eventually the firebrands would even exhaust the war-weary premiers and the matriarch's hopes for peace. Would this entire effort be wasted because a handful of stubborn Niandian women refused to see reason?

"Still!" Matriarch Onedu was on her feet, her hands held out in supplication. "You speak in abstracts. I speak of our *people*. And our Federation is dying as a result of this slow, deadly sickness we call 'war.' We must put aside our petty concerns with trade, with military pride. Most *especially* pride! The children cry out to the Mother. They do not care anymore about territorial disputes with the Green Union. What do a scattering of barren planets along our stellar frontiers matter? Think of the children! Pity them!"

Renee's throat thickened. Visions of those innocent victims crowding the spaceport nursery battered at her. Wounded and dying babies and kids—and wounded and dying adults.

The matriarch was right. The hell with abstracts! The premiers had to be made to feel what their lofty debate really meant. What it translated to in humanoid—and Haukiet—anguish.

Then she, too, was on her feet and speaking. Her. Not Renee-Tae. Her own words. "Honored premiers, Most High, Eminence: I, Renamos of the Sisterhood of the Nine Worlds, ask you to hear me. My companions, Martil of the Bright Suns and Tae of the Green Union, and I have come here to aid you. We have traveled a very great distance to do so. And we have been patient. But the matriarch advises you well. She holds the soul of Niand in her gentle hands, as the nurturer should. She cares for her people as a mother for her children. Creators of life, premiers, can't you see that life itself is at stake in this discussion? And life must not be thrown away in the pursuit of chauvinistic pride. Niandian life hangs in the balance. And the lives of your enemies—and *their* children. In your pride, will you destroy life? See what you have done, what is even now being done, in the name of your pride.''

She reached out, and Martil and Tae were on either side of her, their fingers gripping hers. Renee tried to put her entire being into those fleshy extensions of herself. One hand clasped Martil's bony, beringed one. The other was in Tae's huge paw. She gathered her strength for the ordeal she knew was coming. Martil's eyes were brighter than she could ever remember them.

Tae's mind touched hers, skimming the surface. She had no trouble at all hearing his thoughts: "Our Ka-Eens make it possible. And they are now three. It will be much easier for Martil and me this time, since you have joined us.''

Her vision blurred. And then she was seeing as the Ka-Eens did, leaping the light-years, to Arbiter Central, once more watching those holograms that were so agonizingly, stunningly *real*.

All about her, in the palace assembly room, Renee heard sounds. Her gaze came back into focus for a fraction of a second, showing her the source of those noises: the premiers and their associates gasping, choking on tears of horror, writhing in their chairs. Under an emotional and intellectual assault past any Niandian's imaginings. Missiles of fact, scoring direct hits.

A re-creation of the Arbiters' very specialized holograms had formed in the middle of the room. They formed an irregular circle, weaving between the floating daises, everywhere at once, ensuring that not a single assembly participant could avoid seeing the three-dimensional figures and scenes.

Real. Death. War. Here in this room. Blotting out the illusionary scenery on the walls. Gripping the watchers by their brains, hearts, and guts.

Death and suffering almost beyond bearing—here in their midst. It engulfed the assembly people riding their platforms.

Niandians—dying.

The Green Union—dying.

Life, being destroyed.

And the premiers and their subordinates felt every individual death. Every wound. The torment of bereaved survivors. Of the helpless, enslaved captives. Of the soldiers, trapped in a "glorious conflict" with no way to escape.

Like that endless discussion preceding this exhibition, the extraordinary holograms seemed to go on and on. In actuality, Renee knew, time was being compressed, millions of incidents consolidated into an incredibly small glimpse of an interstellar, interspecies disaster, but the *effect* was interminable. The minutes necessary to accomplish that effect were rather brief.

She was in a limbo, borne on the shock wave of the holograms the Ka-Eens were feeding into the conference room. Renee had no control over the scenes. Nor did Martil or Tae. That wasn't how the system worked. She and they had cooperated with the Ka-Eens to "summon" the realistic images. They might have dialed Arbiter Central to do so—using the Ka-Eens as living switchboards.

It was finished.

The truth, the *reality* had been forced home to every Niandian here, even the guards posted at the doors. Sight and sound and emotions had roared over long-existing barricades of racial hatred and obstinate pride.

The holograms vanished. Abruptly, Renee was once again back inside herself. She had ceased to be part of an unseen projector ten thousand light-years in length. Trembling and sobbing, she collapsed into Martil's arms, felt him shuddering with the same devastating reaction. Tae embraced them both, his big arms a haven.

She had deluded herself, thinking this would be a kind of high-tech trick. It wasn't the Arbiters' version of futuristic magic. No simple, casual flicking of a switch to create those images, those overpowering holograms with their stunning super-whammy.

The demonstration had taken a terrible toll on the three of them. Tae was as shaken as she and Martil were, though his strength helped him bear up better during the aftermath. Renee longed to crawl away somewhere and hide, have a good long bawl, let down all the remaining reserves and cleanse her bleeding soul.

"No," Martil said, his voice hoarse. She raised her head, snuffled, and peered at him as he went on, "Not yet. We can do that in a while, but not yet. We will have to conclude the demonstration. *You* will have to conclude the demonstration. With words."

Of course. That was her job. The female member of the team had to score the clincher—sewing up these opening truce negotiations with the Niandian matriarchy.

"O-okay." Tae caressed her hair, sending a bit of spine-stiffener her way. Renee took a deep breath and repeated, "Okay. Sorry I fell apart. It's just that . . . that it's an awfully lot stronger when those holograms aren't a rerun."

chapter
13

THE Niandians were in shocked disarray. Some of them were sprawled in the thronelike chairs atop the platforms. Others, agitated and unable to stay still, had jumped down from their daises and were pacing or even running about the room. They were trying to escape from the wrenching experience the Arbiters had put them through.

Renamos wiped away her tears and examined the assembly. Onedu, Zia, the premiers and their aides, the cabinet ministers—everyone had been deeply affected. Only a very few looked as though they'd resisted the worst trauma of that storm of emotional and thought-grabbing holograms. She couldn't understand how they'd done that; any holdouts must have hearts that were diamond hard and cold as glaciers. And even they were badly shaken, just not so severely as the rest.

She counted, assessing. A parliamentary matriarchy. Renamos had learned, by now, as much as she needed to about the way the Niandians' political system worked. Onedu had the deciding vote, but the matriarch had to go with majority opinion if she expected to continue her rule at its most effective level. The important thing was— did the peace party have enough numbers to swing the assembly's conclusions solidly into truce negotiations?

That was difficult to tell. The male Niandians, in particular, were tough to read. They'd learned to smother their true feelings under stress. Not all of their feelings, however, not in circumstances like these. The men plainly were stunned by what they'd just witnessed. The women were easier to assess. At least most of them were. A few struggled frantically to hide their reactions and put on a facade. Probably they didn't want their political opponents to seize on this opening and hit them when they were vulnerable. The assembly's war-party members were digging in their heels, yet on a downhill slide, thanks to the impact of the holograms.

But would it be enough to produce a lasting truce? Would it convert the warmongers and push the fence sitters over to the matriarch's side? Renamos worried about that—and about that nagging sensation lurking somewhere in her memories, too deep to grasp. Annoying. And potentially dangerous. They didn't need any surprises at this stage of the arbitration process.

The matriarch leaned on her chair arm and wept brokenheartedly. Chayo sat with his shoulders hunched and his head down. He was racked by violent shudders. Apparently viewing the holograms hadn't gone easy for him, either, the second time around. He hadn't participated in their projection, as Renamos had. But he was among his own people, swept along by their collective shock and emotional feedback. Zia was rigid, standing at the edge of the dais. Her beautiful face was streaked with tears, her eyes wide with panic. She seemed to be searching the room. For what? A place where she could crawl off and hide and weep unseen? Renamos empathized with that urge, and it must be worse for someone of Zia's status, someone rarely out of the public spotlight.

"Hon-honored col-colleagues and . . ." the matriarch began, then broke down, sobbing. Once more, she attempted to call the conference back to order, and failed again. "R-Renamos, you must g-give us time . . . we . . . we cannot . . ."

"The peace proposals are best considered now," Martil said. His words weren't as steady as usual. Cooperating to create the terrible images had taken plenty out of him, too. Tae, his rugged face solemn, touched the smaller man's shoulder, sharing his mood.

Renamos stopped her partner before Martil could really get into his laying down of the law. "Please. They need some breathing space to glue themselves together. I don't think they have the Haukiets' recuperative powers." Tae smiled wanly, confirming her guess. She went on. "Let them have a short recess. If any of them balk at the negotiations later on, we'll throw the holograms at them again—harder."

Martil's eyebrows arched. "Can we?"

She set her jaw in a stubborn line. "Yes, *we* can."

"All right. All *right*!" His momentary flicker of irritation and uncertainty died as quickly as it had flared up. "You're probably correct."

Renamos told the matriarch, "We understand, Most High. You wish time to calm your hearts and minds before you vote."

"I—I thank you for your patience, Arbiters." Onedu took the Earthwoman's hands briefly, relaying her gratitude. When the matriarch announced the recess, many of the Niandians hurried into comfort stations and lounges connected to the big room. All of the propaganda images had vanished from the walls. Now there were only doors, providing access to privacy niches. From some of those alcoves issued sounds of vomiting and horror-stricken cries. The Arbiters' holograms followed the assembly even into its hiding places, sickening them, hammering home the necessity of peace. For long minutes, there could be no business progress. It was going to take a while for the matriarch's conference to be in any condition to make rational decisions.

Gradually, things cooled off a trifle. Shaken and jittery officials emerged from the lounges and wandered about, talking to one another in muted, chastened tones. Renamos, Martil, and Tae waited on the sidelines, watching. This was a new experience for her, and an achingly familiar one for her partners. None of them felt any malicious satisfaction. Nor did they have a sense that they'd taught the Niandians a lesson. They'd simply done what they had to to save this sector of the galaxy. If reason prevailed, the ordeal was well worth it. Serious nuts-and-bolts discussions concerning a cease-fire could begin. There would be the inevitable inertia to overcome, getting the ball rolling. Undoubtedly, more people would die before the truce was finally in place. But hopefully the numbers would be fewer and fewer, day by day, until both sides were trading words, quibbling over terms in the instrument of peace and not trading bomb strikes and salvos between space fleets.

Every minute of delay held risk. It not only meant more innocent victims in this conflict. It held the terrifying possibility that a remaining "victory or death" diehard would become desperate to the point of suicide and pull the trigger on the Bender Principle weapon.

Little wonder they'd be desperate. Fanatics, realizing their last chance for continuing this brutal war was slipping out of their reach.

The Arbiters had to persuade everyone to disengage as quickly as possible. A balance beam separating peace from holocaust teetered on a fulcrum—this conference. The holograms had been designed to push the scales toward peace, before irrevocable steps were taken in the other direction.

A few yards from the Arbiters, the matriarch began holding court, of a sorts. One by one, her ministers and the premiers came by her in a shambling parade. Whispering with her. Occasionally glancing fearfully at Renamos and her partners.

Chayo took the arm of a fat deputy premier and led him gently toward the Arbiters. The older man's belly heaved with sobs, and tears coursed down his mauve-colored, plump features.

"Tell them," Chayo prodded. "Do not be afraid."

"Oh, if—if we had only known!" the man cried. "If we had only known. How terrible it is! Terrible!"

Renamos nodded sympathetically. The deputy premier seemed startlingly familiar. Why did she remember him so well?

"Those—those Green Union infants . . . the poor, poor things! And all those others—dying. Bleeding. Horrible! Unbearable! If we had only known. If Esher had only known, she would never have been so . . ."

The nagging something that had been hiding in the depths of Renamos's thoughts went *click*! Pieces fell into place rapidly, memories rocketing into reach. She grabbed Tae's hand and shoved his fingers against her head, begging him to pick up on what she was discovering. Maybe he could hasten her train of thought along.

"It was you," she said. "Everybody else spoke to her just once. But you spoke to her twice."

"Wh-what, my Lady?" the mauve-faced man exclaimed, taken aback. "Spoke to . . ."

"Her Eminence. Zia. The first time, you babbled about a trade agreement with the Sush worlds. But the *second* time you called her 'Daughter of Onedu,' and said that Esher requested something. When you did that, Zia looked around and waited for Beyeth to break through the crowd and rescue her. Because her Eminence had heard what she needed to hear," Renamos said, an awful sinking feeling seizing her. "I thought she was just being impatient. But it was a great deal more than that. You'd tipped her off so she'd know Lady Esher and the Gevaris were set. When we arrived at the spaceport, they were ready to kidnap me and start trying to twist my point of view around to match theirs."

"N-no . . ."

Martil leaned toward the cowering little man, studying him intently.

"Yes," Renamos retorted. "I would have remembered sooner, if my memories hadn't been messed up by all those drugs they fed me. But it's coming clear, finally. You gave Esher's message to Zia . . ."

Chayo's expression was aghast. The matriarch, overhearing the confrontation, hurried toward the Arbiters. She and her son were both struggling to deny the obvious. Renamos rounded on Onedu, demanding, "What relation is Esher to you? Chayo called her 'beloved of my mother.' What does that mean?"

"She was Premier Kilar's second in command," Chayo said, his voice cracking as understanding overcame his earlier refusal to accept logic.

The matriarch stammered, "Esh-Esher was my mother-sister—daughter of my mother."

"Zia's aunt." Renamos glared accusingly at the fat man. Tae and Martil were already doing so. She said, "Zia. Esher. Equally devoted to last-ditch protection of their people, their children. Devoted to the point of utter fanaticism. Zia's gone beyond your normal maternal caring instincts, Onedu. Taken them to deadly lengths. When I watched her, after you'd seen the holograms, I thought she was looking for a place where she could cry in peace. Instead, she was counting noses—votes. And figuring out that her faction will lose. The princess wants the war to go on.'' The matriarch shook her head, appalled, mouthing denials. Renamos had no time to be gentle with the woman. ''It's a fierce desire to guard Niand at all costs. Zia's convinced that's only possible, now, if she takes charge and destroys the enemy totally—despite our warnings. Lady Esher wasn't the top Gevari. Zia is!''

''Are you certain?'' Martil asked, his manner steely tense.

''Positive! Oh, damn! She isn't here. She's already left the conference area, and I don't think she went to do anything as frivolous as powder her nose. She can't allow a truce, not from her twisted way of seeing the universe.''

''She will seek a fait accompli,'' Martil said, nodding.

Common sense told Renamos that he couldn't have used a French idiom, but that was the way her Ka-Een translated it—into terms handiest for her. She exclaimed, ''There has to be a *fifth* Bender Principle weapon! One the security people haven't found. Maybe one nobody but the Gevaris know about. And after she's fired it, Zia believes peace negotiations will be pointless—because she'll have wiped the Green Union into dust.'' Whirling, she clutched at Chayo's shirt. ''Where would she hide that weapon? We've got to stop her, before it's too late!''

Mother and son hesitated for a heartbeat, staring at one another, their mutual terror tangible. Then Onedu blurted, ''It—it must be in her suites, in the southwest wing. But she wouldn't . . . Chayo! Guide them there! Quickly! Save us! *Save* us!''

The prince and the Arbiters raced out of the conference room. Renamos sensed rather than heard the matriarch ordering some of the royal bodyguards to form a detachment and follow. Not that they'd be of much help. By the time they got organized, they'd be long outdistanced. And the four couldn't afford to stop and wait for that uniformed backup.

Tae and the Ka-Eens prodded at Chayo's mind, wanting to anticipate where all of them were heading. No luck. The prince's confused emotional state got in the way.

Renamos galloped, pushing herself hard to keep up with the men. They rushed through interconnecting corridors and up and down numbers of ramp escalators.

I could kick myself, she thought. Female intuition? Hah! Zia faked me out expertly. I was too locked into my own biases. I pegged her as just a beautiful symbol, just as I would have disdained an overly handsome airheaded male fashion plate back on Earth. I've been thinking like a member of a cultural minority instead of like an Arbiter. I've got to grow up and become a full member of the team.

We have to catch her. It's no good arresting her after she's done the deed. By then, the Haukiets will be gone—and so will humanity and all other life for light-years outside the Niandian Federation . . .

There was a line of uniformed men ahead. They formed a living obstacle, blocking the corridor. And they were pointing billy-club guns at the Arbiters and the prince.

chapter
14

Tae shoved Chayo against the wall and Martil and
Renamos dropped flat as the soldiers fired. Red streaks
sizzled harmlessly the length of the hall. With incredible
speed for such a big man, Tae lunged, bowling the Niandian troops over, knocking them cold.

Then he and Martil galloped on, Renamos in their
wake, urging Chayo to hurry up and follow. He did,
though looking pretty dazed. No matter. His guidance
wasn't essential anymore. They *had* to be closing in on
Zia's sanctuary, if those guards had been willing to kill
the matriarch's son to protect the princess's rear. The
soldiers, too, must be Gevaris. Treachery! Right here in
the palace!

Another turn in the corridor, and more guards left disabled by Tae. They were lying sprawled on either side of
a door like dozing library lions. And just beyond, a woman's body was lying at an awkward angle. Half her head
was gone, blasted away by a lethal bolt from a Niandian
gun. What remained showed that the woman had been
spectacularly ugly.

Renamos and Chayo stumbled to a halt and Chayo exclaimed, "Beyeth! No!"

"She was loyal to the wrong ruling person, to the matriarch, rather than to Zia. And obviously it cost Beyeth

her life. Get moving! Or she's going to be only the first of billions. Which way?''

Chayo gulped down his nausea and pointed.

Running. Lungs laboring. Throat aching. Renamos's Ka-Een pulsated in sympathy with her stress. But to her relief, they were gaining on her partners.

Up ahead, Martil and Tae were having a grunting, panting argument with more treasonous guards. The struggle was taking place at such close quarters that guns were a hindrance rather than a help. Man-to-man fisticuffs. Chayo charged in eagerly, venting his anger and frustration in old-fashioned muscle-stretching.

The guards weren't alone in blocking the corridor. Just beyond that point—and in a better position to take aim with a gun—stood Pasyi, the Gevari agent who'd masqueraded as a med staffer and helped kidnap Renamos. One other escapee from the earlier roundup of rebels, Hij, was in the middle of the brawl.

Pasyi raised a billy-club gun, her expression icy. Plainly, she didn't care if she shot down Hij and the guards as well as the Gevaris' opponents. Just so long as Zia, the rebels' leader, was left free to complete their last, terrible act of defiance.

Renamos envisioned General Vunj's operatives, the men Pasyi had shot at the spaceport. And she made herself respond as though the weapon in Pasyi's small hand was no more than a training stinger.

Outside yourself.

She steered on automatic, as Soh had taught her, touching reserves of energy Renamos didn't know she possessed.

Leaping. The billy-club gun's shaft brushing harmlessly past her as she dived beneath Pasyi's outstretched arm.

Seizing the Gevari agent, crashing to the floor . . .

I weigh more, Renamos thought, but I can't count on that.

The Gevari's face contorted with rage. Pasyi fought to get her arm free to shoot her assailant.

Renamos slammed her hands against the smaller woman's ears, derailing the rebel's struggles for a moment. And as Pasyi screamed in shock, Renamos grabbed the woman's silky ponytails and used them as a sling to whip her opponent's head onto the floor so hard that Pasyi's skull bounced. The tiny figure went limp.

Sucking in air, Renamos snatched up the gun and jumped to her feet. She was alone. The doorway behind her was cluttered with the unconscious forms of Hij and the guards. Somewhere ahead, around a bend in the corridor, she could hear the clatter of her partners' boots and Chayo's. They'd hurried on, assuming Renamos was capable of taking care of herself—and of Pasyi.

As she had!

But there was no time to gloat over that accomplishment. This wasn't over. Not at all!

She raced along the hall, cursing her short legs. She couldn't let Martil and Tae get too far in advance of her. She was part of the team, and they were in this together.

The corridor ended in a long ramp escalator. Renamos jumped onto it and kept running, swaying wildly as she tried to maintain her balance.

At the foot of the ramp, the men were arguing with a closed door. Or Martil and Tae were. Chayo stood to one side. He looked somewhat punch-drunk. No wonder! He must be under assault by an emotional and intellectual avalanche. His sister—a traitor. *The* traitor! He'd been the peacemaker, risking his neck to bring the Arbiters into this and stop the war. And all the time Zia had been working behind the scenes to keep the war going on a bloody marathon to destruction.

Tae's enormous strength mastered the door, and it gave suddenly, locks snapping. He and Martil rushed forward.

Thanks to her position on the descending ramp, Renamos could see over their heads and past them, into the chamber beyond. Zia stood there, out of the men's reach, and she was pointing a billy-club gun. They had no weapons, though Chayo did. He must have picked one up from the supply dropped by the guards the three of them had overpowered earlier during their mad dash.

But he wasn't moving! Wasn't making any move to counter his sister's murderous defense.

"Stop her, Chayo! I can't shoot from this angle!"

It was too late. A dazzling red glare lit up the scene

in the room for a fraction of a heartbeat, and Martil and Tae fell.

Pain ripped at Renamos. Pain more awful than anything she had ever borne, had ever imagined. Not physical pain. Worse. Deeper. Part of her very being ripped out of her. Part of her . . . essence.

But what remained forced her on. She reached the bottom of the escalator, leaped off, running into the chamber beyond the broken door. The red afterglow from Zia's shot still brightened the room. When she had fired, something had resisted the deadly bolt with awesome, alien strength before it collapsed, and the radiance was the fallout of that resistance.

Renamos dodged to one side, ducking behind a bank of Niandian machinery. She peered around a corner and tried to draw a bead on Princess Zia.

Chayo was entering the room, crossing it. He was wide-eyed, walking like a zombie. And he came between Renamos and his sister. Behind him, Zia was raising her arm, pointing. And Chayo followed her, moving further into the chamber, still shuffling like an automaton or someone trapped in a hypnotic spell.

The two of them halted by a large display, a Niandian computer of some sort. Renamos knew with terrifying certainty what the thing was.

But now Chayo had stepped aside, and she had a clear view of Zia. Renamos rose and aimed the Niandian gun she'd confiscated from Pasyi.

If only I can make this thing work! she prayed, desperately.

And abruptly, she knew how. Skills she alone couldn't have commanded. Fire lanced out of the weapon's tip, streaking toward Zia. Halfway there, it was stopped. Splattering against an invisible barrier, splashing to the floor, a beautiful shower of melted red energy.

Renamos emptied the billy-club gun in vain. Zia didn't even glance around at her. The princess was busy. Bending over that computer. Chayo gawked at her and took one tentative step in her direction. His sister turned to him, fury etched on her lovely features.

Abandoning the useless gun, Renamos ran to the invisible barrier. She couldn't hear what brother and sister were saying, but she could see them quite clearly. Chayo put out a hand, pleading. Zia slapped him so hard that his teeth popped. Then she was screaming at him, though no sound reached Renamos on the other side of the force field. Chayo dropped to his knees, bowing his head, his lips moving in a mumble of apology and his hands clasped in abject submission.

He couldn't do it, could he? The weapon he'd been carrying lay on the floor, forgotten.

She was his sister. His absolute superior. He loved her, and he'd spent a lifetime being poured into a cultural mold that prevented him from breaking the psychological hold binding him. He couldn't defy her, overpower her, kill her. Not even to save the peace.

Zia's hands were on the computer once more. Her lips were moving, too, but not in apology, as Chayo's were. The princess was sending the command, setting an irrevocable process in motion.

A process that would destroy the Haukiets and all other life within their sphere of influence and between their stellar regions and the Niandians'.

Earth. A cinder. Evy, Susan, Tran Cai, Maria, Deputy Mayor Lupez, gone. Never knowing what had hit them. Innocent victims. A few among billions, perhaps trillions of innocent victims of Zia's "victory or death!" hatred.

The barrier was unbreakable. Renamos couldn't reach her—physically.

But the princess had to be stopped. Now.

Our weapon is a scalpel, Martil had said: The dealer of death will be dealt death.

Martil was wounded, perhaps dead. Renamos couldn't sense his presence. Tae? She sought him with her mind and touched a faint, fluttering something that might have been his essence. But he was *really* mute, at present. No guidance. No help.

She was utterly alone.

No, not alone. Another essence was entering the picture, enveloping her. Becoming her. They were one. And time did not exist, nor did the limitless extent of space. Renamos was swept up in an incredible expansion as she and that other part of her grew infinitely strong. A second essence. Also female. Asking her: *"Must it be? It will mean loss. A severing of life. Must it be?"*

"Yes," Renamos replied without speaking.

Time seemed arrested. Zia's hand was moving so slowly, so very slowly, toward the doomsday control.

The symbiotic essences that were Renamos could not be kept out by any force field. She was in that Gevari command center, beside Zia, entering Zia's thoughts, probing. Seeking knowledge. Names. How many other Gevaris remained? Which ones would never bend? Which would continue this cosmic destruction, even should Zia fall?

Zia knew them all. Her loyal adherents. Her fellow die-hards and would-be slaughterers of countless multitudes. Names of power, of important Niandians scattered throughout the twenty-five worlds of the Federation. Living mines, nursing the seeds of an endless war in their beings.

If Zia failed, they would carry out her final mission, nevertheless. They would permit no truce with the Haukiets. No cessation of hostilities—ever.

Names. Names Renamos could have tossed in her hands. Names that meant lives—which would take other lives.

The Gevari were ruthless. They would not hesitate to blot out all existence but their own, for a space of fifty light-years surrounding Niand.

In a nanosecond, it would be too late to use the Arbiters' scalpel.

However, time was nothing. Renamos could be everywhere at once. She was more than herself. Infinitely more. And a third essence was joining that dual presence of Renamos and her Ka-Een. This additional non-anthropomorphic ally was disoriented, torn out of its normal rapport. It anchored itself with Renamos's Ka-Een. They were asking her analysis of the situation: *You are humanoid. You are able to think and feel as Zia does. You must tell us what the Haukiet Tae would, if he were able. You must make the choice . . .*

The answer came from a pit so deep within Renamos that spoken words could not have expressed it: *The fa-*

natics have to die—and so must their Bender Principle weapon.

The scalpel cut. Bloodlessly. Painlessly. Instantaneously. Throughout the Niandian Federation. The Gevaris' names were taken from Zia's mind—an invasion that seared Renamos's innermost conscience, that. And wherever the rebels were, those ones who were immovable, murderously and permanently committed to death and destruction, fell. They ceased to exist. Spirits, winking out. Hundreds of candle flames, pinched off, and darkness descending. All their minds were probed, another terrible invasion, but necessary, to assure that only the evil was excised. No one innocent, or salvageable, would be struck down.

And as the Gevaris, so the very destructive device and its connecting network. A technology Renamos alone could never have mastered—smashed.

Then she was herself again, though not alone, and abyssal despair ripped at her. Gradually, she became aware that she was hammering on that force field and sobbing helplessly.

Abruptly, the invisible barrier collapsed. Renamos fell forward onto her hands, wincing with pain as they made contact with the floor.

Chayo knelt beside her, murmuring, "M-my Lady?"

"Had to. We had to," she said, staring at her bloody palms. She'd hit the transparent wall desperately, again and again, in her reflexive attempts to break through it physically and stop Zia. The force field had been proof against flesh, as no doubt it would have turned aside most weapons. But the Gevaris' leader couldn't have known the field was no protection against the Arbiters' nonhuman partners.

"Had to," Renamos repeated. "She was activating the Bender Principle weapon. In a fraction of a second more, it would have been too late. We couldn't let that happen."

Chayo looked utterly drained. His handsome face was haunted. "My Lady, Zia is dead. My mother-sister is . . . is dead."

chapter
15

Nᴜᴍʙ, Renamos gazed at him. He might or might not forgive what she—they—had done. But that wasn't important at this moment. Another matter demanded her attention.

She staggered across the room. Chayo hurried to help her, despite her attempts to shrug him off. Help her! Even now! Even after she'd participated in his sister's execution!

"Martil? Tae?" Martil was lying on his back. His eyes were half-open, his chest covered with gore. Tae was lying beside him, prone, one big arm stretched out, his fingers touching Martil's shoulder. A puddle of pink foam was spreading out beneath Tae's head and body.

Renamos bent over them, hoping against hope. "Please be alive."

Then she gasped, stricken. The remains of a pseudo-metallic chain clung to Martil's neck and tiny fragments of gold wire lay here and there, dotting the blood covering his dark shirt. She saw no trace of what the gold wire had held.

"My Lady, what is it?"

She pulled free of Chayo's concerned grasp and bent over Martil, caressing the broken chain. That pain! That feeling that her very core was being ripped out of her. She moaned. "His Ka-Een. It's gone! It doesn't exist anymore. When Zia shot them, it tried to shield him, and it—oh, Martil!'' She remembered his words—that he couldn't envision life without his Ka-Een partner.

Presences. Reminding her of what had to be done.

Renamos dried her tears and touched Martil's throat. There was a pulse, rapid and dangerously light, almost a fluttering. She turned to Tae and forced herself to slide her hand through that pool of pink blood, reaching under his body, searching. Her fingers closed on a small pseudo-metallic cage and sensed the Ka-Een within it.

Regret. Apology.

Tae's Ka-Een hadn't realized what was about to occur until it was too late.

''It's all right,'' she whispered comfortingly to two symbiotic and pulsating gray-green-gold essences. ''It's all *right*! Oh, Chayo! They're badly hurt, maybe dying.''

''I'll get doctors.''

She caught his arm. ''No. Niandian doctors can't help them, particularly not Tae. They wouldn't know how to begin to repair a Haukiet converted to humanoid form. And Martil . . . he's lost his Ka-Een. I don't know if he can hang onto life without it.''

''Here. Give him mine.'' Chayo fumbled at his vest-tunic and pulled a chain over his head, holding out a Ka-Een pendant for Renamos to take. She'd almost forgotten. They *had* given him one, hadn't they? He laid the pendant in her hand and said, ''Take it, my Lady.''

''How can you *bear* it?'' she exclaimed, appalled. Chayo returned her stare with bewilderment. She and those two essences—no, three now—reached out, probing. He didn't feel any loss. No aching, pit-deep desolation. ''I see. You weren't really possessed, apparently. It's—thank you.'' Renamos gently touched Chayo's face, wishing she could explain, and pitying him.

Then she picked up Martil's limp right hand and nestled Chayo's Ka-Een there, forcing his bony, beringed fingers around the pendant. She had to re-create the action of him embracing the little being.

''It'll have to do,'' Renamos said. ''Chayo, wait. Please. Ask your mother to wait, too, until I come back. Don't let her make any decisions before then.''

''Come back? Where are you going, my Lady?''

"I hope I'm going to the Arbiters' nerve-center world," she replied, "and taking Martil and Tae with me."

How had they done it, when they were piggybacking Chayo to safety out of the ruined city of Hell-All? Touching. That was vital in these circumstances. Especially since Martil had only a borrowed Ka-Een to transfer his essence. And Tae needed to be touched as well, because he was so badly wounded.

She clutched Martil's hand, ensuring he didn't drop Chayo's pendant. Tae was already touching Martil, so that contact link was in place. Renamos placed her bleeding fingers against Tae's blond head.

Chayo gawked as she started to expand outside herself. Three presences, non-anthropomorphic, one of them still a bit vague and unsure of its position in this symbiosis.

You must possess Martil. He needs you.

Reaching further. Two more presences joined the circle. Very weak presences. One a great, amorphous being, caged in a humanoid body. The other a thin, dark, quicksilver-natured . . .

No!

She had felt herself moving into Martil's and Tae's unconscious minds. And she didn't want that. All she needed was their essences.

Being swept around and around. Chayo's face and the room out of focus, disintegrating in an assortment of dots, a wirephoto seen close up and then receding, pulling further and further away from her. Renamos clung to a mental image with all her inner strength: a room with big hassocks and out-of-synch people. Particularly female out-of-synchs carrying big, lovely medical bags over their shoulders, bags full of wonderful tricks to heal that terrible hole in Martil's chest and stop that pink foam from leaking out of Tae's head and body.

You have to get us there. I don't know the way. You've been there before. Do it just as you would for Martil and Tae.

There was nothing. Blackness. A blackness more total than anything in the real universe. She shouldn't be able to see anything, but she did: A glittering dance of gray, green, and gold.

And then there was a hard, shiny floor beneath her, a fancy linoleum floor, and a big room surrounding her. The furnishings were big hassocks. Out-of-synch people were hurrying toward her, Martil, and Tae.

"Thank you," she whispered.

We must be in time. For their sakes . . .

"Martil?" His eyes remained partially open, though unseeing; Renamos could detect a glint of hazel irises through the parted lids. A pulse in his throat moved. So making a leap across ten thousand light-years using a borrowed Ka-Een hadn't killed him outright. Was that because of what Martil referred to as her affinity for the essence?

"Tae?" She thought his lips twitched, but that wasn't likely. He wouldn't speak to assure her he was alive. Renamos sought his presence. It wasn't strong, but it existed.

Out-of-synchs were swarming around them. She stood up and edged back to give them room to work. Their forms were blurry, but she seemed to see them in a new light. Renamos and her Ka-Een could sense each and every one of them. Fellow team members. Fellow Arbiters.

They knew what she had done. She had used the Arbiters' power and their weapon, which was a light-year-spanning scalpel. She had destroyed lives, a lot of them. Every Gevari who would have endangered the Haukiets and the numberless unknown species in the stellar regions dividing Haukiet and Niand.

Renamos had killed. The Ka-Eens had given her the choice, and she had made it. Martil had said that she was free to choose, as the Sisterhood had fought for that right, on the planet where she had been born.

Choice. But actually there hadn't been much of a choice. And she hadn't been able to save lives without first taking lives.

The Many-Voice was speaking to her. "You were ready for that responsibility. It was yours."

"I must go back. We're not through there, yet."

"Understood," the Many-Voice of the Arbiters agreed.

Renamos couldn't keep herself from glancing anxiously at the place where the out-of-synch doctors were laboring to save Martil and Tae.

"It is not finished," the Many-Voice nudged her. "You have said so yourself."

"Yes. I have to take care of that cosmic picture." She braced herself, stepping into that symbiosis she was feeling more and more at ease with.

There were only two of them, this time. A female essence was asking, "Where to?"

Martil and Tae might know stellar coordinates. They could accurately locate a particular world among thousands scattered across the void. Renamos of the Sisterhood of the Nine Worlds couldn't, not yet. She had to depend on the non-anthropomorphic member of their reduced partnership. "Where we came from," she said softly. "To the chamber with the doomsday weapon."

The room with the big hassocks vanished. Total, heartstopping nothingness.

And then there was light again. Right on target! The spot her mind had sought beyond ten thousand lightyears. The spot her Ka-Een had brought her to. "Good girl," Renamos murmured.

The matriarch was standing over the body of her daughter. Chayo was nearby, his handsome face an expressionless mask. Guards circled them. When the soldiers saw Renamos they stiffened and leveled their guns at her. Chayo threw up a hand and ordered them to hold their fire. Wary and nervous, the uniformed Niandians did so, maintaining a close watch on the Arbiter.

Renamos studied Chayo. He walked toward her, his pace hesitant. Now and then he glanced back at his mother. When he was within arm's length of the Arbiter, he bowed slightly and said, "My Lady Renamos, I have waited." His voice was strained. He sounded as though he badly needed a drink.

The matriarch turned, staring at the two young people. The ruler's gaze fastened intently on Renamos. The Arbiter saw no hate in the Niandian's eyes. That would have hurt. She had come to admire that imperious woman bearing the burden of her people on her thin shoulders. "Honored—honored Arbiter, you have done this to my daughter?"

Zia, in death, was lovely. She had fallen in a graceful way and her features were serene, not contorted with agony. Because she had suffered no agony. That wasn't necessary. If she had to die, the scalpel would cut cleanly and mercifully. Renamos sighed and said, "No, I did not kill her. She killed herself."

"Yes. Yes!" General Vunj was sitting in the room's shadows, tended by a couple of med staffers who were hovering over his Niandian wheelchair. Renamos wondered if he'd been brought here to see his daughter's body. Or had those who still suspected Vunj of being a traitor thought that this jolt would make him confess to treason? The former motive seemed to be the one the Niandians had acted on. General Vunj's attendants were very solicitous, the soldiers' glances in his direction sympathetic. "Tried to . . . tried to . . . dangerous!" Vunj exclaimed. "She would not listen. Not since she was very young. Could not be . . . I knew something was afoot. Couldn't ferret them out . . . not fully out. Her people . . . too loyal. Impossible to bribe or break. Dangerous! Death! She wouldn't believe that it is death to harm an Arbiter . . . death!"

Chayo shook his head, concentrating his focus on Renamos. "My Lady, I know you did not . . . did not kill my mother-sister. You couldn't have. The power screen was on. Your weapon could not penetrate that. And yet . . . she is dead. All at once, Zia was dead. I am certain she did not kill herself. I was beside her . . ."

"Yes, you were, weren't you?" Renamos didn't hide the scorn in her tone. Chayo met her stare unashamedly. He'd done—or had *not* done—what he had to. Just as she had.

"Arbiter," the matriarch pleaded, "do not hurt us further. We are beginning to receive the reports. From our sister worlds . . ."

"You will receive many more," Renamos warned. "From every part of your Federation."

"You have struck us so deeply! People we never dreamed were Gevari—dead!"

"Fools," General Vunj interjected, peering into nothing. "I told her it was death to employ the Ja-Yan device!"

The matriarch closed her eyes a moment, struggling for control. "I should have realized. Yet I was blind, as only a mother can be to her daughter's flaws. But, could this not have been handled otherwise, Arbiter? I would have restrained her."

Renamos didn't mention Chayo's failure to "restrain" his sister. "Zia killed herself, Most High," she said again, "by her act of using the Ja-Yan device, as you call it. The Arbiters have disabled that device as well, an intervention we find very distasteful, but which was necessary. Zia's own hatred destroyed her. She could not yield to peace, nor could the Gevari we were forced to strike down with her. Martil of the Bright Suns told you of this danger, when we first arrived on Niand. Zia chose to defy that danger, and her rebels have paid the price. Most High, you have complained that the Gevaris have been a thorn in your side, politically. That thorn has removed itself. You are free to initiate a cease-fire. Make it a permanent one."

The Niandians were listening fearfully. It was not the sort of fear that might turn, in time, to a lust for revenge. Rather it was terror of something beyond comprehension. Childlike awe of omnipotence.

"Death to challenge the Arbiters!" Vunj shrieked.

"Don't!" the matriarch cried, addressing Renamos, not Vunj. "My assembly of premiers is reconvening now. The war party has been swept away by this—by Zia's death. Those who resisted peace negotiations are in disorder." Renamos guessed that a better term would have been "scared shitless." The older woman vowed, "No more killing! We will send our emissaries to meet with those of the Green Union. At once!"

"No further disputes over territory," Renamos said. "No excuses to renew this conflict."

"No! I swear! Speak to the assembly, Arbiter. Tell them."

The Earthwoman shook her head. "From this point on, you must go forward on your own to achieve peace. We have helped you to take the important first step. For the good of Niand, you must act alone now. As the Haukiets must. This is as it should be. We do not govern for others. It is regrettable that Zia's murderous scheme forced us to intrude as much as we have. But in a way, her death brings you all a chance for life.''

Grieving, the matriarch burst into tears anew. Renamos longed to comfort her, but knew she dared not. Niand was going to be far behind her soon, as Earth was. She had to let go.

''My Lady?'' Chayo's eyes were reddened, but he wasn't weeping now; he was holding his mother, giving her a shoulder to cry on. A compassionate young prince. He looked questioningly at Renamos, his thoughts terribly obvious.

''I can't stay,'' she said kindly. ''You don't need me. But Niand needs you. That large and loyal faction of yours will have to help heal the wounds. Your leadership will be vital, to your mother and to the Federation. Put them on a solid footing, for peace.''

''My mother will have others to aid her,'' Chayo replied. Not resentful. Just stating the facts, biologically determined. ''Now that Zia is dead, my mother's sister Wisi will inherit.''

''Perhaps. Or perhaps it will be a granddaughter. There just may be a capable, highly intelligent Niandian bride in your future.'' Her Ka-Een probably translated that somewhat differently than she had expressed it, but Chayo got the idea. He frowned, skeptical. Renamos went on. ''You're quite a catch, you know. Come on. Don't be so damned self-deprecating all the time. Have some pride. You deserve to. Make the choice to stand on your own two feet, as you did when you first contacted the Arbiters.''

A glimmer of confidence shone in the prince's pale eyes. But she hadn't anticipated his next reaction—a spark aimed in her direction. ''My Lady, I would rather serve you.''

Did her Ka-Een dabble in double entendre? Renamos stood on tiptoe and kissed Chayo. A friendly good-bye kiss, nothing more. He was handsome, likable, and courageous—up to a certain line. But she was keenly aware of the divisions between them, which would prevent anything heavier than a sexual dalliance. And she wanted a lot more than that. Chayo was outside her affinity. Unpossessed by a Ka-Een. Not his fault. Yet he'd always been a stranger because of it.

"I'm sorry. It wouldn't work out," she said. "I'm fond of you, but you lie too much."

He was bewildered, though he didn't argue. Instead, he accepted her decision, edging back a pace. Symbolic. She'd soon be edging away from him. She spoke wordlessly to her Ka-Een, tuning up for another mind-boggling leap. The matriarch lifted her head and blinked, staring apprehensively at the Earthwoman.

"I leave you now, Most High," Renamos explained. "I advise you to make peace. And do not rebuild the Ja-Yan device, because the Arbiters will be watching."

Niandians paled and blurted oaths, promising to obey. Even Chayo went through those forms, despite the fact that he knew that Niand was comparatively small potatoes on the Arbiters' galactic scale. The prince had seen what peace meant, during his visit to those remote worlds of the Arbiter culture. As a result, he was now the Arbiters' man-on-Niand. He'd have the strongest possible motivations for keeping his mouth shut and allowing his people to believe that the Arbiter "Big Brothers"—and "Big Sisters"!—truly *were* watching everything that went on here. With that daunting sword of Damocles hanging over them, Chayo could subtly guide his species toward a lasting peace.

"We will be watching," Renamos repeated. I lie a bit myself, occasionally, don't I? she thought as she moved into rapport, one with her Ka-Een.

Nothingness. And then—home.

It really is home to me, this Arbiters' nerve-center world, she realized. However long I live, I'm part of the team. If the team still exists.

Out-of-synchs were eddying around her. Renamos asked, "Where are Martil and Tae?"

A cold object touched her neck, and lethargy swept over her. She was being supported, led to one of the big hassocks, gently lowered onto it.

"N-no, it wasn't that much of a strain, finishing the mission. Don't put me to sleep yet . . ."

A shimmering female figure bent over her. A medic. A sequined flashlight hypo was clutched in one of the alien's appendages. Renamos got the oddest impression that the medic was grinning at her triumphantly—the way doctors usually did when they'd slipped one over on a recalcitrant patient.

Like giving the patient a knockout shot for the patient's own good.

"That—" Renamos yawned hugely. "—was a damned dirty trick." But she couldn't hang on to the thought. Giving up, she sank down into the enveloping warmth of what felt like tons of wonderfully soft cotton.

chapter
16

ONE of the huge medical-monitor cats was lying on Renamos's hassock bed. Sitting up, she met the animal's examining stare and responded silently.

I'm well. Very refreshed. No hangover. My hands aren't bleeding. My stomach doesn't hurt. I don't have a headache. Report to Central that all my functions are normal. And ask them how Martil and Tae are.

The cat jumped off the hassock and disappeared through a wall.

Renamos grimaced in annoyance. Well, the beasts *were* rather primitive empath-telepaths, of course. As hospital aides, though, they were great; no waking you up to stick a thermometer in your mouth or give you a sleeping pill.

She dressed in a silken jumpsuit that had been draped over the room's handy valet rack. The garment was designed with a V neckline. How thoughtful, allowing her to accent her best points. Her costume complete, she headed for a wall, sensing that her Ka-Een was steering her toward one particular area in order to make their exit. As they did, Renamos almost tripped over Tae. He was lying in the hall just outside the room and playing with one of the big Siamese medical-monitor cats.

She knelt beside him, caressing his yellow hair and putting a finger under his craggy chin. Renamos winged a suggestion that he turn his head so she could look him over, and he cooperated willingly. The right side of his face, which had been pillowed in that ooze of pink blood, was as good as new. So was the rest of him. He grinned broadly.

"Where's Martil?"

In answer, he stood and reached for her hand. "I can walk, thanks." Shrugging, Tae turned and led the way down the corridor. Renamos's spirits seemed to skip in his wake. Martil had to be alive! She'd feel it, picking up grieving wavelengths from Tae and the Ka-Eens, if the fox-faced Arbiter weren't.

Typically, Tae was eating up space with his stride, and she was having some trouble matching his pace. But that was better than being bounced on his hipbone or dragged along like a comet's tail.

Finally, they walked through a wall into another of the Center's "motel rooms." Martil was lying on the sole hassock occupying this chamber. A monitor cat sat on the foot of the bed, or rather at Martil's feet. Either the Arbiter didn't have any reservations about nudity or the out-of-synch doctors didn't; he wasn't wearing a stitch, any more than Renamos had been while she was zonked out. She was mildly surprised that she felt no embarrassment at finding him naked. In fact, it seemed perfectly normal, given the circumstances.

Martil's chest was bright blue. Some form of shimmering, painted-on bandage. Much better than bloody-red! His vulpine face looked abnormally thin, and there were dark circles under his eyes. Closed eyes. Gently, Renamos brushed the black bangs away from his forehead, relieved to find that the skin was cool, not feverish.

He blinked, peering up at her.

"Sorry. I didn't mean to wake you." She perched carefully on the edge of the hassock near him. Tae flopped down on the other side, making both her and Martil bounce. The cat glared, and Martil gave his friend a mock scowl of disapproval. Seeing that made Renamos want to cry—tears of joy, of release, that both men were well enough once more to play their teasing games with each other.

Martil's bony fingers closed around hers and he said, "I'm all right." The cat gazed at him skeptically.

"I know Tae is," Renamos replied. "I fell over him outside my door." She tentatively examined the blue paint on Martil's chest.

"One of our miracle drugs. Our people are very efficient, if they get to you in time," he explained. "Actually, Tae presented them with much worse problems. He had a brain injury. And he's lost some memories. His *dirnows* files will have to help him relearn those areas."

Renamos shook her head. "I don't know what *dirnows* files are."

"Yet," Martil amended. "Eventually your Ka-Een will guide you into an understanding of that, along with many other facets of our culture." He exchanged a glance with Tae, then went on, "But you have already learned a very great deal. Fortunately for us, and for the Niandians and the Haukiets. And for your people of Earth. You did superbly. I told you that when you were ready for full Arbiter status, you would be the first to know it."

"Actually, my Ka-Een was the first," Renamos said. She traced invisible patterns on the hassock, feeling sad. "I was forced to kill Niandians. A lot of them. Oh, I know what would have happened if I hadn't stopped Zia and the other Gevaris. I had to make the choice to stop them, to save billions of other beings. Back on Earth, I used to be contemptuous of those who claimed that it was sometimes necessary to sacrifice a few to save many. I found that hard to believe. I wanted to save everybody. Well, nearly everybody. But now I've lived through a situation where there was no option." She took a deep breath. "The Bender Principle weapon, and its operator, had to be dismantled. I never realized I could move at a thousand—a million!—times the speed of light."

"We can't. No humanoid can. You couldn't have done it alone." Martil was rubbing absentmindedly at the mole on his chin. Renamos smacked his hand. The monitor cat growled. But when Martil grinned sheepishly, the animal shut up, mollified.

"You ought to have that damned thing zapped off," Renamos scolded. "Can't the out-of-synchs do that for you?"

"Of course. I choose to keep it. A personal idiosyncrasy. My choice. We are free to follow our own desires, when those do not harm others.'' Renamos nodded, the light moment drifting away from her and depression returning. Sensing what was troubling her, Martil said, "It had to be done. You mustn't feel guilty.''

"I don't. Not guilt. Just sorrow. I didn't kill Zia and her fanatics out of pettiness or anger or any other shallow motive.''

Martil and Tae smiled, amused. "You wouldn't have been able to,'' Martil said. "Not for *petty* reasons.''

"The Ka-Eens know when we're ready for such a terrible responsibility,'' Renamos agreed.

Hungrily, Martil sought for the pendant lying at his throat. He held the tiny pseudo-metallic cage and its entity in a kind of one-handed embrace. "Yes,'' he murmured. "The Ka-Eens know.''

"Is it . . . how is Chayo's Ka-Een working for you? Okay?''

"Very well. We are adjusting to the rapport with far less difficulty than I would have expected. It seems eager to join with my essence. Apparently Chayo and I have something in common.''

"You both lie a lot, for sure!''

He waggled an eyebrow. "Plainly, it had developed no permanent rapport with him. I gather he yielded it up to you quite easily.''

"For your sake. Yes, he did. A generous gesture, but one that didn't cost him anything personally. Maybe he'd never needed a Ka-Een in the first place,'' Renamos said. "I brought him home safely from Hell-All the same way I brought myself through to Niand riding your lead beam. My affinity with the Ka-Een essence gives me a special boost.''

"You could not have carried me in the same way. Chayo wasn't bleeding to death when transport occurred.''

Aghast, Renamos exclaimed, "And you were? Lord! I was afraid it was really bad, but . . . I'm damned glad Chayo's pendant worked. Even more than I was before I knew what the situation was.''

The ghost of a smile tugged at his mouth. "Indeed. Thank you for your gifts, and your wisdom in assessing what was needed. If we ever have occasion to visit Niand again, I will thank Chayo.''

''I doubt any of us will see Niand from now on,'' Renamos said. ''We're not essential to the peace process there, anymore. Their choices have been made, finally. The right choices.''

''We have been briefed as to what happened after we were disabled,'' Martil told her. Briefed. While they were unconscious and recuperating. Just as the ''briefing material'' must have been extracted from her mind while she was recuperating. The Arbiters certainly had an efficient system for tidying up loose ends. A woman could get used to that—and a lot of other advantages the Arbiter culture offered. ''It was well done, Renamos. All of it.'' Tae nodded a second, his Haukiet blue eyes gleaming.

Renamos stared into nothing, remembering. ''When push came to shove, Zia would have killed Chayo without hesitation, if he'd tried to stop her. But he couldn't have killed her. Too much affection. And a lifetime of conditioning as a cultural minority. I know the feeling. On Earth, I had to reach deep inside myself to break those same ground-in patterns. Unequal humanoid social systems are both pervasive and addictive. After existing under them for hundreds of generations, people assume that's the only way things can ever be. We can't see that whether or not biology is destiny, it's the humanoid mind and our individual abilities that have to determine what we are and how we should be perceived.''

Martil managed a sly smile. ''You want Chayo to establish a so-called men's lib on Niand.''

''Maybe he will,'' Renamos snapped. Then she sighed. ''I'm still kicking myself a bit because I let matters get so out of hand there. I could have gotten to Zia sooner, before no options remained, if I'd just spotted her scheming. When Chayo tried to call her for help, when we were being attacked at Hell-All, she got his message, all right. She just used it to confirm that he—and we—were there, and told her Gevaris to pour it on and kill us. She sent the bomb strike on his apartment, too, after we'd first landed on Niand; he'd checked in with her, like a dutiful brother and a proper cultural minority, as soon as we entered his quarters. Why the hell didn't I put the pieces together then?''

"Because none of us is perfect," Martil said. "We should have detected her plot ourselves. But we did not."

"I'm female!" Renamos cried. "I should have felt it."

"Spoken like a cultural minority? Relying on your alleged female intuition. What did you just note? That it was individual mind and ability which should determine a humanoid's status. And her or his ego, I might add. Zia was a fanatic," Martil said, his expression grim. "And fanatics are notoriously difficult to fathom."

"And yet, there's a part of me that knows how she ended up in that victory-or-death corner of hers. She suffered from an excess of caring, of matriotism, in Niandian terms. Her own point of view became the only one possible. She cared so much it blotted out any possibility of compromise. Zia couldn't back off, rein in her anger, and see if there wasn't a path out of the problem that wouldn't harm others—and her own . . ."

"She had not learned the true victory, as Soh puts it," Martil commented. "No *unnecessary* blow."

"One gets caught up in the passion of caring," Renamos went on, opening an old wound, letting the pain flow out of her being. "Seeing the enemy all around. The callous. The abusers. The drug dealers and amoral criminals who feed on other people's miseries. The politicians who are only interested in maintaining their authority. The cheating businesspeople, endangering the public. Everyone who forgets what being a member of an intelligent species is all about."

"But you did not resort to an attempt at wide-scale murder, as Zia did," Martil consoled her. "You would not have done so, even had you possessed Zia's power and her weapons. That is not your nature. It never has been."

Remembered anger, from a previous life, and final twinges of uncertainty faded. Renamos said, "Well, I had good guidance. My parents. Evy and my friends. You weirdos. With so much help, how could I fail to learn my own potentials and learn how to live without trampling on other beings' choices."

"Indeed!" Martil exclaimed. "And you chose to complete the mission as it had to be completed. Now Niand, Haukiet, your origin planet, and countless others have the freedom to make *their* future choices. And in time, many of them will achieve the free culture of the type we Arbiters enjoy.''

"If Earth doesn't blow itself up first," Renamos said, growing gloomy again. "Or destroy the ozone layer and create an uninhabitable greenhouse world. Or poison its water and soil past reclamation. Or overpopulate itself out of a food supply. Or . . .''

Martil's eyebrows disappeared under his bangs. "What a marvelous species you come from! How did someone of such a background ever adapt to our system? After all, the Arbiters can offer you none of the 'privileges' to which you are accustomed—including the position of a cultural minority.''

Stung, Renamos said, "I've got news for you. Both of you. I refuse to be a cultural minority, on Earth or here! And this Arbiter team is now really *balanced*. My Ka-Een *is* female. So ha!''

"You're being chauvinistic," Martil chided, his eyes twinkling mischievously. He was exceedingly weak, yet. If he tried to get out of bed, no doubt that monitor cat would yell for help, telepathically, and the doctors would zap Martil with a hypo and make him behave. Nevertheless, the fox-faced Arbiter's sense of humor was fully recovered, and his tongue worked just fine.

"I am *not* being chauvinistic," Renamos said, irked. "Not really. And if I am, it's a special brand of chauvinism. Long overdue. Call it Renamos pride, and get used to it. I intend to hang on to it indefinitely, as far as I can go into the future.''

Martil shammed a weary sigh. Tae laughed, his huge body shaking and making the hassock jiggle like a waterbed.

Underlining her point, Renamos went on, "You grabbed me off my world, away from my friends and coworkers. Now you have to provide a viable replacement. I don't know, exactly, when I stopped thinking of myself as Renee Amos and became Renamos of the Sisterhood of the Nine Worlds. But that's what I am now. And I'm going to *remain* Renamos. Permanently.''

"Since we can't send you back, I suppose we'll have to make the best of it," Martil said. The twinkle in his eyes resembled twin stars. "Even if you do have this quaint, cultural-minority instinct to fight for your rights before checking to see if you might already possess those rights. Or indeed if they are rights which you really want to have. You might prefer to discard them, and assume other, much more desirable ones. Such as total choice, and a partnership in an Arbiter team."

It took her a split second to detect the teasing note under his solemn statement. He and Tae were eagerly awaiting her reaction. In a minute, that monitor cat was going to give all three of them—plus their Ka-Eens—hell. Who cared? Renamos giggled helplessly and muttered, "Oh, shut *up*, you weirdos!"

About the Author

JUANITA COULSON began writing at age eleven and has been pursuing this career off and on ever since. Her first professional sale, to a science-fiction magazine, came in 1963. Since then she has sold seventeen novels, several short stories, and such odds and ends as an article on ''Wonder Woman'' and a pamphlet on how to appreciate art.

When she isn't writing, she may be singing and/or composing songs; painting (several of her works have been sold for excessively modest prices); reading biographies or books dealing with abnormal psychology, earthquakes and volcanoes, history, astronomy—or almost anything that has printing on it; gardening in the summer and shivering in the winter.

Juanita is married to Buck Coulson, who is also a writer. She and her husband spend much of their spare time actively participating in science-fiction fandom: attending conventions and publishing their Hugo-winning fanzine, *Yandro*. They live in northeastern Indiana, surrounded by books, magazines, records, typewriters, and other paraphernalia.